ADVANCE ACCLAIM FOR *SAFE IN HIS ARMS*

"Colleen combines a rich, historical setting with real characters who reach out and grab ahold of you from page one. You won't want to put *Safe in His Arms* down until you turn the last page. Then you'll be sad the story ended so fast! I love Colleen's books and look forward to the next one!"

—LYNETTE EASON, AWARD-WINNING, BEST-SELLING AUTHOR
OF THE WOMEN OF JUSTICE SERIES

"Colleen Coble is an amazing storyteller who weaves stories I can't put down. In *Safe in His Arms* she combines a heroine I wanted to take to tea with a misunderstood hero and placed them in a historical setting I thoroughly enjoyed. Mix in romance and a touch of suspense and it is the perfect book."

—CARA PUTMAN, AWARD-WINNING AUTHOR OF *STARS IN THE NIGHT*
AND *A WEDDING TRANSPIRES ON MACKINAC ISLAND*

"I so enjoyed the strong heroine and enigmatic hero in Colleen Coble's *Safe in His Arms*. What a fun story of learning to love, to trust, and to be safe in the arms of God, no matter the circumstances. You'll want to keep turning the pages on this one to discover what happens next!"

—MARLO SCHALESKY, AUTHOR OF THE CHRISTY
AWARD-WINNING *BEYOND THE NIGHT*

"A fiery redhead, a mystery man, and plot twists galore. What's not to love? Colleen has done it again . . . created a page-turner. Don't miss it!"

—STEPHANIE GRACE WHITSON, AUTHOR OF
THE QUILT CHRONICLES SERIES

ACCLAIM FOR COLLEEN COBLE

"Colleen is a master storyteller."

—KAREN KINGSBURY, BEST-SELLING AUTHOR OF
UNLOCKED AND *LEARNING*

"Suspense, action, mystery, spiritual victory—Colleen Coble has woven them all into a compelling novel that will keep you flipping pages until the very end. I highly recommend *Without a Trace*."

—JAMES SCOTT BELL, AUTHOR OF *DEADLOCK* AND *A HIGHER JUSTICE*

"Coble's books have it all, romance, sass, suspense, action. I'm content to read a book that has any one of those but to find an author like Coble who does all four so well is my definition of bliss."

—MARY CONNEALY, AUTHOR OF *DOCTOR IN PETTICOATS*

"Coble captivates readers with her compelling characters. Action-packed . . . highly recommended!"

—DIANNE BURNETT, CHRISTIANBOOK.COM

"Coble wows the reader with a fresh storyline. Readers will enjoy peeling back the layers and discovering this is more than your average romance book."

—*ROMANTIC TIMES*, 4-STAR REVIEW OF *THE LIGHTKEEPER'S BALL*

"Coble's historical series just keeps getting better with each entry."

—*LIBRARY JOURNAL*, STARRED REVIEW OF *THE LIGHTKEEPER'S BALL*

WHAT READERS ARE SAYING

"I have always been a hopeless romantic . . . When I began reading your books I couldn't put them down. I love not just the romance but the connection I feel with God when I read your books. It really is incredible!"

—JENNIFER

"I just finished *Blue Moon Promise* and it was outstanding! I am so looking forward to *Safe in His Arms*! Thank you for sharing your God-given talent with us."

—NANCY

"I love your books! I am a big fan :) You are by far my favorite author."

—KATELYN

"I wanted to let you know that I am reading *Blue Moon Promise* and I can't put it down. I love the way you write! I've read your Lonestar series and I can't wait to read *Tidewater Inn*."

—JEAN

"You are such an amazing writer and person. I've been dealing with lots of health issues, and on my 'bad days' I turn to your books to keep me inspired, to keep me thinking positive thoughts, and to help get me through the tough times. Thanks for being an inspiration and for all that you do to include your reader friends in your life."

—BECKY

"I just read *The Lightkeeper's Daughter*, *The Lightkeeper's Bride,* and *The Lightkeeper's Ball*. I could not put them down. I also read the first two books of the Lonestar series and I can't wait to get my hands on the next two. I loved them all!!"

—ADELE

"I finished *Lonestar Angel* and just loved it!! Sure would love for that series to go on and on, keeps getting better and better."

—TERESA

"I just finished the Rock Harbor series . . . I loved it. You should see my house, laundry, dishes, etc. I haven't done a thing in days. I literally couldn't put the books down. I am off to find *Alaska Twilight*. You are by far my new favorite author. I am from Indiana too, and have visited the UP before. I could almost smell the woods, feel the wind, and hear the waves. Thanks for a truly amazing series."

—TANYA

"I just wanted to say thank you for writing the Rock Harbor series. I lost my son in a car accident 12 years ago this month. They waited to bury him when I woke from a coma. I don't remember the accident or barely the funeral. It felt like a nightmare, very unreal and out of body. In your book, she got her little boy back, but she also learned to not be so angry with God. That is something I will always have to work on. I feel very guilty for that, but I am angry. Your book has helped me with that some. I look forward to more in the series, strangely it gave me a peace."

—TIFFANY

"I am so very excited about your new books coming out! I have read almost everything you have put out in the last five years! I am counting down the days till the next Rock Harbor book comes out, and I am pre-ordering *Cry in the Night* this weekend! Thank you so much for all you do! Not only have I enjoyed the story lines, I feel like it's a daily devotional as well!"

—BESS

"I just finished your *Lonestar Sanctuary* novel and LOVED IT! I am a HUGE cowgirl/rodeo fan at heart and worked with troubled children so it really spoke to my heart. I am so glad I have discovered such a wonderful author and will highly recommend your books to my friends and book club!"

—KIM

SAFE IN HIS ARMS

ALSO BY COLLEEN COBLE

SAFE IN HIS ARMS

An Under Texas Stars Novel

COLLEEN COBLE

THOMAS NELSON
Since 1798

NASHVILLE   DALLAS   MEXICO CITY   RIO DE JANEIRO

Published in Nashville, Tennessee, by Thomas Nelson. Thomas Nelson is a registered trademark of Thomas Nelson, Inc.

Thomas Nelson, Inc., titles may be purchased in bulk for educational, business, fund-raising, or sales promotional use. For information, please e-mail SpecialMarkets@ThomasNelson.com.

Publisher's Note: This novel is a work of fiction. Names, characters, places, and incidents are either products of the author's imagination or used fictitiously. All characters are fictional, and any similarity to people living or dead is purely coincidental.

Scripture quotations are taken from the King James Version of the Bible.

Library of Congress Cataloging-in-Publication Data

Coble, Colleen.
 Safe in his arms : an under Texas stars novel / Colleen Coble.
  p. cm. — (Under Texas stars ; 2)
 ISBN 978-1-59554-914-3 (trade paper)
 1. Texas—Fiction. 2. Christian fiction. 3. Love stories. I. Title.
PS3553.O2285S24 2013
813'.54—dc23   2012038219

Printed in the United States of America

13 14 15 16 17 QG 6 5 4 3 2 1

For Scott and Carolyn Johnston,
who lovingly tell us all that we are safe in His arms

DEAR READER,

I hope you enjoy reading *Safe in His Arms* as much as I did writing it! There's a lot of me in Margaret. Growing up, I always felt awkward and unattractive. I was taller than every boy in my class until I was in the seventh grade. I hated my wavy hair and ironed it when I got to high school in the sixties. I wanted blue eyes, not brown. My feet were too big, and so were my hips. Sound familiar? ☺

Women are indoctrinated from infancy about beauty. We feel we must be Superwoman and have it all: beauty, brains, a good work ethic, great with children, a good cook. The list is long, isn't it? I think it's particularly hard for women to accept the unconditional love God offers. We are so used to being held to such a high standard—and failing—that we feel we can never measure up.

What a blessing when we realize that we don't have to. God loves us, warts and all. We are safe in his arms. Safe to tell him our dreams, our fears, our failings. Safe to relax in his unconditional love.

I love hearing from you! E-mail me anytime at colleen@ colleencoble.com.

Love,
Colleen

ONE

The town of Larson, Texas, was busy on this warm February day. Cowboys in their dusty boots eyed the women attired in their best dresses strolling the boardwalks. Margaret O'Brien strode down the boardwalk in front of the feed store toward the mercantile. Things seemed to change daily with new stores sprouting like winter wheat. Every day more cowmen arrived in Larson, drawn by the lush grazing land and the water of the Red River.

Pa should be around here somewhere. She nodded to the ladies clustered in front of the general store, the familiar discomfort washing over her. Why couldn't she look like them? No matter how hard Margaret tried, she remained what she was: too tall and more at home with her hands gripping horse reins than a teacup. She ducked into the store and inhaled the aroma of cinnamon, bootstrap, sweat, and pickles. She busied herself with collecting material for their housekeeper, who had a bee in her bonnet about making curtains.

A cluster of women were talking in hushed whispers about the latest Zulu atrocity in Africa. These early months of 1879 had been full of bloody battles. Hearing such things always made Margaret wince, remembering her brother's death at the hands of the Sioux. At least a national monument had been established earlier this year in memory of those who fell during the Battle of the Little Bighorn.

The women fell silent when Margaret paused. "Good morning," she said in as confident a voice as she could muster. "Anyone know what kind of material to buy for curtains? I thought this was pretty."

When she held up a lilac-flowered fabric, one of the women tittered, a tiny blonde Margaret had never seen before. Her face burned, and she put the bolt of fabric back.

"How about this one?" a woman said behind her.

Margaret's heart leaped at the sound of her friend's voice, and she whirled with a smile. "Lucy, I didn't know you were in town today. Should you be riding in a wagon in your condition?"

The blond woman laughed again at Margaret's indelicate mention of Lucy's pregnancy. Lucy linked arms with Margaret. "I feel fine. You like this pattern? I think Inez will love it."

Margaret eyed the red-and-white plaid. "It's a little . . . loud."

"Cheerful," Lucy corrected, smiling. Her head high, she led Margaret out of the group. "Silly twits. Now, don't start moaning about how they don't like you. They don't know you." Lucy shook her head. "And they won't bother to get to know you if you don't take a little more care when you come to town."

Margaret smoothed her hands on her rough skirt. They had come after cattle feed, and she had work to do in the barn when she got home, so she hadn't bothered to change. She should have put on a nicer dress. "It was too much bother since I had to help load feed."

"It's worth it, Margaret." Lucy glanced at the watch pinned to her dress. "Nate is going to be looking for me." She hugged Margaret. "I'm so glad I saw you. You're coming to the party, aren't you?"

"Sure. I'm not going to dance, but I'll come keep you company." Smiling, Margaret watched her friend waddle away. Dear Lucy. She had barreled past Margaret's prickly exterior, and they'd become fast friends. Lucy was easy to trust. She was all heart.

Margaret had her purchases put on account, then stepped out into the sunshine.

Cattlemen had driven herds of cattle through here more than an hour ago, but the dust and odor still lingered in the air. Her father motioned to her from in front of the stagecoach station. Calvin stood close behind him.

She started toward them, but the man beside her father arrested her gaze. He was tall, even taller than her father, which meant he had to be at least six foot three or four inches. She guessed he was in his early thirties. The man's Stetson was pushed back on his head, revealing shiny brown hair, and his bronzed face was chiseled with planes and angles that spoke of confidence and determination. He cast a lazy grin her way.

Immediately Margaret's hackles rose. That kind of self-assurance—arrogance, really—always reminded her of her uncle. She'd had to assert herself strenuously with him around the ranch because he thought a woman's place was in the kitchen, not in the stockyard. This man was the same type, the sort of man who would demand to be catered to and obeyed. No one who looked that strong and proud would listen to a woman.

She forced a smile. This man was probably nothing like her uncle. But her trepidation slowed her steps. Her father motioned her forward, though, and she reluctantly moved to join them.

Her father put his hand on her shoulder. "Here's my daughter, Margaret."

The man's gaze swept from the top of her head down to the dusty boots just peeking out from underneath her serviceable skirt, and Margaret's lips tightened. People in Larson were used to her attire, but this man's eyes widened. He'd probably never seen a woman dressed for ranch work. She wore a man's chambray shirt, and her red hair hung over her shoulder in a long braid. The bits of cow manure on her skirt and boots didn't add much to the general picture either. He'd really be shocked if he saw her in her britches when she was helping with the cattle.

She lifted her head and stared him down. His dark eyes betrayed none of his thoughts. She didn't think she'd ever seen eyes that shade. Like a buckeye nut, they were a rich brown color. Heavy brows accented the strong planes of his face.

Margaret thrust out her hand. "Pleased to meet you. And you are . . . ?"

He could have stared over the top of her head without taking notice of her at all. But he didn't. He gazed straight into her eyes, and her breath caught in her throat as she felt the magnetic pull of the man.

"Daniel Cutler." His handshake was firm and as self-confident as his appearance.

Margaret pulled her hand away. "You been in town long, Mr. Cutler?" He'd given his name but not his business here in Larson. Pa seemed almost proprietorial toward him, but she clamped her teeth against the questions clamoring to escape.

"He just got in today," her father put in eagerly. "He's our new foreman."

"New foreman?" Margaret's heart dipped like a bronco about

to arch its back to the sky. "We don't need a new foreman, Pa. I can handle things by myself. I've spent the last ten years of my life proving it."

Their ranch hand Calvin straightened as well. "That ain't right, O'Brien. You said if I did a good job, you'd promote me. This shavetail"—he gestured toward Cutler—"ain't what the ranch needs."

Her father glared at Calvin. "Get that feed loaded and keep your nose out of my business." Her father skewered her with an even sterner stare. "Now, Margaret, I told you it's time you let go of some of these notions about running the ranch by yourself. I'm getting too old to be of much help, and I'd sure like for you to set your mind to finding a husband and giving me some grandchildren."

Her father's gaze traveled over Margaret's apparel and displeasure shone in his eyes. "Though what man would have you when you make no attempt to look like a woman is another concern altogether."

She had begun to find her composure, but at her father's words, blood rushed to her face. They didn't need to air their disagreements in front of this stranger. Pa had never understood how his words burned her spirit like a brand. She never let on how he hurt her, and she didn't now. She narrowed her eyes at this stranger who was set to disrupt her life.

Daniel Cutler seemed to be taking it all in with interest, and a small smile played around those firm lips of his. He probably agreed wholeheartedly with her father's assessment. Like all the rest of the men in her acquaintance, he would be looking for some dainty young thing with a simpering smile and golden curls.

She tossed her head and glared at him. His smile faltered, and she felt a stab of satisfaction. "I'm sorry you've come all this way for nothing," she told him. "But we really don't need a foreman. Not you and not Calvin."

"The thing's done," her father said. "Toss your belongings into our wagon, Daniel. We'll head back to the ranch as soon as we get this feed loaded."

She caught her breath at her father's blatant dismissal. "Pa . . ."

He held up his hand. "Enough, Margaret. Daniel is here. Zip your tongue and help get the wagon loaded."

I will not cry. Biting her lip, she walked to the back of the wagon.

Daniel threw his satchel into the wagon. He didn't wait to be asked but went to the pile of feed sacks and began loading them. His muscular arms handled the heavy bags with ease. For a moment Margaret stared at the muscles in his back as they rippled beneath his shirt. In spite of her dislike of the man, he was a fine specimen of masculinity. Other women strolling by paused and cast surreptitious glances his way. Glances he seemed not to notice.

She helped load the sacks, but he threw the heavy bags into the back twice as quickly, with not even a labored breath. She bristled at his strength. He was probably trying to show her up in front of her father. She'd teach him she didn't need his help—not for loading feed and not for running the ranch.

She and Daniel worked side by side for several minutes until all she could smell was burlap. Daniel tossed the last of the feed into the wagon and turned to her with a grin. "What now, Boss?"

Boss. The way he said the word with a hint of mockery made her grimace. Just as she opened her mouth to put him in his place, shots rang out down the street. Five men, their revolvers blasting at anything that moved, rushed out of the bank and mounted their horses. The horses came thundering toward Margaret.

"Get down!" Daniel tackled her to the dusty ground.

The breath puffed out of her as he fell on top of her. She struggled to free herself, but his strong body kept her pinned beneath him. She could smell the clean scent of soap underneath the scent of his skin. Never in her life had she felt so helpless and dependent. And protected. The word whispered through her brain with a gentle allure.

FRANK WAS GOING to ruin everything with his impatience. It was all Daniel could do to hold his anger in check. "Stay here." The young woman glared at him, but at least she stayed under the wagon where he'd pushed her.

He spit the dust from his mouth and rolled out from under the wagon. Shots rang out again, but he didn't duck back into safety. The gang wouldn't shoot at him. Slipping along the side of the building, he made his way to the back of the bank. The last person he expected to see was the beautiful blond outlaw staring arrogantly at him from her perch on a palomino.

"Golda," he said tightly. Her beauty had stirred him once, made him leave a lucrative job in the Austin area and take up a life of crime.

"I didn't expect to see you, Daniel."

Her voice was husky with a smoky quality that froze men in their tracks while she devoured them at her leisure. He moved away, reminding himself that he was no longer her prey. "I don't know why. That was the plan. You moved in too soon, though. I just got here."

She shrugged her slim shoulders and urged her horse closer. "You know my brother. Frank likes to keep everyone off kilter. I think he wasn't sure you'd really show. You've been gone awhile, and he's not sure he can trust you."

"I told him I had a place to scout out the banks, and I do. But I'm going to need a little time."

"I'll tell him."

More shots sounded from out front. "You'd better get out of here." He didn't wait for her to call him back because he wasn't sure of his strength to resist.

MARGARET WIPED DUST from her tongue. She couldn't believe she was still crouching here under the wagon. For more years than she could count she had taken care of herself. She wasn't some squealing miss who ran at the first sign of gunfire. The sooner that bear of a man learned that, the better.

She rolled out from under the wagon as shots rang out again, followed by the sound of men's voices.

Daniel materialized in front of her. "Stay still." He stared down the street. "I think it's safe now."

He gripped her arm and helped her up as though she were a delicate miss dressed in a fine silk dress. Margaret dusted off her skirt and tried to think of something to say to put him in his place. He ignored her as he stared down the street. Several men ran out of the bank, with the bank president, Orville Parker, bringing up the rear.

Orville's cravat was awry, and his black hair stood up in spikes. "Help! We've been robbed!" He waved his arms. "Come on, all of you, we have to catch them."

The sheriff, freeing his revolver from his holster as he ran, came rushing from the other side of town. "I need all the men who can ride and shoot. We might be able to catch them."

Margaret turned to stare at Daniel, but he just stood there placidly as men all around him grabbed horses and guns. She narrowed her eyes at him.

Then Daniel nodded at her pa. "I reckon I'd best ask your leave to join the posse."

Her pa shook his head. "They have enough men, and we need to be getting back to the ranch."

Margaret eyed the relief on Daniel's face. He must be a coward in spite of his hefty size. Why else would he not want to join the chase? If she were a man, she would have been the first one to volunteer. She turned abruptly and began to clamber onto the seat of the wagon, but before she could climb up, Daniel's large hands spanned her waist and lifted her as though she weighed no more than a feather duster.

Margaret jerked away from his grip and would have tumbled to the street except for his steadying hands. "I've been climbing in and out of this wagon for years by myself," she snapped. "I don't need your help."

"Just being mannerly, miss." Curls had escaped Daniel's hat and lay plastered against his broad forehead.

The mirth in his dark eyes set her teeth on edge. She would see him fired and gone from her property if it was the last thing she did. She didn't want him laughing at her every day. Snide smiles behind her back were something with which she was quite familiar, and she didn't need any more of it from the *foreman*.

"Margaret, quit fooling around. We need to get on the road." Her father climbed up beside her. When Daniel settled next to him, his bulk caused the springs of the wagon to groan.

Her father's voice held a trace of petulance, and she knew he was tired and needed to rest. It was selfish of her to make more trouble. She settled herself on the seat and leaned forward to grab the reins, but before she could seize them, Daniel had them in his large fists.

"Giddup." He slapped the reins against the backs of the horses, and the wagon lurched forward.

Caught off guard, Margaret nearly tumbled into the back of the wagon with the feed sacks. She scowled at Daniel, but he didn't seem to notice. Gripping the side of the wagon, she pressed her lips tightly together.

She glanced back at Calvin and saw him glaring at the back of Daniel's head. At least someone else was hankering to get rid of the man. Daniel clearly thought he was the biggest toad in the puddle, but Margaret would soon set him to rights.

TWO

❧

Several shacks were scattered round the small clearing where Charlie Cutler poked at the fire, but most of them were empty at this time of day. The gang had scattered to various perches to watch for the posse. Sparks flared into the air and a bit of ash floated aimlessly in the wind. He'd been like that ash with no purpose. But no more. He finally belonged.

He heard a step behind him and turned to see Golda Munster coming toward him. She had turned every head in camp, and no wonder. Charlie had never seen skin so fair and smooth or lips so full and red. He couldn't take his eyes off her, and neither could the other men. She was ten years older than he was, but he didn't care. Her silky blond hair and big blue eyes mesmerized him.

She lifted her blue skirt clear of the mud puddles. A scowl marred her beautiful face. She scowled more often than not. About the only time Charlie had seen her smile was when she was flirting with someone, but it only added to his fascination. Probably most of the gang longed to bring a smile to her face, to see her white teeth gleaming behind painted red lips.

She settled on a log one of the men had dragged close to the fire. The hem of her skirt was thick with red dirt. "Anything to eat?"

He grabbed a rag and lifted the skillet from the fire. "Got some flapjacks."

She grimaced. "I'm tired of such paltry fare. I'd love a thick beefsteak or poached fish. Just because we're in camp doesn't mean we shouldn't fill our bellies with decent food. I was at the mercantile before the bank robbery, and things were pretty plain there too. Typical of a wide spot in the road like this." Lifting the lid, she sniffed at the aroma, then wrinkled her nose again. "Who made these?"

"Your brother."

She shrugged and grabbed a tin plate, then forked a flapjack onto it. Charlie watched her take dainty bites. He could watch her for hours, her movements, her expressions. She always left him tongue-tied, but he was here because of her.

"I remember the first time I ever saw you," he blurted out. His face burned when she lifted a brow and smiled. "I mean, who wouldn't. You sauntered onto the porch looking for Daniel, and I told Pa you were the prettiest thing to ever wear a boot. You and your family had just moved in down the road. I was about twelve, I think."

Her small white teeth gleamed as she leaned forward. "Do tell me more, Charlie." Her sly expression said she knew she was fascinating.

"You never noticed me, since I was a kid, but I'm grown now. I'm a better man than Daniel. And I'd never leave you like he did. I'd follow you anywhere, Golda."

She didn't need to know he had nothing at home to draw him back, not like Daniel. Once Mama was gone, there was nothing holding him in that lonely mansion where he'd been nothing more than a lackey to a demanding father.

Golda sighed, clearly bored. "I saw your brother today."

He straightened. "Where?"

"In town. He about had a conniption that we hit the bank before he got set up."

Charlie leaped to his feet. "He's rejoined the gang? You're joshing me."

Daniel had disappeared for over a year, and Charlie hadn't heard from him. Charlie assumed something had happened with Golda, and Daniel had gone slinking back to Austin to their father. Otherwise, Daniel wouldn't have left her.

"Of course he has. He can't stay away from me."

If his brother were here, Charlie would have leaped on him and pummeled him. This was *his* place now. Daniel had no right to come back here. It was all Charlie could do to stand there with his plate in his hands.

Golda finished her meal and dropped the plate onto the ground. "I thought I heard a ruckus out here earlier."

Those big blue eyes on him drove all thought from Charlie's head, and he struggled to remember the fracas. "You did. Hugh rode in to tell us the posse had all the main roads covered. We're safe here, though. It's pretty hidden."

She rose and touched his shoulder as she sauntered back to the cabin and went inside. Charlie's shoulders sagged. She was always doing that. Small pats and caresses that kept him from leaving even though he knew he had no future with her. It was as if she could read his mind.

A horse neighed nearby and he glanced to the grove of trees to his right. Sunlight hit the clearing, and Richard dismounted from his horse.

Richard tipped his hat back with a thick forefinger, revealing a thick thatch of gray hair. "You hear how much the haul was today?"

"Not enough. Frank was pretty grim. Where were you?"

Richard shrugged. "Frank got a little high on his horse and moved before I arrived. Saw your brother, though, and got a message for you."

"There's nothing Daniel has to say that I want to hear." Charlie started back to the campfire, but Richard grabbed his arm.

"You're acting like a fool," the older man said, curling his lip. "Now shut up and listen. Daniel wants to meet you before he rejoins the gang."

"No." Charlie jerked his arm away, but Richard blocked his path. "I'm not a kid he can order around. I make my own decisions."

"Don't get all huffy. He just wants to talk."

Charlie gritted his teeth. "There's nothing he can say that I haven't already heard." Richard didn't reply, so Charlie shrugged, an idea beginning to form. "I'll see him, I guess. When and where?"

"Friday night. At the river ford."

"I'll be there. What are you going to do? Does Frank know you're here?"

"Not yet. I'm going to see him now." Richard's sharp gaze pierced him.

"He's liable to shoot you for not showing up when you were supposed to."

"And I suppose you'd be glad of it? It would leave the way clear for you with Golda."

Richard was Golda's second choice, the man she flirted with when Daniel wasn't around. Charlie looked down. "I don't want you hurt. When are you going to see Frank?"

"Tonight. I'll be back later."

"What about Daniel? When's he going to show his face? I think Frank's been watching to make sure neither of you double-cross him."

"I'll let him tell you about his plans when you meet him in two days. I'm just the messenger."

Richard mounted his horse and wheeled away. Maybe Charlie would just settle Daniel's hash when he saw him. Get him out of his hair once and for all. As Charlie went around the bend of the trail, the door to the cabin opened and Golda stepped back outside. She beckoned to him and he was glad to answer.

SHE WAS A mighty prickly woman, this Margaret O'Brien. Daniel glanced at her from the corner of his eye, then stared straight ahead. Fine figure of a woman, though. She'd give some lucky man sons and daughters worth having if they had her fire and determination. Her red hair and green eyes betrayed her spirit and passion for life. She had no use for him, though, and Daniel couldn't say he blamed her. He wouldn't cotton to someone waltzing in and taking over a job he had all picked out for himself either.

But he had a purpose for being here, and not even a woman like the rancher's daughter would distract him from it. His mission was too important. He'd just been glad Charlie wasn't among the robbers who rushed past him.

Paddy O'Brien pointed out the lane to the ranch, and Daniel turned the horses down it. From here the rolling meadows of Triple T Ranch spread before him. Lush grass for the cattle intermingled with rugged red buttes under the blue skies. The beauty of the place tugged at Daniel's heart, almost as though he were coming home, although that was ridiculous. He'd never been in this part of Texas. But this Red River Valley was beautiful, no doubt about that. He thought he'd heard a song about it once, but he couldn't remember the words.

The ranch house and outbuildings came into view. A low, stuccoed home crouched beneath two cottonwood trees. Several barns and corrals surrounded the home, and he could see herds of longhorns grazing on the hills around the ranch.

"Mighty pretty place," he told Paddy.

Paddy was a big man, though age had stooped his shoulders and shriveled his skin, and he lifted his head high, clearly pleased by the compliment to his life's work. And rightly so. The Triple T spread out before them in all its bustling glory.

Daniel cast another glance at Margaret. A smattering of freckles shimmered on her nose, and her chiseled face with its high cheekbones gave her a regal bearing as she glanced around the Triple T. He didn't doubt she had helped make the ranch a success and had earned that look of proud ownership.

Her hair was bound in a thick red braid nearly as big around as her wrist. What would it look like released from the confines of the braid, gleaming in the sunshine? Like red fire, most likely. He dragged his thoughts away from the intriguing woman and pulled the team to a halt. His job didn't entail casting longing eyes at Margaret O'Brien.

"Margaret, show Daniel to his quarters," Paddy said.

Margaret didn't look at him. She jabbed a finger at the bunkhouse behind the house. "It's in there."

"Margaret," her father said in a warning tone.

Her lips compressed, Margaret wheeled around, and her braid

flipped Daniel in the face. Her hair left the faint scent of mint in its wake. He suppressed a grin as he followed her across the yard. Her stiff back proclaimed her outrage, but she didn't say anything. Daniel was sorry for that. He would have liked to listen to her voice some more. Low and throaty. It reminded him of wind in the trees back home.

She shoved open the door to the bunkhouse and stepped inside. Daniel followed her. It took a moment for his eyes to adjust from the bright sunshine to the dim coolness of the room. The large room was utilitarian with bunks along the walls. The floor was rough wood and scratched from years of boot heels. Dishes overflowed the dry sink. He'd been in many rooms like this one.

Margaret stepped to a door on the left side and opened it. "This is the foreman's room. It's got a private entrance off the back of the bunkhouse to the privy."

He peered past her at the small room, furnished with a metal cot with a sagging mattress, one battered chair, and a dresser that held a porcelain pitcher and bowl. "Looks comfortable." He dropped his satchel on the floor and shut the door behind him.

She backed away from him, but Daniel reached out and held her arm. "I'm not a threat to you, Margaret."

She jerked her arm from his grip. "It's *Miss* O'Brien."

He pocketed his hands and nodded. "Miss O'Brien, then. From what I can see, this is a pretty big spread and you can use the help. I'm not sure how I managed to get your back up, but can we call a truce?"

Color bloomed along her cheeks, and she narrowed her eyes. "I would have thought my father would have taken one look at you and realized the person he needed to be wary of was you. You may have fooled my father, Mr. Cutler, but you didn't fool me for a minute."

"What burr do you have under your saddle about me? You don't know me yet."

She waved in his direction. "Look at you, with your fancy pants and shirt. No self-respecting foreman would think of wearing a shirt like that. The thorns and briars would puncture your skin right through those clothes. And those boots look like you just bought them before you boarded the stagecoach. You're no brushpopper, that's for sure."

Daniel glanced down. She wasn't far wrong. He had bought them just for this job. "So you don't like my new duds? I'd of thought a pretty women like you would be agreeable to a man getting gussied up for a new job."

Astute woman. He'd have to be on his guard that she didn't figure out why he was here. He'd grown up in Austin and had learned finer ways. It astonished him that she'd seen a polish he thought the gang had knocked off him.

She leaned closer. "Your manner is way too cocky and your hair is much too stylish for ranch work. In short, Mr. Cutler, you don't belong here. And I don't want my pa to get dependent on a city man like you. You'll only let us down when the going gets tough."

She would make a good detective. Daniel reached out and touched her cheek. She flinched but held her ground. He grinned at her glare.

"You'll kindly keep your hands to yourself!" She wheeled around to leave but Daniel caught her in his arms.

She stared up at him, her eyes wide with alarm. Her skin was warm as sunshine and smelled spicy, as though she'd rubbed something on it. The moment stretched out and he saw an answering flicker of awareness in her eyes. She caught her breath and struggled to get away.

He instantly released her and she scrambled back. Her green eyes snapped with anger. She drew back her hand to slap him, and he caught the blow in midair. But he wasn't expecting an attack from another quarter. Margaret kicked him in the shin, and he bent over double with the pain.

"Yee-ouch." He rubbed his shin. "It was only a touch, Miss O'Brien, not an attack on your person."

Her chest heaved and her eyes glimmered. "You are despicable! Are you in the habit of accosting women who find you repugnant? I am a believer, Mr. Cutler, a Christian woman. My—my caresses will be saved for the man who will one day respect me enough to marry me. They are not to be bandied about like currency on the open market."

Daniel felt like a heel when he saw tears sparkling on her lashes. And for the first time in his life, he thought that marriage might not be such a bad proposition with the right wife. Someone with fire and passion like Margaret O'Brien.

He reached toward her to reassure her that his intentions were honorable, but she flinched and ran from the bunkhouse. Great. She would probably tell her father that he'd manhandled her, and he would lose his job before it started. He squared his shoulders. He had to stop that from happening. Too much depended on this central location.

He rushed after her, but her tall form wasn't running for the safety of the house and her father. She was hurrying toward an orchard grove behind the barn. She disappeared into the trees and he followed. He found her facedown on the grass, her shoulders heaving with her sobs.

Daniel knelt beside her and hesitantly touched her shoulder. She buried her head farther into her arms. "Go away."

He drew his hand away. "I'm sorry, Miss O'Brien. I was way out of line." He waited to see if she would respond to his gentle tone.

She gulped and scrubbed at her face. "Go away," she said again. This time her voice was resigned and full of sadness.

Daniel didn't understand why one touch should have produced this reaction. He reached to pat her shoulder, but she quickly sat up and shrugged away his hand.

"Don't touch me." Her face was red and blotchy from weeping.

Daniel fished a handkerchief out of his pocket and handed it to her. "I'm sorry, Miss O'Brien. Truly. I don't know what got into me. All I can say is you're a beautiful woman, and I've wanted to touch you from the first minute I laid eyes on you. It won't happen again, I promise."

The color ran from her face, and she stared at him as though he'd just grown horns. "Don't mock me, Mr. Cutler," she whispered.

He frowned at her. "I wasn't mocking you. And if no one has ever told you that you're beautiful, then I have to wonder about the men in this valley." He rose and brushed the twigs from his trousers. "But believe me, I would rather hug a polecat than you after that display of female hysteria. You can be sure it won't happen again."

The color came back into her pale face and she rose to face him. "It certainly won't happen again. I understand now the type of man you are, and I won't let my guard down again."

"I suppose you'll go running to your father. You're not woman enough to face your problems on your own."

Her eyes flashed and she tilted her chin. "If I were going to tattle to my father, I would have gone to him at once. You're not a problem, Mr. Cutler. You're no more important than a rogue bull that has to be put down. I can handle you with one arm behind my back."

For one crazy moment, Daniel was tempted to show her that he wasn't to be underestimated, but sense reasserted itself and he politely stepped away from her. "We shall see, Miss O'Brien, we shall see."

He felt a stab of satisfaction at the way her cheeks colored and her eyes darkened with trepidation. Her emotions showed so readily in her face. She had translucent skin that colored easily, and it would be tempting to spend his time provoking a reaction out of her. She was a match for him in more ways than one.

THREE

Cattle dotted the rolling acres under the blue bowl of sky as far as the eye could see. Margaret sat on the porch step with a bowl of peas she was shelling in her lap for supper. She looked up now and then to admire the sights.

Every time she took a moment to look around the ranch, she was struck anew with its beauty. The ranch house nestled in the valley where it sat surrounded by barns, corrals, and a garden. A well-tended, prosperous holding she had been instrumental in making successful. The rosebushes she'd planted several weeks back had taken hold at the base of the low porch that ran the length of the house, and she caught a whiff of their sweet blossoms. *Hers.* This place was hers.

She touched her cheek where Daniel had touched it. *Beautiful.* Though she'd heard no mockery in his voice when he said the word, there had to be some reason for his lies. What was he doing here with his city clothes and ways?

A horse neighed and she looked up to see a wagon lumbering up the rutted track. It stopped in front of the house. She squinted in the sun as a familiar figure climbed down from the wagon. She smiled at the sight. "Lewis, I wasn't expecting you." She turned to the open window. "Pa, Lewis is here."

She and Lewis were close to the same age, and he'd always been more like a brother than a cousin. His father had died when he was fifteen, and he often spent summers with them. He was about two inches taller than her with brown hair that curled over his collar. His slim stature masked the strength in his muscles. She'd seen him rope a bull and bring the animal to its knees in an instant.

She put down the bowl of peas and rushed to meet him as he came toward her. "What are you doing here?"

He swung her into a hug that lifted her feet off the ground, no small feat with her height. "I missed you too much to stay away."

When he set her feet back down, she tucked her hand into his arm. "How long can you stay?"

His eyebrow lifted. "Permanently. Uncle Paddy didn't tell you?"

Something about his manner made her stop and look up at him. "Tell me what?"

Lewis's hazel eyes were troubled. "I think you'd better talk to your dad. I thought you knew . . ." He bit his lip and looked toward the house as the screen door opened.

Her father let the door slam behind him as he hurried to join them. He clapped Lewis on the shoulder. "Good to see you, boy. You made excellent time."

She didn't like the way her father wouldn't look at her. His face was red too, like a little boy caught in a misdemeanor. "Pa, Lewis says he's staying permanently. What's this all about?"

"Now, Margaret, don't go getting your britches twisted. The ranch needs a male hand. It's only proper that he has a stake in the ranch. My pa would have wanted me to do right by Ray's boy." Her pa's voice was full of bluster.

Uncle Ray had died before Grandpa, so the ranch had passed to her father. If Ray had lived, the ranch would have been split between the two men, and Lewis would have inherited when his father died. What her father proposed was fair.

"I'm not disagreeing with that, Pa. But why am I just now hearing about this? You could have talked it over with me."

"We're discussing it now, aren't we? You run on in and put on some coffee. We can finish talking about it in the parlor. I'm sure Lewis is mighty thirsty. We got any of that ham left from dinner last night? It's a spell until supper, and I'm sure the stagecoach ride left him hungry."

"There's some in the icebox. I'll make sandwiches." She'd been dismissed like she was the housekeeper. Now that her pa had a man on the ranch and a new foreman, did he plan to relegate her to the kitchen? She wasn't about to allow that. She hurried to the icebox and prepared the coffee and food.

When she came into the parlor, both men went silent. What was going on? It seemed like more than just bringing Lewis in to share the ranch. She was fine with that—as long as she wasn't made to feel like an employee. Lewis took a sandwich and a cup of coffee and so did her father. She set the tray on a table and sank onto the sofa beside her cousin. Her throat was too tight to think of swallowing anything.

Her father cleared his throat. "It's like this, Margaret. It's time you settled down and got married. If you keep on the way you have, no man in the valley will be interested. Running the ranch, wearing men's dungarees—it's not suitable. I'm thinking about sending you off to finishing school."

She gaped. "You'll do no such thing, Pa! I'd go live with Aunt Agnes first."

Her father pointed a finger at her. "Look at yourself, daughter. You're dressed like a man. Your hair is hanging down your back like a hooligan. Those boots belonged to Lewis once, didn't they?"

She stared at the tips of the boots peeking from under the dusty britches. "It's practical, Pa. I can hardly round up cattle in a skirt."

"Exactly my point. I want you to start acting like a lady. Start wearing pretty clothes. I want some grandchildren to dandle on my knee."

The muscles in her jaw ached from clenching it. She swallowed and focused on relaxing. Her father was never swayed by shouting and anger. Even though he blustered about getting his way, he usually gave in to her.

"I want that too. But, Pa, look at me. Men want a dainty woman who looks good pouring tea in the parlor. I'm taller than most men I know. I'm not going to find a husband."

"That's not true," Lewis said. "Any man would be proud to call you his wife, Margaret. You'll be a real asset to any ranch. Look at that garden out there. You're growing enough food to feed an army. You've done a stellar job running this place. I think you're beautiful."

She smiled at his defense. "The most I can bring to a marriage is hard work."

Her father waved his hand in the air. "Having Lewis and Cutler here will give you a break so you can work on more womanly pursuits."

There was going to be no dissuading him this time. She'd

never seen her father look so determined. No matter. While she loved Lewis, he was no ranch hand. And Daniel Cutler wouldn't last long either. She'd still be here when they were both long gone.

DANIEL HADN'T MISSED the tension at dinner. He'd listened to Margaret and Lewis talk about ranch work and family, but he caught her staring at her hands several times. She'd changed into a skirt for dinner and her hair was down. It was just as pretty in the lamplight as he'd imagined.

After dinner the cook gathered the dishes to wash. Margaret grabbed a jacket and slipped out the back door. Lewis didn't seem to notice, so Daniel followed her. He watched her approach the corral. A sorrel horse trotted toward her. She propped one boot on the lower rung of the fence, then dug into her pocket and offered something to the horse. Her husky voice was a soothing murmur as she petted the horse's nose.

"Nice horse," he said, stopping five feet behind her.

She jumped but didn't turn around. "This is Archie. I raised him. His mother died when he was born."

"He's your baby."

"He is." Her boot came off the fence rail and she turned to face him. "What do you want? I'll give you your orders tomorrow—if you're still around. I have no idea why Pa even hired you since he brought Lewis out too."

Her gibe didn't bother him. She'd had a lot thrown at her today. He stepped nearer. "You seemed upset at supper. You don't want your cousin here?"

"This is none of your business." Her voice was cold.

"No, it's not. I'm new here and trying to get my bearings, figure out who my boss is."

She lifted her chin. "*I'm* your boss."

"I got that part already." He couldn't keep the amusement from his voice. It had to be hard for a competent woman like her to feel like her father didn't appreciate her work.

The stars were brilliant in the dark sky, sparkling like droplets of the purest water. "Look!" He took her shoulders and turned her to face the western horizon. "It's the first glimpse of the young moon. It usually happens about twenty-four hours after the new moon."

"I can just barely see the outline," she said. "What's a young moon? I've heard of a new moon but never a young one."

She stood in front of him and her hair brushed his chin. The hint of mint in the air came again. When he'd first met her, he wouldn't have guessed she put anything scented in her hair. His hands were still on her shoulders, and he was in no hurry to let loose.

He dipped his head to inhale another whiff of her. "It's just after a new moon when there is a sliver beginning to show. You have to look hard for it." He pointed. "Did you know that a new moon is thought to be the best time for courtship?"

She jerked away and stepped out of his reach. "You overheard my father?"

"He wants you to get married." It didn't take a professor to guess why her father had hired him and asked his nephew to come help out at the ranch.

She turned back to pet the horse. "I'm happy like I am. I don't need another man finding fault with me."

"You have a lot to be proud of, that's for sure. The ranch looks as fine as cream gravy."

The tension in her outline seemed to ease. She moved her hand over Archie's nose in a soothing caress. "I had an older brother who was killed in the Indian Wars. I was fifteen when he died, so I stepped in and took over."

"Losing someone can change a person." Like it had changed him. Remembering the things he'd done in his life made him cringe. And the things he'd failed to do were even worse.

She stared at him. "You say that like you've lost someone you loved. A wife?"

He didn't smile. "No, I've never been married. My mother died five years ago, and it was my fault. She asked me to take her to the doctor, but I was too busy with my own life. It would have messed up a big deal for me. I told her I'd take her the next day if she still didn't feel well. She died that night." He didn't try to hide his self-disgust as he held her gaze.

"I'm sorry."

"I don't usually talk about it." Strange that he'd told her. "But about the ranch . . ."

Her chin jutted out. "Pa turned things over to me ten years ago. I've done a fine job. A *fine* job."

She sure was pretty standing there with her hands on her hips as if daring him to find one thing wrong with the job she'd done. He dipped his head. "I'm not disagreeing with that. But some things are more important to a man than money."

"Like what?"

He wished he could comfort her. "Like grandchildren and a legacy. I think your pa is feeling his age and wanting to make sure things continue here."

She backed away until she was leaning against the fence again. Archie nuzzled her neck. "I don't know what to do." Her voice was a whisper as though she spoke to herself.

"What do *you* want? We've been talking about what your pa wants. I'd guess you want to run the ranch yourself." The wind ruffled her thick curls.

She turned and patted her horse's nose. "Of course I want to run it. It's what I do. I take pride in seeing the cattle fat and content. I make sure the barns are in good repair and our workers are taken care of."

"In other words, what you do matters."

Her eyes glimmered in the starlight. "I reckon that's what I mean."

"So your cousin is going to take charge now?"

"No!" Her hair swung as she shook her head violently. "Well, to be honest, I'm not sure what Pa has in mind. He wants to make sure Lewis shares in the ranch somehow. That's all he told me."

"You think he'll split up the ranch?"

"He's worked his whole life to make it bigger. I can't see him splitting it up. But Pa has me flummoxed." Her gaze was fixed on him. "Why am I talking to you? You're not going to be here long, and this isn't your business."

"What makes you think I'm not going to be here long?"

"It's clear you're no ranch hand. What are you *really* doing here, Mr. Cutler?"

"Call me Daniel." When she didn't smile, he shrugged. "I needed a job, Margaret."

"*Miss* O'Brien." She took his hand and turned it over. "The only calluses you have are from reins. These hands haven't held a rope or a branding iron. At least not recently."

He tried not to put too much stock in the fact that she'd touched him. "I'll prove myself to you."

She dropped his hand. "There are lots of jobs more suited to your soft hands. Why here?"

"The ad sounded intriguing. A big ranch, room to roam." He could see he wasn't making any headway with her. "I reckon I'll head to the bunkhouse and unpack." He tipped his hat. "See you tomorrow, Margaret."

"Miss O'Brien," she called after him.

FOUR

Margaret reined in her horse and wiped her face with her bandana. The sun beat down from the blue bowl of sky above her. Her gaze strayed to Daniel in the valley below as he herded the cattle. Margaret longed to probe beneath the surface and discover the new foreman's secrets. And secrets there were, she was sure, but over the past couple of days, she couldn't figure out anything new about him.

She didn't know which was worse—to think about the way the new foreman had touched her or to know it wouldn't happen again. She hated him, but in spite of herself, he intrigued her. His apology had been sincere, but his assertion that she was beautiful had left her confused about his intentions. And the way he'd talked to her last night at the barn—like he really knew her and cared. Was what he said about his mother even true, or was it designed to gain her sympathy?

And in spite of his poor choice of clothes, he was no slacker. His broad shoulders easily muscled their way into milling cattle, and he wielded a hammer with authority as he tackled the barn repairs. But she still had a sense that this was not his usual line of work. His smooth-edged veneer hinted he would be more comfortable in a fine hotel than the rustic bunkhouse he now called home.

Oh, he was comfortable on a horse, but he didn't ride like a cowboy. She couldn't put her finger on what the difference was, but it plagued her just the same, and she feared he was some sort of chiseler. Eventually she would discover where he came from and what he was doing here. Lewis had joined them, but he'd been working on the other side of the pasture, and she had only caught glimpses of him.

Calvin rode up to her and pushed his hat to the back of his head. "Can I talk to you, Miss Margaret?"

She twisted in the saddle. "You're upset about Daniel. I am too. Don't worry, Calvin. I doubt he'll be here long."

"Your pa had no call to bring him in here. And Lewis. He ain't treatin' you right." His voice was fervent.

It wasn't the first time she'd seen something in Calvin's eyes, something that made her wary. She thought he had designs on the ranch and thought to get it by wooing her at some point. And he wasn't a bad-looking man. He was in his early thirties, and his sandy hair and blue eyes held some appeal to her, but she didn't care for the way he bullied the other men. No man would bully *her* like that.

She shook her head. "I'll handle my pa. Is that all?"

He leaned close enough that Margaret could smell his sweat. "If you need me to take Cutler down a notch or two, you just let me know. Your pa might need a talkin'-to as well."

She tensed and eyed his intent gaze. He wasn't dangerous, was he? Could he have had something to do with the attack on her father? "Thank you. I'll keep it in mind." She wheeled Archie around and cantered toward the milling cattle.

She mulled over Calvin's words as she worked with the men cutting out cattle, then finally dismissed her unease. He was just trying to get on her good side.

Dehorning was a job she hated, but it had to be done. The red dust coated her clothing and parched her throat. The cattle bawled and thrashed as they were divested of their horns, and she felt half sick by the time it was over. Her head thumped like a Comanche drum. Daniel had worked alongside her without a complaint, taking the brunt of the wrestling of the cattle. And she had to admit she'd been glad for his help.

"Calling it quits?" he asked when she took her hat off and used it to fan her hot face.

For some reason the question made her decide not to go inside like she'd planned. With all the men watching, she couldn't let it get back to Pa that she'd quit on the job like some greenhorn fresh off the stage from New York.

She raised her chin and shook her head. "Just taking a break."

"You look tired," Daniel observed. "We can finish up here. Inez will be ringing the supper bell any minute."

"I'll stay until the work is done." She slapped the dust from her hat, then tossed her braid over her shoulder and put her hat back on her head. He could keep his sympathetic glances to himself. Born and bred to this life, she could outwork him any day. He was a city man, and she would do well to remember that. He'd soon tire of this life and go back to the bright lights.

"Anyone ever mention you're as stubborn as a mule?"

"I get the work done," she snapped. Her headache thumped again, and she was afraid she was going to be sick right on Daniel's boots. His face wavered before her eyes, and she swallowed. Swaying, she put a hand to her head, and a small groan escaped her clenched throat.

His fingers gripped her arm, and he propelled her toward the house. "You'd best get out of this sun."

Margaret protested feebly, but she knew she was finished. Humiliation added to the sick feeling in the pit of her stomach. What must he think of her? He'd likely use this to secure his position with Pa, more proof that she was too weak to be running the ranch.

Daniel opened the front door and ushered her inside. The cool darkness of the house welcomed her like a soothing balm. At least the bright sun no longer stabbed like knives behind her eyes. She sank into the rocker by the fireplace and leaned forward with her face in her hands. She hated feeling so weak and—and vaporish. The next thing she knew, she'd be fainting or fanning herself with an ostrich-feather fan. The thought stiffened her spine, and she raised her head.

Daniel was regarding her with sympathetic eyes, and the kindness in his gaze nearly brought tears to her eyes. Even Pa never looked at her that way, as though he wished he could take her pain away. Pa had no patience for womanly weakness, and she tried never to allow any hint of weariness or sickness to show to him.

"Want a cold rag? My sister swears it helps." Daniel looked determined. "Where would I find some cloth?"

Margaret directed him to the buffet that held the linens, and he soon returned with two wet compresses. He nudged her braid out of the way and pressed a cold cloth to the back of her head, then handed her another. "Put that one on your forehead."

She did as he asked, and the relief was immediate as the pounding eased a bit. "Thanks," she whispered.

"Go lie down. I'll handle the rest of the dehorning."

She wanted to protest, but she still felt too wobbly to object. As she went down the hallway to her room, she heard the front door shut behind him. The window in her bedroom was open, and she lay on the bed with a breeze wafting across her. Daniel's voice drifted through the open window.

"What did you find out?" he asked.

At least that's what she thought he said. She got up and moved closer to the window as she struggled to make out the words.

Another voice answered, one Margaret didn't recognize. "Charlie agreed to meet with you. Friday night at the river ford. Midnight. He's probably having to help stash the loot somewhere. The posse from Clarendon is still on their trail."

"Frank made a fatal error. He was supposed to wait for my report. Now the law in three counties is looking for him."

She put a hand to her mouth. They were talking about the bank robbers. There had been a rash of robberies lately, everything from banks to stagecoaches. That explained why Daniel hadn't wanted to join the posse the other day. He was one of them.

She squeezed her eyes at the sharp disappointment. No wonder he'd made up to her—he wanted to allay any suspicions she had. His sweet words and flirtatious ways hid the heart of a criminal. The disappointment she felt in Daniel surprised her. Why should she feel hurt? She'd known all along he wasn't what he seemed. But she hadn't expected something like this.

She had to tell Pa. Pain stabbed her head when she moved toward the door, and she went back to her bed with a groan and grabbed the wet cloths. Nothing was going to happen for a few days. Maybe she'd better find out more information before she involved her father in the mess. He was likely to go straight to Daniel and tip their hand. He trusted Daniel already. It would be best to ferret out the truth herself. When she knew enough, she could go for the sheriff.

She closed her eyes and willed the headache to go away. There was too much to do to take time for this weakness, but her body didn't seem to want to cooperate. She napped fitfully until the supper bell rang. When she sat up, she discovered the pain in her head had subsided to a dull ache, and she felt full of purpose. Her disappointment was gone with the headache. This would prove she was right all along, that Pa had been taken in just as she'd thought.

She shook her hair loose from its braid and quickly plaited it again. The men were seated around the table by the time she got to supper, and the only place left to sit was beside Daniel. She slipped into the chair.

"Feeling better?" He scooped mashed potatoes on his plate, then handed her the bowl.

"Yes, thanks." She took the potatoes and deposited some on her own plate. Daniel fell silent as they passed the food around. How could she get him to open up? She needed proof, not just some overheard snippets of conversation. If she could foil a bank robbery attempt, vindication would be hers.

"Hey, did you hear there's going to be a barn dance Friday at the Stantons'?" Lewis asked. "Everyone is invited."

"We're all going." Margaret couldn't wait to spend more time with Lucy. The men began to joke and talk about seeing some of the single girls in the area, and her initial rush of happiness faded. It was always the same. No man thought first of her as a possible partner. Even as tall and conspicuous as she was, it was as if she were invisible. She was too much like one of the men to even be considered as an eligible wife. Why Pa thought she had a choice about marriage was beyond her.

Daniel said something, but she'd missed his words. "I beg your pardon." She turned toward him. "I must have been woolgathering."

Daniel's dark eyes probed her gaze. "I said I'd be proud to escort you, Miss Margaret, unless you already have a date."

"You got no call to be annoying Margaret like that."

"Hush, Calvin." Margaret sent him a quelling glance, and he ducked his head.

A refusal to Daniel's invitation hovered on her lips, but after a moment she forced herself to smile and nod. "I reckon I can put up with your company for one evening, Mr. Cutler." What better way to find out more? If she could get him to trust her enough to let down his guard, maybe she could gather the information she needed to go to the sheriff.

"Why are you so formal? I think we've gone way beyond that. My name's Daniel."

Margaret's face burned at how accurate his words were. He persisted in calling her Margaret when they were alone, but she wasn't about to trust him. And the last thing she wanted was to get closer to him now that she knew he was in cahoots with the bank robbers.

A moment of unease assailed her. What if he tried to shut her up—permanently? Bank robbers were desperate characters, and she would be alone with him on the drive to Lucy's. Maybe he would arrange an ambush that would ensure she didn't tell anyone her suspicions.

She gave herself a mental shake. Melodrama, that's what she was indulging in. Pure melodrama. Daniel wouldn't hurt her.

Everyone would know she was with him, and they would expect him to take care of her. She was perfectly safe.

Then why didn't she feel safe? He made her feel as though she were in danger every minute she spent in his company. It wasn't the physical danger that frightened her. Her thoughts were way too bound up in this man. His pleasant facade hid his true nature.

"Very well, Daniel," she said finally. It would be best not to give him any reason for suspicion. She would be courteous and lull him into a false sense of security. But why did she feel so bad about the thought, so dishonest? Pushing away the feelings of guilt, she turned her attention to her supper.

FIVE

Dust motes danced in the shaft of sunlight from the open doors. Daniel tossed another pitchfork full of fresh hay for the horses in the barn. The scent of hay was strong inside the building. He'd been here just a few days but the place already felt too much like home. And he wasn't staying that long.

Paddy hung the bridle on the wall and smiled. "You're doing a fine job, Daniel. I know my daughter got a little het up about your arrival, but she'll get used to you soon. She's a little high-strung." He took off the red handkerchief around his neck and wiped his brow.

Daniel leaned on his pitchfork and wiped his brow. "You're lucky to have her. She's done well here."

"Oh, no doubt, no doubt." Paddy studied Daniel's face. "But things are going to change around here. Margaret won't cotton to the changes much."

"What kind of changes?"

"I'm leaving my ranch to Lewis."

Daniel straightened. "You cut Margaret out of the will?" It was none of his business, but he wanted to object most mightily.

Paddy grabbed a pitchfork and threw hay to the horses. "I'll settle a sum of money on her when she marries."

Daniel went back to throwing hay as well. "I reckon that's not the same thing. There's no mistaking how much she loves this spread. Have you told Margaret the full details of what you plan?"

"I will. When the time comes."

Daniel tossed a forkful of hay with more force than necessary. Margaret deserved better than this. "It's not right, Paddy. She's worked hard for you and this ranch. How do you think she's going to feel when you toss her aside for her cousin?"

"She should be relieved that she won't have the burden anymore."

"You know better than that. This ranch is her life. She loves it with all of her being."

Paddy's jaw had a truculent thrust. "It ain't right for a woman to be so focused on the ranch. She needs to be worrying about young'uns and her own home."

It all made no sense to Daniel. "Did Lewis talk you into this?"

Paddy's scowl darkened. "Of course not. Lewis tried to talk me into splitting the ranch into two." He snorted. "Like I'd chop up the place I've worked my whole life to build."

Exactly what Margaret had said. She knew Paddy would never piecemeal his ranch. But when she found out what her father was doing, the fireworks would light the entire county.

DANIEL WASN'T SURE what awakened him. He sat up and swung his feet to the floor. In his dream he thought Margaret had called for him. He was the last person she would ask for help. He went to the window and looked into the corral. Earlier today Paddy had penned up a pregnant cow. In the dim light of the moon, Daniel saw Paddy kneeling over the cow. It must be giving birth.

Should he go help? While he didn't know much about birthing cows, he could fetch whatever Paddy might need. After yanking on his jeans, he stepped into the yard as Margaret exited the house. Her braid reached nearly to her waist, and her bare feet peeked from under the hem of her robe.

She stepped toward the gate. "I can help Pa, if that's why you're up."

"Another pair of hands won't hurt."

He followed her to the corral. The cow lowed in distress, then a faint moan came. "Paddy?"

Margaret raced past him and yanked open the gate. "Pa!"

Lying on the ground, Paddy moaned again and tried to raise his head. "Somebody hit me."

The cow's legs thrashed near his head, and Daniel jumped forward to drag the older man out of harm's way. "Take care of him and the cow. I'm going to look for an intruder."

He stared at the shifting shadows around the barn and out-buildings. Was that someone under the oak tree? "Who's there?"

Vegetation rustled, and he ran toward the spot. If only he'd grabbed his gun. When he reached the perimeter of the stockyard, he found nothing but mashed-down grass. The best thing to do would be to wake the men and have them help him search.

He ran for the bunkhouse and roused the men. One bunk was conspicuously empty—Calvin's. The men lit lanterns and headed out to fan into the shadows and look for an intruder. Two men ran into the barn with their lanterns aloft. Daniel scoured the perimeter of the trees at the back of the yard. When he heard a shout, he turned.

One of the hands emerged from the barn yelling. "I tripped over a shovel and dropped my lantern. The barn's on fire!"

THE SCENT OF fire lingered in the small bedroom as Margaret adjusted her father's pillow. "You look terrible, Pa. There's a huge lump on your forehead and it's still bleeding." She tried to mask her anxiety with a smile.

"I trust you are finished haranguing me?" He jerked his arm away. "If the intruder didn't kill me, your fussing will."

She'd rarely been in his bedroom. Inez took care of cleaning, and his door was usually kept shut. It was smaller than she'd thought, barely twelve feet square. The only furnishings were his bed atop a faded blue rag rug, a battered chest of drawers, and a wooden chair. The whitewashed walls were dingy and bare. Not a very appealing room, but then, her mother had died so many years ago that the house had never had a feminine touch. She dragged the chair to his bedside and settled on it.

Her father lifted a brow. "What do you think you're doing? It's nearly ten, Margaret. Go to bed. I'm fine."

His gruffness made her eyes burn. "I'm going to stay with you tonight, Pa. Someone tried to kill you. What if he tries again?"

Her father's eyes softened. "I suspect it was a thief. He probably just hit me in his haste to get away."

"You nearly died. If he came into the yard, on our own property, he'd break into the house as well. I have to keep you safe."

"You're being melodramatic." He rolled to his side, facing her. "Go to bed. Having you staring at me all night will keep me awake."

She sighed and slumped against the back of the chair. "I'll go in a little while. Once you're asleep."

His eyes were heavy, and he suddenly looked old to her with his grizzled chin and gray hair. How old was he? Sixty? Growing up, she'd thought him the most wonderful person alive, next to her older brother, Stephen, of course. Pa seemed as strong and powerful as the Red River in flood stage, forcing his will and way on all of them. She suspected it was the only way he knew to show love. For all his bluster, he was a softie.

She studied the picture of her mother on his dresser. Margaret's life would have been so different if her mother had lived. She would have had a role model, a female to guide her. Lucy Stanton was her first real female friend.

She directed her attention back to her father. "The men are placing wagers on whether or not you'll split the ranch between us."

He snorted. "Ridiculous. You know better than that."

She nodded. "You spent your life building this place." She leaned forward. "I thought we could build Lewis a house of his own in the valley. For now, he might want to live in Grandpa's old cabin, but we could make something nicer. We'd be close enough to see it but not so close that we would annoy any wife he chose to bring here. We could work the ranch together. I don't think he'll have an issue with taking orders from me."

Her father's brows drew together. "You've got it all figured out, do you?"

He seemed a little defensive to Margaret. She smiled reassuringly. "It makes sense to do that. He wouldn't want to have a wife here in our house. She'd feel displaced. I'll make sure she feels welcome. Lewis too. You don't have to worry."

Her father sat up and fluffed his pillow. "You'll marry someday, Margaret. Your husband will provide a home for you. Then Lewis will have no qualms about bringing a wife here."

She exhaled and shook her head. "I'm never getting married. I'm nearly twenty-six, a spinster by any measure. I've never had a single beau."

"There was Nate."

Margaret laughed. "Lucy's man? Nate never courted me, Pa. We just assumed it would happen because it made sense to join our ranches. There was never anything between us."

"You were in favor," he reminded her.

"Because I didn't know any better. When I see the way he looks at Lucy, I know the difference now. And who is going to look at me like that?"

Her father lay back against the pillow with a sly grin. "Daniel seems to like you fine."

It was on the tip of her tongue to tell her father what she'd learned about his new foreman, but she bit back the words. No sense in riling Pa when he was recovering from such a shock. And she needed more information. She clamped her teeth together and shrugged.

"You've nothing to say about Daniel?"

"I don't think he'll be around long. And any interest he might be showing is not genuine. I suspect he sees the value of the ranch and covets it. Not me."

Her father stared at her. "You're not inheriting the ranch, Margaret."

Something squeezed in her chest. "You're not leaving me the ranch?" Her throat was almost too tight to force out the question.

He sat up and fussed with his pillow. "I'm leaving Lewis the ranch. I changed my will when I invited him to come."

Margaret shook her head to clear it. "I don't think I heard you right."

"I was perfectly plain. Running a ranch isn't a job for a woman. You've done well these past few years. But for the ranch to grow, it will need a man's hand. I've decided that man is Lewis. He even reminds me a bit of Stephen."

Margaret sprang to her feet. *I will not cry.* Tears were for the weak. "And what about me, Pa? I'm to stay on here as a poor relation?"

"Of course not. I'll settle a handsome sum on the man you'll marry."

"I'm not *getting* married!" She rushed to the door and slammed it behind her, then stood in the hallway with her back pressed against the wall. Her chest heaved and she swallowed back the sobs welling in her throat.

Castoff. It seemed she wasn't good enough no matter how hard she tried. But she would stop this. Somehow she would prove her worth.

SIX

The kitchen was dark as Margaret felt her way along the wall. She wore her nightgown and robe, and the wood floor was cool on her bare feet. She found the kerosene lamp and lit it. The warm glow brought no comfort. This would no longer be her kitchen, her home. Lewis would own it. The thought squeezed her chest. She was born in this house. Every nook and cranny was familiar to her. Every chip in the floor, every nick in the plaster.

She got out a pan and poured milk into it, then set it on the warmer at the back of the woodstove. When it was warm, she added cocoa and sugar. Maybe it would help her sleep. Right now she knew if she tried to curl up in her bed, she would lie there with her eyes open. There had to be something she could do or say to change her father's mind.

She carried her hot cocoa to the table and sat down. Cupping it in her hands, she inhaled the aroma and tried to think. Maybe she should take a look at the old homestead. She hadn't been there in years. If she could draft a plan that would allow Lewis his own place, maybe Pa would relent.

"Care to share?" Lewis stepped out of the shadows and came toward her. He was in his nightshirt and had bare feet. His hair stuck up on end.

A flood of emotions rose in her chest. Love, betrayal, admiration, despair. Lewis was as close as a brother. Did he despise her? She'd always thought he loved her like a sister. How could he do this to her?

"What's wrong?"

She set down her cup. "Pa told me. About leaving the ranch to you and not me." She hated the way her voice broke. She wanted to be calm and reasonable about it.

"Oh." He plopped down in the chair with his shoulders slumped. "That wasn't my doing, Margaret." He stared at her with earnest eyes as though he was willing her to believe him. "I tried to talk him out of it."

"I believe you. I've lived with his stubbornness."

He reached across the table and took her hand. "You'll always have a place with me, though."

She sighed and clung to his hand. At least she knew he loved her. "You and I both know I'm not getting married, Lewis. And I don't want to live with you. Would you be willing to let me have this house? You could build a bigger, nicer one for your wife. Or if you really want this one, maybe we could fix up the old homestead for me."

He withdrew his hand. "How about we share this one until that time comes? If I ever marry, we'll talk about it."

She ruminated on his words. There was much he wasn't saying. But like most men of her acquaintance, he assumed he knew what was best for the womenfolk in his life. "I'm happy to share with you. Pa is apt to change his mind again. It's not unheard of.

So shall we agree that whatever happens, we'll make sure the other one is part of the split?"

"Absolutely." He slipped his hand across the table again. "Deal?"

She grabbed his warm fingers and shook. "Deal."

He leaned back and grinned. "So, you're going to the dance with the new foreman. I thought you disliked him."

"I suspect he's not all he seems, Lewis. I overheard a disturbing conversation." She told him about her suspicions.

He lifted a brow. "I'm in a good position to keep an eye on him. Are you sure it's safe to go to the dance with him?"

"He's not going to hurt me. At least not in front of everyone."

"Well, I'll make sure to stay close to your side just in case."

She smiled at him over the top of her cup. "I'm not sorry Pa brought you back to us."

There was pain in his eyes. "I've never felt like I belonged much of anywhere. Now I do. I love you, you know. I would never do anything to hurt you. You're my family. The only family I have."

"I needed you as much as you needed me." She swallowed the last of her cocoa and stood. "We're getting maudlin."

"That we are." He grinned and rose. "Guess I'll go to bed. It's late. I have to round up strays in the back pasture in the morning."

"Is Daniel going with you?" She pumped water into the cups and rinsed them.

"Yes."

"Be careful. And see if he slips off to meet anyone during the day."

Lewis picked up his candlestick. "I will. You suspect he'll try to meet the rest of the gang?"

She washed their cups and turned them upside down to drain. "Someone named Charlie wanted to meet him Friday night."

"Are you sure you heard it all correctly?"

"The meeting is at midnight, but the dance might still be going on. That's why I wondered if he would have changed the time of the meeting. The river ford is not far from where you'll be tomorrow. It would make sense."

"I'll watch him. But what is he doing here if he's a bank robber? Have you figured that out yet?"

"Where better to hide than in plain sight at a respected rancher's spread? People will get to know him as the Triple T foreman. That carries some status."

His eyes were intense. "You're smart, Margaret. Smarter than most of us give you credit for."

His words warmed her and she curtsied. "Thank you, cousin."

"No wonder the ranch has thrived under your care. I think we are going to make the Triple T the best ranch in Texas."

She followed him out of the kitchen to the stairs. It might not be so bad to share things with Lewis. It was better than being alone.

HER FATHER WAS better in the morning, and he ordered Margaret not to work. To hear him talk, one would think it took a whole day to get ready for a silly dance. With nothing to do until time to get ready, she decided to ride to the old homestead to check it out.

She saddled Archie and mounted. Daniel saw her and frowned.

He jogged over to intercept her. "I hope you're not going anywhere alone. Not after what happened to your pa yesterday."

"I'm not going that far. I'll be fine. I have my rifle." She stared at him. "I haven't had a chance to thank you for organizing the fire brigade last night."

He inclined his head. "You're welcome. I'm just sorry we couldn't save the barn."

She nodded. "Well, I'd better get to work."

He grabbed her reins. "You're not going alone."

She jerked the leather from his hand. "I've had the run of this ranch since I could walk. Mind your own business. If I don't come back in a couple of hours, then you can worry." She dug her boot heels into Archie's flank and took off out of the yard at a canter. The nerve of the man. He had no right to tell her what to do. She resisted the impulse to look back and see if he was watching her ride away.

Once out of sight of the ranch, she slowed her horse to a walk and lifted her face to the breeze scented with sage and wildflowers. She needed this time alone, craved some space to absorb what had happened. Her life had been turned upside down in the space of two days. But her solitude was short-lived. She heard a shout and hoofbeats. Looking back, she saw Daniel riding toward her. Her first impulse was to try to outrun him, but it was futile. Someone would have told him how to find the cabin.

She turned her back on him and rode toward the original homestead, now only a hundred yards away. When she reached the hitching post, she dismounted and tied up Archie. "I won't be long, boy." She stepped onto the low porch. Some of the floorboards were rotted, and a wasp nest was high on the door. The yard was overgrown, and nothing was left of the garden where her grandmother had shown her how to grow roses. Not a hint of the sweet flower was left in the air.

She stepped back off the porch as Daniel arrived. "I told you

I didn't need any help." She ignored him and went around to the back.

He followed. "I'll just hang around and make sure no one else followed you here. I'll leave you alone."

His mere presence disturbed her, but she couldn't tell him without revealing that she had too much interest in him. And maybe she could learn more about him. If Lewis saw that Daniel had accompanied her, he would be concerned, but Daniel didn't scare her.

She said nothing and went to the back door. There was no wasp nest on this one, so she twisted the knob and pushed it open. The dank smell of disuse rushed to meet her, and she wrinkled her nose. Debris littered the floor. Dirt, pieces of old dishes, the remains of some furniture that had been left behind. She could see daylight through the roof over the dry sink.

"Kind of a mess."

She turned to see that Daniel had followed her inside. "I thought you were going to let me look around in peace."

"I was curious."

She glanced around at the rotted wood and peeling paint. "This place is a wreck. It'll take a lot of work to make it livable."

His dark eyes held compassion. "Your pa told you, didn't he? That's why you're looking here. You don't want to live at the ranch house after Lewis takes over. I told him it was wrong."

She let the words sink in. Daniel had dared her father's wrath on her behalf. Why? Did he only want to woo her if she was to inherit? "What did he say?"

Daniel grinned. "Pretty much what you'd expect. Basically told me to mind my business." He shoved his hands in his pockets and looked around. "Your grandparents lived here?"

She nodded. "My grandfather fought in the Texas Revolution

and was granted the land in 1835. He came here in 1850 and built this cabin with my grandmother. He was forty when they arrived. My parents came with them when my brother was small. I was born here. When I was ten, they built the big house and left this one. No one has lived here in eighteen years."

"When did your grandparents die?"

She led him into the small parlor. The old stove, blackened with soot, was in one corner. It had been so long since she'd been here. Nostalgia filled her. "My grandmother died before Grandpa. She fell into the river at flood stage and drowned. My uncle died in a—an altercation. Grandpa grieved, and Pa thinks he wasn't paying attention when he was dehorning some cattle. One of them kicked him in the head and he never recovered."

"So if your uncle had lived, your grandfather would have split the ranch between his two sons. I don't understand why your father won't do the same."

"He's added on to the ranch. It's twice the size it was when he took over. He has taken pride in how large he's grown his holdings. I think he can't bear to tear it apart."

Daniel gestured to the hall. "And that way?"

"Two bedrooms. One for my grandparents and one for my parents." She walked to a ladder. "My brother and I slept here in the loft." She tested the strength of the old structure and craned her neck to look into the tiny space where she'd shared her secrets with her brother.

He grabbed her hand when she put her foot on the first rung. "I don't think it's safe, Margaret."

She let him pull her away, not sure she was ready to face the ghosts of her memories. She still missed Stephen. The last time she'd been here, he was still alive.

"You're thinking about restoring it?" he asked. "Living out here all by yourself? I reckon that's a bad idea."

"I can take care of myself."

"I don't doubt that. But you're a beautiful woman. I wouldn't want you to be alone here."

Beautiful. She wished she could believe the earnestness in his eyes. She turned and made her way out into the sunshine.

SEVEN

The interlude with Margaret at the old homestead had been sweet. Daniel liked the way she'd shared the family history. He'd talked her into going back to the ranch, then went to what was left of the barn. The ruins were still smoking and warm. Paddy didn't remember much except being hit on the head while he was caring for the cow, but Daniel wanted to find out if the attacker had left any clues in the barn.

Lewis stood in the shade of the springhouse. "What are you doing out here?"

Daniel wiped the soot from his hands on his jeans. "I reckon I'm trying to figure out who might want Paddy dead." The sun was bright and hot overhead.

Lewis shrugged and stepped out of the shadows. His face was red and damp with the heat. "Uncle Paddy thinks it was likely a thief." He pulled his handkerchief from his pocket and mopped his brow.

"I don't think so." Daniel stared at him. "Calvin was upset when I was hired. But upset enough to get revenge? He wasn't in the bunkhouse when I roused the men to fight the fire."

"You're a more likely suspect than Calvin."

Daniel went back to sifting through the charred debris. "I didn't hurt him."

"So you say. Where were you when he was struck?"

"I woke up and saw him with the cow, so I decided to see if he needed any help. When Margaret and I got there, he was on the ground. Ask him if I struck him. He'll tell you I didn't."

The undercurrent to Lewis's questions puzzled Daniel. As far as he knew, the two of them were strangers, yet Lewis seemed to have a personal stake in his accusations. "Why the questions?"

"I know who you are. What I can't figure out is what a *bank robber* is doing playing cowboy."

Daniel held the man's gaze. How did Lewis know about his past? Had he recognized him from an old wanted poster? "I don't think you know me as well as you think you do."

Lewis lifted a brow. "You deny you've robbed banks?"

"If Paddy has questions, I'll answer to him. Not to you." He kicked some timbers out of the way, then paused when he saw a hole under them. "What's this?"

Lewis glanced at it. "A hole."

Daniel lifted more of the timbers out of the way. "Looks like someone has been digging."

"Probably putting out hot coals."

Daniel didn't argue with Lewis, but the hole was deeper than it would have been if someone were simply shoveling dirt onto the fire. The hole was about two feet in diameter and about four feet deep. He glanced around and saw the handle of a shovel sticking out from under the debris. The metal handle was hot to the touch, so he kicked it loose with his boot. "He used this."

"Like I said, shoveling dirt on the fire."

Daniel shook his head. "I think someone was digging here, looking for something." He stared at the piles of timber, stone, and leather. There was nothing valuable in a barn. Unless . . .

He stared at Lewis. "Could Paddy have buried something out here to protect it?"

"What, you think someone was digging for treasure in the barn?" Lewis's voice held disgust.

The man was determined to dismiss Daniel no matter what he might find. Daniel walked away from the smoldering ruins and stalked back toward the house.

Lewis jogged to catch up with him. "Listen to me, foreman. You stay away from Margaret. She's precious to me, and she's more fragile than she looks."

Daniel stopped and stared at the smaller man. He couldn't blame the man for being protective when it was clear he knew about Daniel's past. "I don't intend to hurt anyone. And as I said, I reckon Paddy is my boss, not you. He seems pleased I'm escorting Margaret to the dance. If you have a beef about it, take it up with him."

"I know what you're up to. You took one look at this ranch and decided to marry Margaret to get it. That would be the only reason a man like you would look twice at a woman like Margaret. You'd never see past her manner to the sweet woman she is inside."

Daniel clenched his fists. "Are you saying I don't cotton to beautiful women or that no one would marry Margaret for more than her money?"

For the first time, Lewis looked uncertain. He must have caught the suppressed rage in Daniel's voice. "A man like you could turn Margaret's head, and I don't want her hurt."

"You keep saying 'a man like me.' What do you mean by that exactly?"

"Your type usually has a beautiful woman on each arm. Margaret can hardly compete with the kind of woman you're used to. She's been around ranch hands all her life. She's not used to sweet-talking men. You could turn her head, then leave her and make her a laughingstock."

"Margaret is the most beautiful woman I've ever laid eyes on. The men in this county must be crazy not to see that."

Lewis studied him through narrowed eyes. "I don't know what your game is, Cutler, but I'll be watching you. She's more fragile than she looks. And if Uncle Paddy is harmed in any way, I'll see you're hanged."

Daniel wished he could explain his mission to Lewis, but all he could do was nod and turn away.

MARGARET EYED THE sun in the sky. She was a pure loony for counting the minutes until it was time to get ready for the party. Her anticipation discomfited her. She tried to tell herself it was because of seeing Lucy, but her innate honesty forced her to admit that the thought of spending so much time with Daniel was the thing that appealed to her most.

Five o'clock finally came, and she went into her room to get ready. Their housekeeper, Inez, already had the tub filled with hot water, and Margaret thanked her as she went to her room and peeled off the rough clothes of the day. She stepped into the hot water and slipped down until the water came to her chin.

Inez scrubbed Margaret's back for her and helped her rinse her long, thick hair. She held out a towel for Margaret to step into. She dried off, then put on her robe.

"*Señorita* Margaret, no," Inez protested when Margaret began to braid it again. "Is fiesta tonight. You must wear it in more attractive way. Let me." Inez pushed Margaret's hands out of the way and brushed her hair out again. "We let it dry while you get dressed, then I will arrange it for you. What dress will you wear?"

"Oh, anything will do." Margaret jumped from the chair and swung open the door to the wardrobe. Several worn dresses hung on their hooks. "I don't have much worthy of a party, do I?" The pang of disappointment made her bite her lip. What was the matter with her? She usually didn't care what she wore. Tonight should be no different. She'd long ago quit trying to compete with other women with their dainty forms in pretty ruffles.

"I know just the dress." Inez gave a serene smile. "I will be right back." She rustled from the room.

While Inez was gone, Margaret stared at herself in the mirror. Oh, why hadn't God made her differently? The Bible said he had formed her in her mother's womb and created her just the way he wanted her, but when she met him, she intended to ask what he'd been thinking of to make her look this way. A heavy sigh escaped her lips. This evening was a mistake.

Inez came hurrying back into the room. From her arms draped a dress in a deep shade of emerald. A triumphant smile played about her lips. "Your *mamá* look lovely in this dress, just as you will. She wear it to a party in Boston before she marry your *papá*. Every man in the room look at her."

That certainly wouldn't happen to Margaret. She wished she'd known her mother. People said she looked like her mother, but they also talked about what a lovely lady she was. If she really looked like her mother, why hadn't she inherited her mother's beauty? "Where did you get it?" Margaret stroked the silken fabric with one finger.

"These many years I have saved it for you, for just the right occasion. Today it is right when I see the stars in your eyes for Mr. Cutler."

Heat crept up Margaret's cheeks. "Mr. Cutler means nothing to me. I intend to get rid of him. We have no need for his help."

"My señorita says one thing, but her eyes say another," Inez said with a smug smile. "I press this, then you try it on."

It was useless to argue with Inez. Margaret sat on the bed to wait. Her hair was drying quickly in the breeze through the open window. The splendid weather would soon give way to spring's warmth.

"Now we try this on." With a flourish, Inez held the dress out for Margaret.

Margaret stood and allowed Inez to drop it over her head. Inez buttoned up the back. The whisper of silk made Margaret feel like a princess. She smoothed the fabric over her waist. Never had she worn such a lovely garment.

"Your mamá, she had your lovely form as well. You are maybe a bit taller, but daily you grow more like her. There now, see how beautiful you look?" Inez drew Margaret to the full-length mirror.

Margaret stared at her reflection in awe. When she was a girl, she'd tried to dress like the other girls. Pa had even bought her a ruffled blue dress she'd coveted. She looked ridiculous in the flounces. But the simple lines of this dress looked elegant on her tall figure. "I—I like it."

"It is lovely. Now, you sit and I arrange your hair." Inez pressed her down onto the bench in front of the dresser and picked up a brush. With a few artful twists, Inez pulled the front of Margaret's hair back and secured it with a tortoiseshell comb. She left the back to fall free.

The ends of her hair had curled as it dried in the breeze. "I don't know, Inez. It will probably get in my way all evening." Margaret sighed. "I should probably just braid it." She panicked, thinking she might draw attention to herself by leaving her hair down. She'd found it best to make herself as inconspicuous as possible.

"No, you must not. This style, it suits the dress. Come, it is time to meet Mr. Cutler." Inez tugged Margaret to her feet and pointed her toward the door. "You go and have good time. You will see—Inez is right."

Margaret felt like an ostrich in a ball gown as she hurried out to meet Daniel. What if he thought she had dressed like this to impress him? She gave a mental shrug. Maybe it would serve her purposes if he thought she was interested in him as a man. But it still didn't feel right. She tugged at the skirt of her dress a bit. Her initial anticipation faded as she worried about what people would think. *Lord, help me face this. I can't bear it if they laugh.* Others would probably think she looked as ridiculous and out of place as she felt.

But there was no help for it. She could hear Daniel and her pa talking in the parlor, and there was no time to change or back out. She stepped silently into the parlor. At first neither man noticed her standing in the doorway. Then her pa turned his head and saw her.

For a moment, the color leeched from his face, then he blinked and smiled. "Margaret, for a second I thought it was your mama standing there." He gave a gruff laugh. "You look lovely, my dear."

Her father's praise brought tears to her eyes. His approving words came far too infrequently. Was her appearance all that mattered to him—to anyone? It seemed to be the way of the world. No one cared about who she was inside. No one saw the heart longing to be loved and to give love in return. She sometimes even doubted God's love for her.

"Thank you, Pa."

Daniel's chocolate eyes studied her, and a wave of heat stung her cheeks. What did he think? He said nothing, just raked her with a gaze that made her feel self-conscious and gangly.

He stood and held out his hand. "I'd better take my gun."

Confusion thickened her tongue. "Your gun?"

"I'll have to protect you from the other men." He grinned, but the admiration in his eyes was clear.

Margaret's heart gave a funny hitch in her chest. "You cut a swell yourself."

This man made her feel inadequate and uncertain of his intentions. And he was a bank robber. For a moment she wished it wasn't so, that she could accept his attentions and hope they might lead somewhere. Then reality raised its cold head again. Even if he was who he claimed to be, it wouldn't matter. His head would soon be turned by some pretty little thing in lace and ruffles, and Margaret's heart would be broken. It was a good thing he was someone totally unsuitable. But that did little to stop the yearning in her heart. She should turn tail and run.

"Have fun," her father said.

"Aren't you going, Pa?"

He shook his head. "Inez has promised me a supper fit for a king. I'm going to enjoy the peace and quiet."

For the first time Margaret wondered why her pa had never remarried. He was still attractive, with his rangy height and bearing.

Inez would make him a good wife. Maybe Margaret should talk to him about it sometime. She stifled a smile. Like she had any business talking to anyone about romance. It wasn't something with which she had any personal experience.

Daniel took her hand and slipped it over the crook of his arm. His warm fingers pressed against hers, and she could feel the bulky muscles of his arm under her hand. "I have the buggy waiting outside." He led her to the door and out to the buggy.

She started to clamber into the buggy, but he spanned her waist with his big hands and lifted her with ease into the seat as though she weighed no more than a doll. For the first time in her life, she felt feminine and cosseted. It was a feeling she could get used to. She pushed the thought away and reminded herself of his thievery.

He went around the buggy and climbed up beside her. "Why did you decide to go with me? I thought you hated my guts."

"Who says I don't?" She lifted a smile in his direction.

He grinned. "Do I take that as a challenge to prove you wrong?"

"You decide," she said airily. Her breath caught in her throat at his nearness.

"I reckon I will."

He reached out and touched her cheek with one finger. She knew she should turn her face away, but she so wanted to lift her face. She'd never been kissed before, and she didn't find him repugnant. He would be gone soon too. Why not, just this once, find out what other women experienced?

His breath touched her face first, then his mouth, his lips warm and gentle. His arm circled her waist and drew her closer. Her fingers clutched his shirt, still stiff from hanging on the line.

All thoughts of his nefarious ways flew from her head like thistle-down from a cottonwood tree as she gave herself over to the kiss.

When he lifted his head, she felt cold and bereft somehow. She didn't want to open her eyes, to face how inappropriate her behavior had been. She peeked through half-closed lids to see him smiling almost tenderly.

"I don't think you hate me at all," he whispered.

The amusement in his voice brought her to her senses and she jerked away, though everything in her wanted to fling herself closer. "You flatter yourself. I suggest you keep your kisses for someone who wants them."

"I thought I was doing just that."

She hated him for the laughter in his voice. But could she blame him? She'd encouraged him by allowing him to kiss her. Her face flamed with heat, and she wished she didn't have to turn him in to the sheriff.

EIGHT

T he Stanton ranch was well tended and expansive. Daniel glanced around at the trim fences and barns as they passed under the wooden sign proclaiming it the Stars Above Ranch. Several dogs barked and chased chipmunks in a field to the right of the house, but the main noise came from the laughter and voices drifting from the brightly lit barn closest to the house. He was eager to meet the family.

Daniel had heard the story from other cowpokes on the payroll. Margaret had fancied herself in love with Nate Stanton until his father had brought home a proxy bride for his son. That had been three years ago, and Margaret had withdrawn even more since then. Daniel wanted a look at the only man who had caught Margaret's eye. She despised him, so why did he even care about what kind of man she found attractive? Though for a moment, when she lifted her face for his kiss, he'd thought there might be some hope for him.

"Nice place," he told Margaret. What had possessed him to kiss her? All her earlier warmth was replaced with a wall of ice he found impossible to melt. It was as though she was determined to pretend she hadn't wanted him to kiss her.

But that kiss.

He glanced at her from the corner of his eye when she didn't answer his comment. His first sight of her tonight had been overwhelming. That glorious hair was loose, and he wanted to plunge his hands into those shining curls. How would it feel beneath his fingers? It looked heavy yet silky. He clenched his fists against the need to touch Margaret's hair now. He must be loco to let a woman get to him like this. Especially when he was only here to do a job and get out.

Daniel halted the buggy at the hitching post and got down. He tied up the horse, then went around to help Margaret, but she had already clambered to the ground by herself. She was the most aggravating woman. It was as though she was afraid to let herself be a woman. He offered her his arm. She shot him a look of disdain from eyes as clear as glass but took his arm anyway.

He led her inside the barn. Women dressed in their finery and men tricked out in their best vests spun by in a reel. Laughter floated on the air, and Daniel felt himself relax. Margaret would get over her snit, and they would have fun. Maybe he should apologize. But he didn't feel sorry for that kiss. Not one bit. The only thing he was sorry about was that it had put the wall between them again.

"Margaret!" A young woman waved from near the dessert table. Blond and pretty, her roundness announced the imminent arrival of a baby.

"Lucy!" Margaret waved back and started toward the woman.

This must be their hostess. Daniel followed Margaret's figure through the throng. A man stood beside Lucy, obviously her husband by the way he looked at her. Pride and worry warred for possession of his face.

That had to be Nate. Daniel looked him over. Strong and

handsome, he supposed, though he was no judge of what women found attractive. The gray eyes under his sandy hair radiated good humor and contentment. One thing was certain—he adored his wife even after several years of marriage.

Margaret and Daniel reached the other couple, and Lucy hugged Margaret with enthusiasm. "I've been watching for you," she said. "I've missed you."

"I've been meaning to get over here, but you know how it is on a ranch. Never enough time to get everything done." Margaret linked arms with Lucy.

"You amaze me, Margaret. I'm not much use other than in the house."

Nate grinned down at his wife. "I'm not complaining." He turned to Daniel and thrust out his hand. "Nate Stanton. You must be the new foreman at Triple T I've heard so much about."

"That would be me. Daniel Cutler."

"Where are you from, Mr. Cutler?" Lucy put in.

"Call me Daniel." He could sense the way Margaret grew still as though his answer mattered to her.

He smiled at Lucy and spilled out the story he'd rehearsed. "Born and raised in Texas, ma'am. My pa owned a bank in Austin, and I worked with him until about five years ago when I had a hankerin' to do something other than work in an office." He just prayed she wouldn't ask any more questions. Since he'd become a believer, he hated falsehood. He didn't want to lie, but he'd avoid the rest of the story if he could.

Instead of more questions, Lucy turned and directed a question at Margaret. "It must be wonderful to have some help."

Daniel couldn't hold back a grin. "Not so you'd notice, Miss Lucy. She wants to see the back of me in the worst way."

Lucy's blue eyes widened and she stared at Margaret. Margaret flushed and glared at Daniel. He grinned back at her. See how she liked being on the defensive. He had to admit, he rather enjoyed getting her back up. Those eyes of hers flashed like green fire, and the color came into her face when she was angry or upset. It was a bit like watching fireworks, and he'd always loved a show like that.

"We don't need a foreman," Margaret said. "I can handle the work."

"Sure, you can handle it, but why should you?" Nate asked. "It's hard work even for a man."

"And I'm a weak female, right?" Margaret glared at Nate, and he held up a hand.

"Whoa," he said. "I meant no disrespect. You can work any man I know under the table, Margaret."

She gave a shamefaced smile. "I'm sorry. I'm a little prickly tonight. It's this ridiculous dress. I feel like I must look like a little girl playing dress-up."

"You look wonderful," Lucy said. "Truly. You know I wouldn't lie to you. Your dance card is going to be full."

"I've been trying to convince her of that since we left the Triple T," Daniel said.

Lucy smiled at him. "Maybe if you danced with her, she could believe it."

"Don't talk about me as if I weren't here." Margaret planted her hands on her hips.

"That's a great idea, Miss Lucy." Daniel grinned, then gripped Margaret's arm and pulled her toward the dance floor as the fiddler struck up a square dance. He winked at her, and Margaret began to smile. His heart leapt at the way she was looking at him.

She might not want to admit she was attracted to him, but he could see it in her face.

They stomped and spun their way around the floor. Margaret was laughing up at him as she dipped and twirled. They were both breathless by the time the dance ended. He led her to a secluded alcove. "Wait here and I'll get us something to drink." She nodded, and he went across the room to the refreshment table. He glanced back and frowned when he saw several men heading her direction.

Lucy was sitting in a chair beside the table. "Hello again. Did Margaret run you off already?"

"No, I'm getting us something to drink."

She patted the chair beside her. "Sit down a minute. I want to talk to you."

Daniel arched his eyebrows. Now she had him curious. He settled on the edge of the chair she'd indicated.

"Nate told me not to interfere, but Margaret is my best friend, and I don't want to see her hurt."

"I won't hurt her." Daniel was a little tired of his motives always being called into question, first by Lewis and now by Lucy. Usually people took him at face value, and he didn't like this constant suspicion.

"She's more fragile than she appears," Lucy said. "She puts up a brave front, but she's really a little girl looking for love. Are you a Christian, Daniel?"

"Yes, I am." Not many people cared about that, and his respect and liking for Lucy Stanton grew.

Lucy's face lit in relief. "Then maybe you can guide Margaret. She needs to know God's unconditional love. She's a believer, but she can't seem to grasp the fact that God is the only one we can turn to for that love. I think her father's high expectations have made her doubt his love for her. And the loss of her mother when she was a child added to her self-doubt. Nate's choice didn't help things."

He leaned forward. "I heard a little about that. What more can you tell me?"

"The entire town thought Nate would marry Margaret. He escorted her to a few shindigs, and I think he even thought he would eventually marry her since she knew ranching. Anyone with half an eye can see Margaret would be a hardworking wife. Then I came along, and things changed. I always regretted the way Margaret was hurt. Since then she's rejected any man's attempt to escort her anywhere. Not that many have tried since she's so prickly." Lucy frowned. "Here comes Nate. I'd better shut up." She laughed and winked at Daniel.

Nate came toward them with a young man with red hair, somewhere in age between hay and grass. He had a girl of about six with curly blond hair by the hand, and he carried a little boy of about two who had his daddy's sandy hair and gray eyes. "I don't think you've met the rest of the family. This is Jed and Eileen, Lucy's brother and sister. And the little guy is William, our son."

Daniel shook Jed's hand and teased Eileen for a few minutes, then went back to the refreshment table. By the time he got back to Margaret with punch, she was surrounded by men.

Calvin was coaxing her to dance, and another man asked if he could get her some refreshments. The wave of jealousy that swept over him caught him off guard. He'd better watch his heart. He shouldered his way past the men and handed her the punch.

"Sorry, men, the lady is taken," he told them. Was that relief on Margaret's face? He smiled at her and she smiled back. Elation

COLLEEN COBLE

raced through him. Why had he thought it fun to make her angry? Her smile warmed him like the first hot day of summer.

The men dispersed with a few grumbles, and Calvin glared at him. "Sorry if I was overbearing," Daniel told her.

"You're not a bit sorry. You men get like a bull defending his territory."

"Guilty. Maybe I'm staking my claim to you." He nearly bit his tongue, but the words were out. What claim did he have on her? She would never look twice at him.

Her eyes widened, and she seemed as though she wanted to say something, but then her white teeth clamped against her lip, and she looked away. Her stiff manner came back, and Daniel sighed. He'd messed it up again. This relationship stuff was hard to fathom. One step forward and two steps back. He was much more comfortable with his horse or the cattle.

His pocket watch read eight. This party had to be over in time for the meeting. He glanced around the crowd and straightened when he saw a familiar figure. What was Golda doing here? If the townspeople got wind of what was going on, his job would be even harder.

"I'll be right back," he told Margaret. He put his drink on the floor next to her and hurried toward where he'd last seen Golda.

He stepped outside and looked around, and a small hand grabbed his arm.

He collided with a small figure. "Golda, what are you doing here?"

She wore a blue dress that showed her curves. "I thought I'd enjoy myself tonight. You have a problem with that?"

"Someone is going to ask where you're from and what you're doing here."

SAFE IN HIS ARMS

She tossed back her golden head. "And I'll tell them I'm visiting." Her eyes glittered. "I saw you dancing with that redhead." She leaned closer. "You'd better not be thinking of throwing me over for another woman. I might have to have a little chat with her."

She pulled something from her pocket, and he saw the glint of her gun. Though it was small, she knew how to use it—and had in the past. "You leave Margaret alone."

She stepped close enough to run her hand up his shirt. Her perfume was overpowering. "Don't make me mad. Frank is beginning to question if this plan is a good one. You haven't sent word about which bank to hit next, and he's getting antsy."

He caught her hand and pushed it off him, then stepped away. "I'm doing my job and Frank knows it." But she could easily put doubts in her brother's mind. She was quite good at it. "I just got here. I need a little time to figure everything out. Frank was the one who moved in too soon."

"He doesn't trust you."

"You mean *you* don't trust me."

If he didn't get out of here, he was going to say something he'd regret.

NINE

～⊙⌒⊙～

Margaret clutched the glass of punch in her hand. The coolness of the glass kept her rooted in reality. Stake his claim, indeed. Those other men weren't interested in her, only in her father's ranch. And the only claim Daniel was going to stake was on the bank's money. She had to make sure he failed in that attempt. Still, she wanted to weep, which wasn't like her. Not at all. But then, ever since Daniel had arrived, she hadn't been behaving in a characteristic way. She had a sinking feeling that she was heading for major trouble. The sooner Daniel was exposed and out of her life, the better.

Where could he have gone in such a hurry? She stood and set her empty glass down among others on top of a barrel. Maybe she could overhear something if she found out where he went. She tried to be nonchalant as she strolled around the barn. But there was no sign of his tall figure. She headed toward the back door, then stepped out into the dark night that enveloped the yard. The sweet scent of flowers teased her nose.

She heard a murmur of voices from over by the feed trough. Stepping cautiously, she inched her way toward the voices. Just as she was nearly close enough to hear, she stepped in something. From the way it squished up over her ankle, she knew just what it was. Then the unpleasant odor reached her nostrils, and she knew for certain it was a fresh cowpat. She sucked in her breath and gingerly tried to wipe it off on the grass.

She stumbled into the side of the horse trough, and a pail clattered to the ground. The murmur of voices stopped, and she heard Daniel's familiar deep voice.

"Get out of here before someone sees you. Tell Frank I'll be in touch so we can make our final plans."

A woman answered, "I don't want to talk about Frank. I want to talk about us. I want you back, Daniel."

"Golda, this is not the time or the place. I'll talk to you later."

Moments later the moon illuminated Daniel's white shirt as he came toward her.

"Margaret, what are you doing out here in the dark?" When he saw her trying to scrape her shoe, he grinned. "Need some help?"

She wanted to shout her questions at him, but she forced herself to smile at him instead. "I think I'll go to the house and get cleaned up. Tell Lucy, would you, please?" She needed to get away from him before she said something she shouldn't.

"I'll come with you." He took her arm.

She wanted to shake his fingers off her arm. The only reason he was working at the Triple T was to scout out the job he'd come here to do. It had nothing to do with her or any attraction he might feel. And there was another woman involved, and if her voice was any indication, she was beautiful. He was a good actor. A man in his position would have to know how to lie and cover up the truth pretty well. Daniel was an obvious master at it.

He guided her across the yard to Lucy's front porch. "I'll send

Lucy in to help you." He hurried back across the yard toward the barn.

Margaret should have felt relieved at his absence, but she was furious with herself and her own gullibility. In spite of what she knew about him, she had begun to believe that he really did feel something for her. But that conversation she'd overheard had made it clear he had only one purpose in coming here tonight. She had made a good cover for him to meet with his cohorts.

That was the way it had been all her life. She was never loved for who she was, only for what she could provide. Tears burned the backs of her eyelids, but she fiercely willed them away. He'd be gone soon. Then life would get back to normal, and all these odd feelings that had plagued her lately would be gone. She would take over running the ranch, and life would be good again.

By the time Lucy got to her, Margaret had already managed to get cleaned up. Lucy made suitable noises of commiseration. "I think I'll just go home," Margaret told her. "Could you loan Daniel a horse? I'll take the buggy and go home by myself."

"Oh, don't do that, Margaret! I'll fetch him and let him drive you. It's not safe to go alone."

"I've been doing it all my life." Alone was what she did best.

"Not at night," Lucy said firmly. She stopped and put a hand to her stomach. "Oh dear."

"What is it?"

"I—I think the baby is coming." A puddle of fluid pooled at her feet. "The baby isn't expected for more than a month."

"Stay calm. You get to bed and I'll fetch Nate and have Jed go for the doctor."

"The doctor is here." Lucy clutched Margaret's hand. "I'm

scared," she whispered. "I thought I was ready for this, but it's too soon. What if the baby dies?"

"You'll both be fine," Margaret said, though her heart fluttered at how fragile Lucy looked tonight. She prayed silently and ran for the door. "I'll be right back with the doctor and Nate."

She collided with Daniel on the front porch. A wave of relief so intense passed through her that she shuddered. He put his hands on her shoulders to steady her, and his touch did just that: a sense of calmness quieted her turmoil.

"What's wrong?" Alarm tinged his words.

"It's Lucy. The baby is coming."

He pulled away. "I'll fetch Nate."

"And the doctor," she called after him. "He's at the dance too." She rushed back inside to Lucy.

A confused expression on her face, Lucy sat woodenly in a chair. "I should know what to do, but my mind is empty."

"Let's get you undressed and into your nightgown." Margaret helped Lucy disrobe, then found her nightgown in the bureau. Lucy was trembling when Margaret dropped the nightgown over her head.

"I'm so scared, Margaret. I'm not strong and brave like you."

Strong and brave. That's how everyone saw her. What would they think if they knew it was all a facade? People thought of her as mannish because of her size, so she had obliged them by becoming even more that way. No one seemed to appreciate her feminine qualities, so why bother cultivating them? It was ironic. Lucy wanted to be more like her, and Margaret wanted to be like Lucy.

"You're stronger than you think," Margaret said.

A white-faced Nate burst into the room, followed by Dr. Cooper. Nate knelt and embraced his wife. "I'm here, Lucy. How are you feeling?"

"I—I'm not sure," Lucy stammered.

Nate helped her to the bed, with Margaret trailing behind. The doctor shooed them all out of the room so he could examine Lucy.

Daniel was pacing across the parlor floor with William in his arms when Margaret stepped into the room. Jed was sitting in the rocker with his head in his hands. Eileen sat on the floor beside him. He sprang to his feet when he saw Margaret and Nate.

"She's fine," Margaret said soothingly.

Jed's stiff shoulders relaxed and he sat back down. "Will it be a long time?"

"Probably. Babies take their time." Margaret wanted to go to Daniel and feel his strong arms around her. She needed comfort and reassurance too, but he wasn't the appropriate one to turn to for consolation. He looked solid and strong standing there with little William in his arms. His strong, craggy face looked like the face of someone who could be trusted. Unfortunately, looks were deceiving. Margaret sighed and looked away.

Daniel put William on the floor, and the tot scampered across the room to his father. Nate scooped him up. "You should be getting to bed, little man," he said.

"Baby brother," William announced.

"Maybe a brother but maybe a sister," Nate said. "You'll like either one. Maybe the baby will be here when you get up in the morning. Like Margaret said, babies take a long time. Your new brother or sister might not make an appearance until tomorrow." He motioned to Jed. "Jed and Eileen will tuck you in and read you a story."

Jed took William from Nate and carried him from the room. He was still protesting at being put to bed, but he didn't cry.

Margaret wished the little one could have stayed. It would have given her something to do with herself.

The doctor came through the door, wiping his hands on a cloth. "She's doing fine, but it's going to be awhile. Might as well get comfortable."

"What about the baby?" Nate asked.

"Too soon to know. Perhaps we've just miscalculated the date," the doctor said. "Otherwise, we may lose it."

A lump formed in Margaret's throat. Daniel took her hand, and she looked up in surprise.

"Let's pray together," he whispered.

Pray with an outlaw. The thought seemed ridiculous, but as she bowed her head, Margaret found it made perfect sense.

THE MOON GLIMMERED on the rocks around the river and bounced off the water. Charlie took out his pocket watch and held it up to the scanty light. Well past midnight. Had something happened to Daniel? He chewed his lip and thought about it. Daniel knew too much to get caught by the law. He was much too experienced a rider to get thrown or injured by his horse.

What if Daniel had lured him here to get him out of the camp? Maybe he intended to tell Frank that Charlie was too young to be involved. Daniel had been adamantly against him hooking up with Golda and her brother. Charlie didn't trust him. Not one bit.

He stood and paced along the river. Small pebbles rolled away from his boots, and one splashed into the water. The small sound distracted him. He should leave right now. Make sure there was no funny business going on behind his back.

Another sound came to his ears, softer and more furtive. He yanked his revolver free from the holster. "Who's there? Show yourself or I'll shoot."

A figure stepped out of the shadows. The moonlight illuminated her beautiful face. Golda had followed him? The rush of pleasure at the realization was quickly squelched when he saw the displeasure on her face.

"What are you doing here?" she demanded. "When you sneaked off, I thought maybe you were going to meet Daniel."

"So what if I was?" he countered.

She laughed and stepped closer. Her perfume filled his head and made it impossible to think. All he could do was stare at her full lips.

Her fingers caressed his face. "Don't play me for a fool, Charlie. We both know Daniel is up to something. I want to know what it is."

What did she want from him? If she were to take a man, it would be someone like Daniel. Strong, powerful. Not a guy like him. She had some plan, but Charlie couldn't fathom what it was.

"I don't know anything other than what we both know—he's gathering information about banks in the area."

She stretched up on her toes and brushed her lips across his. Heat whipped through him, and he clutched at her waist.

"Easy, boy," she said in a whisper.

She cupped his face in her palms and kissed him again, a slow, deliberate caress that drove all thought from Charlie's head. His eyes were still closed when she pulled away.

"Now tell me what you're doing out here all alone," she said, "and I might give you another lesson in love."

He took a step toward her, but she danced away, her skirts swinging. "You have to pay for my favors, Charlie."

"My money is back at camp," he said, still relishing the taste of her on his lips. This was headier than any taste of liquor he'd had.

She stepped close enough for him to catch another whiff of her perfume. "Not money, Charlie. Information. Information is power. I don't like to be kept in the dark about anything. Especially not if it concerns your brother. I saw him tonight. Hanging out with some redhead. I didn't like it. What's he up to?"

She'd seen Daniel? Where? He didn't want to look stupid so he just shrugged. "I just wanted to get out of camp a little while. Hugh was getting on my nerves."

Her smile was sultry. "Come now, Charlie. You don't expect me to believe that, do you?"

He swallowed hard when she put her hand on his chest. "That's all I was doing, Golda. Honest. You know how Hugh can get. I get so tired of hearing him talk about the gunfight in Tombstone."

Virgil Earp was a friend of Hugh's. When Hugh learned Virgil had lost the use of his left arm after being dry-gulched, Hugh talked of nothing else but the ambush. He'd tried to talk all of them into heading to Arizona and taking revenge, but no one was interested. Least of all Frank. Not when the richest banks were right here in Texas.

Golda tipped her head to one side and stared up at him. "Surely you've talked to your brother, Charlie?"

"I haven't." At least only through Richard, and Charlie wasn't about to betray their friend. "We didn't part on good terms."

"You have proven him wrong. I don't know what we would have done without you. He doesn't realize you're a man now. A very handsome man." She stepped closer, and her hand slid up his chest to his face.

It was about time someone realized he wasn't a kid. If Daniel could see him now, he'd realize how wrong he was. He thought he heard something and realized he needed to get rid of her.

He took her wrist in his grip and pushed her away. "We'd better get back. Frank is going to come looking for us if we're gone too long."

"Leave my brother to me." She started for the trees, then turned. "You'd better not follow me. We don't want it to be obvious we've been together. The other men might be jealous. And you know how Frank gets."

He nodded. "I'll be along in a few minutes." When the rustling in the trees faded, he whirled back toward the river. "Who's there?" he demanded in a harsh whisper.

Richard stepped into view. "You'd best leave her be, Charlie. She'll chew you up for breakfast."

"Mind your own business," Charlie snapped. "Where's Daniel?"

"He got detained tonight. What about tomorrow night?"

"No thanks. I've changed my mind. I have no interest in listening to more of his lies. Golda herself told me they didn't know what they'd do without me. I know what Daniel wants, and I'm not interested in hearing any of it."

He stalked off to where his horse was tethered and swung into the saddle.

TEN

Through the long night, Daniel found himself watching Margaret and marveling at her calm efficiency as she saw to the needs of everyone in the Stanton household. She fetched boiling water and clean cloths for the doctor, disappeared into Lucy's room occasionally to offer comfort and encouragement to the laboring mother, soothed Nate's frazzled nerves, and helped Nate usher the dance guests away from the party. This was yet another side to the intriguing Margaret O'Brien. And it made him want to know her all the more.

Daniel was dozing on the sofa when a noise awakened him. He blinked sleepily in the lightening gloom of early dawn. What was that noise? It almost sounded like a kitten mewing. Then the sound strengthened, and he realized he was hearing the first cries of the newborn baby. He bolted upright, then jumped to his feet.

His hands gripped together, Nate was standing at the door. An eager smile vied with worry on his face. "Where's the doctor?"

"Sounds like a healthy little one," Daniel said soothingly. He still remembered the night his brother was born.

"Yes, but I don't hear Lucy." Nate paced across the floor, then turned with determination. "I'm going in there."

Before he could reach the doorway, Margaret stepped into the parlor. She was carrying a tiny bundle. "You want to see your daughter, Nate?" She was smiling tenderly at the baby.

"A—A daughter?" Dawning wonder broke over the new father's face. He approached Margaret and the baby with a tentative stride. "How's Lucy?"

"She's tired but fine. You can see her in a few minutes."

Daniel had waited through the long night with the rest, and he deserved a peek too. He crowded behind Nate and peered into the blanket at a tiny, wizened face topped by a tuft of red hair. "She has red hair."

"Just like her uncle Jed," Nate murmured. "What's the doctor say about her?"

"Our prayers were answered. It was a simple miscalculation. He thinks she'll be fine. She's a goodly weight."

"Thank you, God," Nate whispered.

"Here, you hold her." Margaret gently handed the baby to her daddy.

Joy spread over Nate's face. "She looks like Lucy," he breathed. "But she's so little. I might hurt her. I don't remember William being so small."

"She's stronger than she looks, like all newborns," Margaret said. "Just think how tough those new calves are, and you'll be fine."

Daniel watched with great interest. He hadn't been this close to a newborn baby since Charlie was born, and the thrill of new life was amazing. Margaret's face glowed, and so did Nate's.

The baby was sucking on her fist and making small mewling sounds. Daniel glanced down at Margaret and saw the tender look on her face as she gazed at Nate with his new daughter. The expression on her face tightened Daniel's stomach. She'd loved Nate once and wanted to marry him. Did she still love him? Did she wish this child were hers and Nate's? A lump formed in Daniel's throat. Would he ever hold a child of his own? It didn't seem likely, considering his line of work. But he couldn't imagine a greater joy than holding a little girl who looked like Margaret.

Daniel scowled and turned away. "I'll see to the stock, Nate. You spend some time with your new daughter." He strode from the room. Let Margaret moon over Nate. Daniel had more important things to do than watch.

The hard work in the stockyard cleared his thoughts. So what if she still yearned after Nate? The man was married, and she could see that. Besides, Daniel had to keep his mind on this job at hand. Not until it was over could he think about anything else. But what then? Maybe it was time to change his profession. He could put his dangerous past behind him. Margaret would be worth the sacrifice. The thought was alluring.

By the time he went back to the house, enticing aromas were emanating from the kitchen and his mouth watered. Until he smelled breakfast, he hadn't realized how hungry he was. He glanced into the parlor and saw the new baby safely ensconced in a cradle while Jed and Eileen gazed at her raptly. Nate was nowhere to be seen, and Daniel assumed he was with Lucy.

Daniel followed his nose to the kitchen and found Margaret bustling about in an apron.

She jumped at his appearance. "Goodness, you startled me." Her face was pale and strained with exhaustion, and she waved a wooden spoon in one hand as though she might conk him with it for daring to frighten her.

Daniel grinned. "Is that your weapon of choice?"

She flushed and put her arm down. "Are you hungry?"

"Famished."

"Dig in. The kids and Nate have already eaten."

Daniel sat at the table and watched her as she dished him up some potatoes, eggs, and bacon. When she set the plate in front of him, he caught her by the wrist and pulled her down onto his lap.

The look of astonishment on her face made him burst into laughter. Daniel wrapped his arms around her and kissed her. Her lips were warm and so soft. She smelled of sunshine, bacon, and baby. Who would have thought that combination could be so appealing?

Her arms crept around his neck. Then she suddenly pushed at his chest and clambered to her feet. "Would you stop doing that?"

"Why? You know I like you, Margaret. I would like to call on you formally." The distraction from the job before him would be too great, but he seemed unable to help himself when Margaret was near him. He had more and more a sense that she was the one God had planned for him.

"Don't say that!" She whirled and stalked to the dry sink. After pouring water from the pitcher into the dishpan, she scrubbed the pots.

He stood and stepped up behind her. "Why not? It's the truth. I like spending time with you. You're strong, beautiful, and brave. What more could a man ask for?"

She spun around and shoved at his chest. "Stop mocking me! Did someone put you up to this? Is Pa paying you or something?" Her eyes sparkled with tears.

Daniel's jaw dropped open. "Paying me? Is that what you think of me? What kind of man do you think I am, Margaret?"

"I think you're a bank robber!" she blurted out. Her eyes grew round, and she put a hand to her mouth.

"I see," he said slowly.

His thoughts raced. A bank robber. She must have told Lewis her suspicions and that's why he'd confronted Daniel. How had she guessed? And she was closer to the truth than she should be. He'd better back away until this job was over. The thought of putting her in danger was more than he could bear.

He dropped a mask over his face and stepped back. "In that case, I reckon there's no more to say. Are you going to turn me in to the sheriff?"

Margaret's face grew pinched. "Are you admitting it?"

"I'm admitting nothing. But I warn you to stay out of my affairs." He'd better be tough with her for her own good. If they got near her, Frank and Golda would chew her up and spit her out like a discarded pea pod. Daniel couldn't risk that. Better to frighten her into keeping her mouth shut.

She tipped up her chin. "And if I don't?"

"My partners might not take too kindly to interference. You wouldn't want anything to happen to your pa."

She put a hand to her throat. "You're despicable," she whispered.

"So I've been told." Weariness descended, and he turned toward the door. "I'll borrow a horse from the barn and head on back to the Triple T. Give Lucy and Nate my congratulations." He didn't wait for an answer. There was nothing more to say.

MARGARET WAS STILL trembling an hour later. Daniel had practically admitted he was a bank robber and was here for some unknown purpose. But what could it be? Why would he pick the Triple T to hole up in? Larson's bank had already been robbed. What was keeping him from moving on?

She had to do something. She couldn't go to the sheriff. Daniel had threatened her pa, hadn't he? And Margaret couldn't run the risk of causing harm to her father. Besides, she didn't know if she could bring herself to turn Daniel in. In spite of what she knew to be true about him, she had to be honest—her heart was more entangled than it should be. She squared her shoulders. She couldn't let that stop her from doing her duty. If she could discover what the plan was and then foil it, maybe she could rid her heart of this preoccupation with Daniel.

Once things were in hand at the Stanton household, she hitched up the buggy and drove home. Weariness settled on her like a heavy blanket. Would Daniel be there when she arrived? Maybe it would be better if he had slipped away while she was gone. She wasn't strong enough or smart enough to discover his plan and stop it. But her innate sense of right and wrong reared its head, and she had to do what she could. She wished she could confide in someone.

All she wanted to do was crawl in bed when she got home. Helping Lucy all night had been tiring, but her problem with Daniel was even more exhausting. She climbed out of the buggy and walked into the house with dragging steps.

Her pa was sitting in the parlor with his Sunday suit on. "Everyone all right at the Stantons'? The ranch hands told me about Lucy. I wasn't sure if you'd be home in time for church."

Church. She looked down at herself. There was no way she could go looking like this. But in spite of her exhaustion, she needed to go. Maybe sitting in the quiet atmosphere of worship would help her know what to do about Daniel. "Let me get cleaned up first."

"Take your time. You've an hour yet, and I'm still waiting on Daniel. He's going with us this morning."

What a hypocrite! Robbing banks, then deluding innocent townspeople into thinking he was a fine, upstanding citizen they could trust.

Inez helped her quickly bathe, change her gown, and give her hair a lick and a promise. By the time Margaret got back to the parlor, her initial fatigue had dropped away, and she was filled with determination to stop Daniel from harming her valley and those she loved.

She stopped in the doorway when she heard his deep voice speaking to her father. Holding her head high, she waltzed into the room. "I'm ready." She speared him with her glance, but he seemed unbothered by her censure.

Her father went toward the door. "I'll get the buggy."

Daniel rose lazily to his feet, and his gaze swept her figure. "Mornin', Miss Margaret. You look pretty this morning, though I like your hair down better," he said softly.

Heat rushed to her cheeks, and she scowled at him. "Then I shall be sure to keep it in its braid."

His soft laughter followed her out the door as she stalked outside after her pa. The man was truly insufferable. He admitted he was a criminal, yet he had the gall to still flirt with her.

Squashed between Daniel and her pa, Margaret thought the trip to town would never end. Daniel's nearness was a torture, but he would soon be gone. She ignored the bereft feeling she experienced at the thought of never seeing him again.

Church was buzzing with the news of the Stantons' new

arrival. Margaret recounted the events of the previous night while her father and Daniel found a pew. When she made her way to their side, she found her father on the inside while Daniel had saved a spot for her on the aisle. She slid into the seat beside him and tried to ignore the clean smell of him and the broadness of his shoulders.

He cleared his throat and opened his Bible to the passage Reverend Mitchell announced. Margaret silently railed at him for being such a hypocrite. She turned her own Bible to John 13. The pastor began to preach about how Jesus loved Peter even though he knew ahead of time that Peter would deny him three times.

"God loves us in the same way," Reverend Mitchell said. "Not because of what we do, but because of who he is. We can't earn God's favor by working for it. We don't earn it by our beauty or our possessions, for God is the one who gives those things anyway. His love is not dependent on anything. He loved us when we were unlovable, just as he did Peter."

Reverend Mitchell's words arrested Margaret's attention. Out of fear, she worked hard to earn the love of others and dutifully did what she thought God wanted. She was always afraid of not living up to standards she never really understood. Could God really love her if she did nothing—just because he chose to love her—because she was his child? It didn't seem possible. The longer Reverend Mitchell preached, the more agitated she became.

Had she ever given God everything she had, everything she was, everything she did? She didn't think so. And she didn't know if she even could. The one thing from which she gained a bit of pride and satisfaction was her standing in the community. If she wasn't an O'Brien, she wouldn't be worth anything. At least that's how she looked at it. That was probably wrong, wasn't it? But how did she go about laying aside the baggage she carried and clinging only to God? And did she even want to?

Lacing her fingers together, she tried to control her agitation. Finally, with a murmured apology, she stood and hurried from the building. She rushed down the steps and found her way to a picnic area behind the church. Taking a deep breath, she considered all the pastor had said. Unconditional love. It seemed so elusive. Yet how she longed for it! She was tired of struggling to earn it. Tired of wanting to be something she could never be, not for God or for anyone else.

A shadow fell across her arm, and she whirled around. His hands thrust in his pockets, Daniel stood staring down at her. "Are you all right?"

She studied his face and found only concern. But then, he was a good liar. "I suppose you were worried that I'd gone to find the sheriff." Why couldn't he leave her alone?

"Not at all. He's still in the church." Daniel took a step toward her. "Anything I can help you with?"

As if she would tell him anything. "No."

"Was it the pastor's sermon?"

Though a hypocrite like Daniel should be the last person with whom she discussed truth, she was too unsettled by what the pastor said to hide her feelings, and she blurted out the truth. "Unconditional love seems impossible."

"Impossible?" He smiled. "With God, nothing is impossible."

"You're a fine one to talk about God." What did he know anyway? She must be crazy to even discuss spiritual topics with him.

"Even criminals can know God's love," he said gently. "If I didn't believe in God's forgiveness and great love for me, my life would have no meaning or purpose. It's what drives me forward and gives me hope."

Maybe he wanted to turn from his life of crime. Margaret's heart beat quickly, and she leaned forward. "You believe in unconditional love?"

He touched her cheek. "Why do you think you're so unlovable, Margaret?" he asked softly.

Tears flooded her eyes. They were supposed to be talking about him, not her. "Look at me. I'm too tall and gangly. My hair is too red. There are lots of reasons men don't find me attractive."

"You are the most beautiful woman I've ever met. And even if you weren't, God sees beyond the blazing glory of your red hair and the strong children you would raise up. He sees the fierce caring of your heart and the loyalty you give to those you love. He sees the tender heart inside that's crying out for love and approval. He gives it to you freely, Margaret. As I—" Daniel broke off abruptly.

Was that really how God saw her? It would be so wonderful to rest in that love, to feel safe there. And what else had Daniel been about to say? She swallowed hard. "I wish I could believe you." She couldn't think with his thumb running over her jaw.

"Don't believe me. Believe God. He tells you in the Bible how much he loves you. You don't have to take someone else's word for it."

Daniel was an enigma. How could a bank robber be standing here talking to her about God's love? And he'd threatened her father. None of this made sense.

"Who are you, really?" she whispered.

His hand dropped from her cheek, and he stepped back. "Just a man trying to do his best in this world. One who has things in the past he would change if he could."

"Is that why you're here? To change those things?" She held her breath waiting for his answer, her heart pounding in her chest as though it might burst.

"I can't tell you any more. Let's just say I've got more in my past to haunt me than you can imagine. But God loves me in spite of it all, just as he loves you. When are you going to let him take that chip from your shoulder? When will you let go of that guard you put around your heart to keep out everyone, including God?"

"I don't keep people out."

He laughed. "How many close friends do you have, Margaret? Lucy is it, isn't she? And it's because she forced her love and friendship past that wall."

Maybe he had a point, but she wasn't about to admit it to him. What did he know of the pain of constant rejection, the agony of never fitting in with other people? It was all very well to sit in judgment of her, but he'd never walked in her size-nine shoes when all the other women wore size five. He'd never had to listen to the titters of other girls as they giggled behind a door when Margaret sat alone along the wall at every dance she'd ever gone to because no man liked a woman to tower over him.

She was an eel in a pond full of goldfish. And it was God's fault. That was the crux of the matter, she suddenly realized. Why had he made her unlovable to the world? She wouldn't do that to a child of hers, so why had he done it to her?

Daniel studied her face. "Have you ever thanked God for giving you the advantages he has?"

"Advantages?"

"All those things I've already mentioned. You're tall and strong, loyal and brave, kind and loving. You stand out in a crowd and you're a leader. He wouldn't trust those qualities with just anyone. He must love you a great deal."

She blinked at the thought. Could the things she thought were curses actually have contributed to her character? She would have to ponder that. She shook her head again at the way Daniel seemed to understand spiritual things. She didn't understand him, and she was beginning to think she never would.

He looked back toward the church. "Looks like the service is over. I reckon your pa will be looking for us." He offered her the support of his arm.

"How did you learn all this?" she blurted out. "You're a criminal."

He smiled, and the sadness in his smile broke her heart. "Someday maybe I'll tell you," he said softly.

ELEVEN

The landscape was dark and moonless. So dark Daniel lifted his lantern to light his way to the springhouse. When a shadow moved, he paused. "Richard?"

"I'm here." His Stetson low over his face, Richard stepped into the circle of light cast by the lantern.

Daniel glanced back at the house. Nothing moved there. The faint sound of piano music tinkled through the open window. Inez's son, Vincente, had been puttering around on it, so everyone should be occupied in the parlor. "Did Charlie show up last night?"

"He did. I got there just before he left."

Daniel heard an odd note in Richard's voice. "When can we meet?"

"He's changed his mind. Says he's happy there. He's guessed you want him out of the gang, and I think he's afraid you'll persuade him in spite of his determination."

Daniel pushed his hat away from his forehead and exhaled. "What aren't you saying?"

"I saw Golda leave before I got there. She kissed him."

Daniel suppressed a shudder. She'd been one reason he left the gang. "That woman is a snake."

"She's got her good points."

"I don't know what they'd be."

Richard put his hand on Daniel's shoulder. "You're bitter. It's understandable after your experiences with her. But Charlie is young and impressionable. I overheard her asking about you. I think she's using him to get to you."

"Poor Charlie. He has no idea how to deal with a woman like Golda."

"You didn't either, but you learned." Richard's hand left Daniel's shoulder.

Daniel didn't like to remember how young and stupid he'd been once. It shamed him to think of the things he'd done for Golda. She'd reeled him in without any trouble at all. If Daniel didn't fix this, Charlie would follow in his shoes.

"I have to see my brother."

Richard shrugged. "I'll try again, but right now he's saying no."

"Then I'll go there."

"What, you'll just waltz into camp? That won't go over well."

"They're expecting me to show up with bank information."

"But you have no information for them, and the big heist isn't for another month. Frank has too good of a nose for you to mess with the plan. He'd smell a rat right off."

"You have a point." Frank Munster sensed things he should have no way of knowing. It was uncanny. If Daniel tipped his hand, Frank might take it out on Charlie too. Daniel heard that once Frank had put a gang member in the line of fire, then had the rest of the men pull back so the fellow was killed. Daniel never heard what the poor chap had done to get on Frank's bad side. But it was never a good place to be.

"Be patient. I'll talk to Charlie again." Richard gestured toward the blackened barn ruins. "Any idea what happened there?"

"One of the hands dropped a lantern while searching for the intruder who hit Paddy."

"Any idea who hit him?" Richard asked.

Neighbors from all over were due to descend on the ranch in a few days to rebuild the barn. "Not a clue."

"A man like O'Brien doesn't build an empire like this without ruffling a few feathers. What about the nephew?"

"Lewis?" Daniel had to stop and ponder the thought. "I can't see him doing it. He seems to love his uncle."

"He's set to inherit when O'Brien dies. Maybe he didn't want to wait."

"Anything is possible, but I don't think Lewis is our man," Daniel said.

"What about the daughter?"

"You don't know Margaret. She's loyal and loving."

Richard had been pacing. He stopped and stared at Daniel. "You like the girl."

"Sure I like her. She works like a field hand on the ranch. Pretty too." Though pretty was too tame a word to describe Margaret's striking beauty.

"I've only seen her from a distance. Dressed like a man but striking."

"Just because she's had to be. It's practical to wear britches to work in. She's never had a mother around to teach her. She's all heart, though. If her father were in danger, she'd lay down her life for him."

Richard's teeth gleamed in the lamplight when he smiled. "I never heard you talk about Golda like that."

"Golda is a cobra. Beautiful but deadly. Margaret is a flower. The closer you get, the more beautiful she is."

"Kind of poetic. Now I know you're smitten if you're talking like that. I wish you well, Daniel. It's time you quit chasing danger. I don't want you to end up in the calaboose."

Daniel grinned. "You haven't given up danger yet."

"If I found a woman like your Margaret, I might." He took out a packet and began to roll a cigarette. "I'd better get back. I'll let you know what Charlie says. Don't do anything until you hear from me. We've got too much riding on this to have something go wrong now."

"All right." Daniel walked with him to where his horse was tethered. "Tell Charlie it's imperative that I talk to him."

"Hear anything from your pa?"

Daniel had been trying not to think about his father. "Nothing. I wrote a letter last week. There hasn't been time to get an answer."

"How much time does he have?" Richard's voice held sympathy.

"Time enough, I hope. But that's in God's hands."

"And your sister?"

"She should be there by now. My aunt is there as well. I expect she'll write me when she gets the letter."

"That might sway Charlie more than anything."

"I hope so. There isn't much time. Not for my father and not for Charlie to extricate himself from this mess."

Richard mounted the horse and touched the brim of his hat. "Stay out of trouble."

"Always." Daniel watched him ride away and hoped he could

follow the admonishment. He'd give it a few days, but if Charlie wouldn't agree to a meeting, Daniel would have no choice but to force the issue.

THE NEXT FEW days sped by as the ranch geared up for the March roundup. Daniel saw to having the men distribute hay bales to the fields for the cattle, checked the repair of the buildings, and got things ready for the roundup. Branding would take about a week, and he wanted to get it done before any bad storms hit. So far, they'd been lucky, but the rolling thunderstorms were a way of life in Texas. The days had been uncharacteristically warm, and he paused astride his horse to wipe his bandana across his sweaty face.

Margaret had worked hard these past few days as well, but he'd managed to keep his distance, even though he wanted to be around her, to listen to her throaty laughter, to see the sun glisten on her red hair. She despised him, though. He needed to find out how much she knew about his operation, but he was almost afraid to probe too deeply for fear he would discover she knew more than was good for her. And that was stupid of him. Forewarned was forearmed.

It bothered him he might have to consider her an enemy when all he wanted to do was get closer to her. But his life wasn't quite ready for that. He had to get this job done first. He sighed. It wouldn't be over too soon for him. Charlie would change his mind about seeing him, and he had to be on his toes when the word came to move.

The air pressed down on him in a nearly unbearable cloak of

heat and humidity. High clouds had begun to build in the southwest, and Daniel frowned. They could be in for a bad storm. The air had that quality to it. It would bear watching.

The stock milled restlessly too, another sure sign of inclement weather. He dug his heels into his gelding's flanks and turned toward the job at hand. Cutting calves from their mothers, he herded them toward the corral where the other animals waited. Tomorrow they would start the branding, a job he didn't look forward to.

Margaret was sitting on the fence around the corral when he got his small band of calves safely into the yard. Dust streaked her face, and the humidity had caused her red hair to spring to life with curls that had escaped the braid. She looked like she had a curly halo around her face, and he grinned at the sight.

She scowled at him. "What are you smiling at?"

"I like your halo. It suits you."

Her frown deepened. "What halo?" She cautiously reached up and touched the top of her head. She grimaced at the way her curls stood out from her head, then sighed and put her hand down. "I give up."

"You done for the day?"

She nodded. "I was about to go in and get cleaned up for supper." Her face froze, and her mouth dropped open as she stared at something behind him.

Twisting in the saddle, he turned to see a heavy black thunderstorm bearing down on them. Then the thunder rolled toward them. The herd milled restlessly as lightning flashed.

"We've got to stop a stampede!" Margaret shouted.

Daniel nodded. "You go east. I'll go west," he yelled. "Round up any hands you see to help."

"They'll know and be on their way." She jumped on her horse and galloped toward the cows.

Daniel watched her for a moment as she moved among the cattle, distracting them from the storm and herding them out from under the trees. She was a remarkable woman. There had not been a trace of fear on her face when the lightning started.

He shook himself from his reverie and began to move the cattle. A particularly vicious bolt of lightning struck a tree near the largest group of stock. Their eyes rolled in terror, and they grew more restless. Daniel could feel the imminent stampede beginning to build as they turned and started toward the east pasture.

Margaret! He turned in his saddle to look for her. She was right in the middle of the path and would be trampled. A cow near him bawled in terror as the thunder and lightning intensified, and then Daniel's worst fears materialized. Three cows near him started on a run. Soon others joined them, and the mindless rush began to spread.

He shouted for Margaret to get to safety, but it was impossible to make himself heard over the sound of the wind and thunder. He turned his horse's head and raced toward Margaret. Just before he reached her, she realized her danger. Her face whitened as she saw the wave of cattle coming her way. She shouted something, and he thought it was his name.

Just as he reached her side, her gaze locked onto his. She held up her arms, and he jerked her onto the saddle behind him. Archie galloped off, his eyes rolling wildly with terror.

She pointed toward a hillside. "Get a wiggle on!" she shouted in his ear.

The cattle would not be able to run over the boulders and

would turn and run around them. But he was not at all sure they would reach the safety of the mass of stones in time. As the stampede grew nearer, the thunder of the cattle's hooves was louder than the rumble overhead as lightning flared.

Urging his horse forward, they made the final few yards, then he and Margaret tumbled from his horse.

Daniel grabbed Margaret's hand, and they ran for safety. Diving into the ravine behind the rocks, Daniel and Margaret tumbled headlong among the stones and cacti. He tried to protect her from the worst of the fall, but she cried out once or twice. When they hit bottom, he pulled her into the safety of his arms and buried his face in her neck. If the cattle ignored the rocks and trampled them, he wanted his last moments to be spent with her close. The dust of the melee washed over them as they huddled behind the boulders.

When no sharp hooves struck them, he raised his head and peered over the top of the boulders. Just as he'd hoped, the cattle skirted the outcropping and thundered past in moments that seemed to last forever.

When the dreadful roaring of cattle's hooves subsided, a cold rain began to pummel them. Daniel raised his head and stared down at Margaret. Her eyes were closed, and blood oozed from a cut on her forehead. He sat up and pressed his fingers to her throat. Her heart pounded beneath his fingertips. *Thank you, God.* He didn't know what he would do if he lost her.

He ran gentle hands over her arms and legs. Nothing seemed to be broken. She started to stir as the cold rain hit her face. He'd never seen a grander sight than her lids beginning to flutter.

She opened her eyes and blinked. "Are we dead?"

"I don't think so. I hurt too much to be dead."

Her eyes widened and she sat up. "You're injured?" Her gaze wandered over him.

Her anxious voice did wonders for his ego. She cared more than she allowed herself to admit. "Just cuts and bruises. Do you hurt anywhere?"

"My face." She touched the cut on her face, then pulled her hand back and stared at the blood on her fingers. "Is it bad?"

"Just a small cut. We were lucky."

"I hate stampedes." Her green eyes were the only color in her face.

"I kind of like them." He got up and brushed water off his pants. "You have to admit it's exhilarating to face one of them and live."

"Some people aren't as lucky as we were." She took his hand and allowed him to haul her to her feet. "My mother wasn't."

"Your mother died in a stampede?"

Her hair hung in wet curls around her face. She nodded and tears stood in her eyes. "When I was three. She was out helping with roundup just like today. Pa tried to reach her to get her out of the way, but he was too late. I don't think he's ever gotten over it."

Daniel's heart ached for the hurt little girl he saw in her eyes. "I'm sorry. No wonder you were scared."

She tossed her head, but the terror still lingered on her face. "Don't feel sorry for me. These kinds of things are supposed to make me stronger, right?" She brushed herself off. "We'd better get to the ranch house and see if everyone is all right."

He found his horse, now grazing calmly, and helped her mount, then swung up behind her. Her head reached his chin, and he could smell the scent of whatever she used to wash her hair.

She held herself rigid, and he could feel the way she leaned away from him. "Relax," he murmured. "I won't bite."

But she continued to lean forward with her eyes straight ahead. How could he ever get past that wall she'd built around her heart?

TWELVE

M argaret was still trembling when they reached the ranch house. Men and animals thronged the track in front of the house, and she looked frantically around for her pa. Only when she saw his tall, spare form did the tension ease from her shoulders.

She slid from Daniel's horse, then ran to her father and threw her arms around him. "Oh, Pa, there was a terrible stampede."

He patted her shoulders awkwardly, then pushed her away. "My goodness, Margaret, you're a grown woman. I expected more backbone than this. It was just a little stampede. We've seen worse."

Backbone. Margaret stiffened her spine and managed to bring her trembling under control. "I'm sorry, Pa. You know how I hate storms and stampedes."

"And it's about time you got over that fear."

"It's not entirely groundless," she reminded him.

His lips tightened at her words. "But I'll not have you hiding just because your mother was in the wrong place at the wrong time. An O'Brien doesn't run from anything."

"Yes, Pa." Her throat closed with unshed tears. Not one word of joy that she was all right, not one ounce of approval from him. She should be used to it by now, but she still craved a smile of commendation. No wonder he saw nothing wrong with leaving Lewis the ranch. He had no real love for anyone. Had he even loved her mother?

She sensed Daniel's gaze on her. There was probably pity in his eyes, but she didn't want to see it. Right now, her inadequacy was all she could bear. "I'll check and see if Inez and Vincente need help with supper." Rushing away, she gritted her teeth. She would not cry.

All through supper she felt jittery. She jumped at the least noise, and her pa had to ask her twice if she was going to check the horses before bed. The animals were as unsettled as she was.

She grabbed her cloak and went out to the corral. The soft scent of the hay in the corner wafted to her nose, and the sound of the horses' nickers soothed her frazzled nerves. She patted her gelding's nose, then turned to go back to the house.

Daniel was standing in the gate opening. "Are you all right? You hardly spoke at supper, and you're mighty pale."

"I'm fine." In no mood for bantering, she started past him.

He caught her arm. "I believe you should respect your pa, Margaret, but don't take his words too much to heart. There's a lot of hurt tied up in him. And guilt."

"Guilt?"

"He wishes he had been there to save your mother."

"How do you know that? He's never said a word about it. You heard him tonight. He didn't even ask if I was all right. Sometimes I wonder if he has a cowpat in place of a heart." She choked out the last sentence.

He stared at her for a long moment. "I would feel terrible if something ever happened to you. You are becoming important to me."

A lump formed in her throat, and she struggled not to cry. All she'd done was cry since this man came into her life. She was sick of it. He was a criminal, and she had to get rid of him somehow. But a void as deep as the canyon behind the ravine formed at the thought of never seeing him again. But what other choice was there? She could never chuck all she believed to go off with a man like him.

"You could turn yourself in," she said impulsively. "Tell the sheriff all you know. Help him find and capture the rest of the robbers. You'd probably get off if you did that."

"I can't." He let go of her arm.

She clutched his wrist and he didn't pull away. "Sure you can. Put this life of crime behind you. You said yourself God loved you and would forgive all your sins. And the sheriff is a good man. You could trust him."

He gave a faint smile. "Can't you believe in me a little, Margaret?"

She turned from his sober face and ran past him to her room. She rubbed her fists against her eyes. If only there was some way out of this mess for all of them.

An idea bloomed in her head. He didn't want to betray his comrades, but what if she found them and turned them in to the sheriff? Then they wouldn't betray him to the sheriff to get back at him for turning on them. She sat on the edge of the bed and thought about it. Though she had no notion of where the gang could be holed up, she could follow Daniel for a few days and see what she could find out.

She could see that he wanted to change. His face reflected regret and a longing to put his past behind him. It was up to her to help him. She refused to examine her motives too closely. The answers she might find there might be more than she could handle right now.

SATURDAY MORNING, WAGONS loaded with material lumbered to the house. Men on horseback and women carrying baskets of food milled around outside. Margaret stepped into the yard with hot biscuits and honey. She saw Nate and intercepted him on his way to the charred spot where the old barn used to be.

"How are Lucy and the baby?" she asked.

He tipped his hat back with one finger. He looked a little haggard. "Doing well. Little Carrie isn't sleeping much yet, though. We're all tired."

"It's obvious you need some rest. Tell Lucy I'll be over to see her in a few days."

"You can tell her yourself. She's in the center of that bunch of women oohing and ahhing over Carrie."

Margaret gasped. "She shouldn't be out yet."

"You know Lucy. Nothing keeps her lazing around the house." He looked off toward the men carrying lumber for the new barn.

She put her hands on her hips. "It's your job to keep her in line, Nate Stanton."

His grin widened. "Right. You give it a try." He strode off to join the other men for the barn raising.

"Indeed." Carrying the basket of biscuits, she joined the circle of women. Little Carrie's face peeked out from her swaddling blanket. Her eyes moved under the delicate cover of her eyelids. Her little rosebud mouth sucked as if she were dreaming of nursing. Margaret stared hard at her friend. Though Lucy was a little pale, she was smiling and seemed fine. It seemed odd to see her without the round belly.

"Want to hold her?" Lucy didn't wait for an answer but put the baby in Margaret's arms.

Margaret ran her lips over the infant's soft hair and inhaled the sweet scent of a newborn. The child was so light in her arms. She snuggled Carrie close and kissed her small forehead. "She's adorable, Lucy." The nursery for her and Stephen still held their small beds. She'd sometimes peeked in and imagined her own children sleeping there. "What are you doing out of bed? You should still be resting, not gallivanting all over the countryside. Come inside to the rocker."

Lucy smiled and fell into step beside Margaret. "I knew you'd make sure I got some rest today. I couldn't stay home when everyone was here enjoying themselves."

Fanny, Lucy's cousin, came along too. "I tried to tell her the same thing, Margaret."

The parlor held a gray horsehair sofa and two wing chairs grouped around the woodstove. The rug had seen better days. It was threadbare in front of the sofa and had marks from mud Margaret had been unable to remove. The curtains were clean, though, and a breeze lifted them. It filled the room with the fresh scent of newly mown hay.

Margaret put the basket of biscuits on the small table and shifted the baby to her other arm. "Would you like something to drink, maybe Arbuckle's?"

Lucy patted the sofa beside her. "What I want is for you to sit down and tell me about that handsome foreman your pa hired. He couldn't take his eyes off you at the dance."

"Oh hush, Lucy. You couldn't be more wrong. I dislike him very much." Margaret nuzzled Carrie's soft head again. The baby felt so wonderful in her arms. She never wanted to give her back to Lucy.

Fanny laughed and leaned over to take a biscuit. "Do tell us about him, Margaret. If you aren't interested, I might be."

It felt as though someone had stuck a hot brand in Margaret's midsection. How had she come so quickly to think Daniel was hers? The thought of him with another woman brought unbelievable heartache. She needed to root him out of her life. And quickly, before it was too late.

"He's not the staying kind of man, Fanny."

"I don't know why you say that." Fanny nibbled on her biscuit. "He's a foreman. They tend to stay around."

Margaret longed to confide in the other women, but it felt disloyal to Daniel to be talking about him behind his back. But what did she owe to someone who made his living by hurting others? It was ludicrous that she cared one iota about the man.

Lucy was studying Margaret's expression. "What aren't you telling us? Has he kissed you?"

Margaret's cheeks flamed with heat. "What a personal question to ask. I'm quite surprised at you."

"He has, hasn't he?" Lucy's smile was gleeful. "I think the two of you make a lovely couple."

"We are not a couple. He's quite insufferable. And he'll be gone soon. Besides, I have more important things to worry about than a new foreman." Margaret let Carrie curl her small fingers around her index finger as she told the women about her father's decision.

"I can't believe your father would pass you over for a cousin." Lucy held out her arms when Carrie began to whimper.

Margaret hated to let go of the warm little body, but the infant was hungry. "I understand it all too well. When Stephen died, Pa knew the family dynasty he'd hoped to build was at an end. Even if I were to marry and have children, they wouldn't carry the O'Brien name. This way there will still be an O'Brien running the ranch. Lewis's children will be O'Briens."

"But they won't be *his* grandchildren. I think Nate should talk to him. He'll listen to Nate."

Everyone listened to Nate. He was known for being smart and fair. "I don't know. It's Pa's ranch. He can do what he wants with it."

Lucy's blue eyes darkened. "But what would you do? Ranching is all you know."

Margaret tried to infuse her voice with enthusiasm. "Lewis says I can always stay here. If he takes a wife, he'll build me a cottage."

"Don't even try to tell me you'd be fine with that. I know you, Margaret. You value your independence above any woman I know. You'd hate deferring to another woman's views on a ranch that should belong to you. Would Lewis allow you to help the way you've always done?"

Margaret rubbed her head. "I don't know. I'd like to think he sees my value to the ranch."

But how could he when her own father didn't?

THIRTEEN

〜◯〜◯〜

The last nail had been pounded into the barn roof when Daniel wiped his moist forehead. Most of the neighbors had left. His right hand ached from swinging a hammer, and his forearm was knotted. He headed toward the springhouse to wash up.

Paddy emerged from the springhouse with his hair and whiskers wet. "Looks good, doesn't it? This barn's bigger than the old one. The rascal did me a favor."

"You've got good neighbors."

"The best." Paddy's genial smile faded. "That young Stanton had the nerve to take me to task for cutting Margaret out of my will. I must have a word with my daughter. She knows better than to chatter with her friends about my business."

It was none of his business, but Daniel glanced at Paddy and considered his response. He could stay out of it or actually tell the old man he was wrong. The fellow had a temper and it was possible he might fire him. All Daniel's plans would be ruined if he was booted out on his ear. Even as he decided he was staying out of it, he opened his mouth.

"I have to agree with Nate," he said. "Margaret has worked hard here on the ranch. She deserves better from you."

Paddy's thick brows drew together. "You're mighty opinionated for someone who just got here. How would you know what my daughter has or has not done around this place?"

"I've seen the respect she's earned. And I've been here long enough to see how hard she works. I'm not speaking against Lewis. He seems a fine man. But Margaret is your flesh and blood."

"She's a female. And like her mother, she's led by emotion."

"That's hardly fair, Paddy. Margaret is smart. She knows what is best for the ranch, not an outsider like Lewis. What if Lewis decides he doesn't like ranching and sells it? Where would Margaret go?"

Paddy reared back. "Sell it? Why would he do that?"

"He's lived in town all his life. What makes you think he'll take to ranching life? He may hate the unending work. He may marry and his wife will persuade him to sell out and move to town."

Paddy chewed on the idea with a scowl. "Margaret would never do that."

"No, she wouldn't. She loves this place as much as you do. Before you will it out of your family, you should think about it."

Paddy's face grew pensive and he looked off toward the river. "If only Stephen hadn't died."

"I'm sorry about that." And Daniel was. He couldn't imagine losing Charlie. That's why he was here.

Paddy stared at him. "I should fire you for meddling."

"I know. But you won't. You like my work, and you're not an irrational man."

The older man grinned. "You're a bit partial to my daughter, Daniel. You have my permission to court her."

Daniel shut his mouth. He had nothing to say to that. If he said he wasn't interested in Margaret, Paddy would see the lie. Much as Daniel would like to agree to the idea of a courtship, romance wasn't on his agenda. Not now.

"Nothing to say?" Paddy asked with a sly grin.

"I—I don't know what to say. I should think you'd want to merge your ranch with that of another rancher in the area. Aren't there better matches out there for Margaret?" Though the thought of her in another man's arms made his gut churn, he had to ask.

Paddy waved his hand. "It will take a strong man to deal with Margaret. I think you have what it takes. She thinks I'm too old and foolish. That I didn't notice your new boots and citified ways."

Daniel had thought the same. "So why did you let me stay?"

"Your eyes showed a strength of character I liked. And I decided it was time for Margaret to begin to learn more about being a woman and less about being a ranch hand."

"I think she's both."

Paddy nodded. "Not many men see past her mannish exterior. She's worn britches too long, and it's my fault. I should have put a stop to it long ago. I'm going to send her to Sally, the town dressmaker. Get her tricked out in some new dresses."

Daniel wanted to laugh but didn't dare. Didn't Paddy realize his daughter would fight him like a hooked catfish? "Don't change her too much."

Paddy clapped his hand on Daniel's shoulder. "You marry her and I'll think about changing that will, son. You've given me things to think about, and I thank you for that."

Margaret spoke from behind them. "Think about what?"

Don't say anything. Daniel willed Paddy to keep quiet. The last thing he needed was for Margaret to think he had his sights set on the ranch.

"I told young Cutler here that if he married you, I might change my mind about leaving the ranch to Lewis."

Daniel tried to catch her eye, but she was staring at her father with horror. Daniel reached toward her, but she took a step back.

Her green eyes were wide and hurt. "Why not haul me to town and put me on the auction block? Let everyone get a chance at the ranch. The only problem is, they'd have to take me with it." She whirled and ran for the door.

Daniel started to go after her, but Paddy grabbed his arm. "Let her be. She won't thank you for interfering right now. Maybe later."

INEZ'S ROUGH HANDS smoothed Margaret's hair where she sat on a stool in her serviceable blue nightgown. Inez plaited it swiftly. "Your father, he loves you, Señorita Margaret. You must never doubt that. He is man and does not understand feelings of women. Your mama, she die too early to teach him."

Inez's hands in her hair drained some of the tension from her shoulders. Margaret had always missed having a mother, but never more than this moment. What was she to do with her life? If Pa gave Lewis the ranch, she would be displaced, no matter what her cousin said. He had good intentions and would try to make her feel part of the work, but the minute he married, everything would change.

And how dare her father try to bribe Daniel into marrying her? No wonder he'd been pursuing her. She'd thought he was genuinely interested in her. Now she suspected her father had brought him to town for the express purpose of marrying her off. Pa would change his tune when he heard why Daniel was *really* here. When the sheriff and posse rode up to arrest him. Her chest squeezed and she pushed the mental image away. Yearning after a greedy man like Daniel was fruitless. She had to decide her future by herself.

She glanced around her room. The floorboards were wide and could use repainting. The gray walls hadn't been redone in a good ten years. Now that she could buy paint already premixed in a can, she would suggest they repaint in here. There was no personality to this space. Male or female could be comfortable here in the double bed with the rag rug on the wood. The stool was wood with no cushioning. There was only a tiny closet with four hooks in the room. She'd had no need of a larger one since her wardrobe was far from lavish. In spite of its shortcomings, this room was *hers*. How could she bear to leave it?

"All I know is ranch work. I wouldn't know how to earn a living outside of the ranch."

Inez tied a ribbon at the end of the braid. "You keep books for the ranch. Orville, perhaps he would have place for you."

Margaret groaned. "I can't imagine anything worse than being cooped up in the bank all day long. But I may have no choice." She'd have to rent one of those rooms above a store. "I shall have to decide what I want to do with my life, then do it."

The options weren't exciting: teaching, cooking, cleaning. Dressmaking was out. She was very slow and tended to prick her fingers, leaving blood behind on the fabric, and she'd never mastered the sewing machine Inez was so fond of. There were good friends in the area who might hire her as a stable hand. She was good with horses. But then that created another set of problems—lodging. Most hands stayed in the bunkhouse. She was a woman. That would never be allowed, nor would she want it.

Marrying was her best option. She would be able to manage her own household and do things her way. She ran through the list of men she knew who had ranches. Most of them were married, and if they had sons, the sons were too young. But other ranchers came through the area. Maybe she could figure out a way to meet more travelers.

"You will think of something." Inez patted her shoulder. "I can see."

"I was trying to think how I might meet more ranchers who happen to be coming this way. Maybe I can get a job in town. When I was in Larson last week, I saw the café was looking for a waitress. Emma Croft likes me. She might hire me."

"But what of your duties? Your papa depends on you."

Margaret rose from the stool and went to the bed. She folded the quilt back to the bottom of the bed and pulled back the sheets. "Pa would have to get along without me. He has Lewis now. And Daniel. There is plenty of help."

Inez followed her to the bed and dimmed the kerosene lamp on the bedside table. "Mr. Daniel, he has his eye on you."

Margaret fluffed her pillow. "Daniel is only interested in gaining control of the ranch. He is only courting me because Pa might give me the ranch if he marries me."

"You know this to be true?"

"I heard Pa tell him that tonight with my own ears." Talking about it was like probing for a splinter in a sore finger. "I don't want to talk about Daniel. I shall not be marrying him."

"I think you like him."

"He's not what you think, Inez."

"I do not understand."

Margaret rubbed her forehead. "He is duplicitous. His reasons for being here have nothing to do with ranching."

Her maid shrugged. "All people have reasons for what they do. Very confusing. But Mr. Daniel, he is good man."

"There are parts that are not so good." She flipped her braid behind her and sat on the edge of the bed. The springs squeaked under her and the mattress sagged in the middle. There were so many things that could use sprucing up at the ranch, but it wouldn't be her problem.

Inez studied her face, then smiled. "You are tired, señorita. Sleep. You will feel better in morning."

Margaret snuggled into the sheets, smelling of fresh air and lye soap. Inez extinguished the lamp and pulled the door shut behind her. The work Margaret had done today didn't explain her fatigue—it was purely heartache. She would figure out what to do in the morning.

FOURTEEN

⸜◦✦◦⸝

L arson teemed with people. Most everyone was in town today. Margaret let her father out at the mercantile, then drove the buckboard to the blacksmith's to have a wheel repaired. The streets were muddy from the recent rain, and a passing buggy tossed clumps at Margaret's boots. She gave the blacksmith instructions, then walked across the street toward the café.

It was too early for lunch so Emma should have time to talk to her. The sign was still in the window. Margaret paused on the boardwalk and glanced down at her britches. She should have worn her Sunday dress even if Pa had asked her about it. Though she'd never applied for a position before, it made sense that she should look her best instead of appearing in tan dungarees and a faded plaid shirt. She smoothed her hair. At least Inez had put it up for her this morning, though the wind had tugged strands of it loose on the ride to town.

She squared her shoulders. There was no help for it now. If she didn't apply today, it would be another week before she came to town. The bell on the door tinkled when she pushed into the café and glanced around. The dining room was a pleasant place. Red-and-white-checkered tablecloths covered the tables, and the chairs were comfortable. Margaret had spent many an hour enjoying Emma's excellent food.

A couple she didn't recognize was drinking coffee by the front window. The woman kept peering out the window, then glancing at Margaret as if to ask what she was doing standing around instead of taking a seat. Margaret smiled at them before going through the door and down the hall in the direction of the aroma of roasting beef. Today's special was beef stew.

The kitchen was at the end of the hall. A wooden table still held traces of flour from Emma's famous homemade sourdough bread. The wood floor was spotless. A couple of pie safes and cupboards stood along the wall opposite the stove. The huge stove belched out heat.

Emma stirred a large pot on a woodstove. Her olive skin was smooth, but she'd owned the café for more than thirty years, so she had to be at least sixty. She didn't take any guff from the men, and most of the trail riders knew better than to say a smart-mouthed word to her. Which was another of the many reasons Margaret held Emma in high esteem. As far as Margaret knew, Emma had never married. She'd forged a path for herself, just as Margaret intended to do.

Emma turned with the wooden spoon in her hand. She put it down and dried her hands on the large red apron she wore over her gray dress. Her hair was up in a tight bun. "Margaret, surely you're not hungry at this hour of the morning. What can I do for you?"

Margaret walked into the room and stopped by the worktable. "I see you are still looking for a waitress."

Emma's eyes brightened. "I am. Doing this by myself is more

than I can handle. It's hard work, mind you. Twelve-hour days, six days a week. I pay three dollars a week, plus the men are fair tippers. Who are you recommending? Anyone I know?"

Twelve-hour days. There would be no time to help at the ranch at all. "What about half shifts?"

Emma put her hands on her hips. "What is this all about, young lady?"

"I'd like to apply for the job myself, Emma."

The woman didn't even gasp. She looked Margaret over and nodded. "No one could say you aren't a bold one. I suppose you aren't going to tell me why you're thinking of leaving your ranch?"

Margaret held her head up. "It's Pa's ranch, not mine. He has other plans for its settlement, so I find myself in the position of needing to secure my future." She gestured to the kitchen. "You built this business all by yourself. I'd like to learn from you."

Emma's gaze swept Margaret's figure. "You'd have to wear a dress. I can't have you working in my establishment dressed in those dungarees like a man. Men might think you aren't quite proper."

Though the comment was as she expected, Margaret's smile faltered. "It will take me some time to acquire dresses. I don't have anything serviceable for work."

"The mercantile got in a shipment of ready-made dresses."

Ready-made. Those would never fit, but Margaret nodded. "I will see what I can do. Now about the hours. Is there any flexibility?"

Emma chewed her bottom lip. "Your pa doesn't know about this, does he? When he finds out, he'll be mighty upset."

Margaret's throat squeezed. "So you won't hire me?"

"I didn't say that." Emma turned back to stir the pot. "Paddy doesn't scare me. But I don't think you'll be able to deal with being cooped up inside all day. You're used to fresh air."

"I won't let you down, Emma. Please." Margaret was ready to abandon the thought of asking for shorter workdays if it meant she could go back to the ranch and tell her father she had a job.

Emma turned back toward her and smiled. "We're already shorthanded. Whatever hours you work would be welcome. Breakfast isn't so bad. I have flapjacks and bacon cooked up ahead of time. I can handle that by myself. How about you come in at twelve every day and work through until eight? That will give you time to help with morning chores. And it will let us both see whether you're suited to this work."

"Thank you, Emma, I'll work hard."

Emma turned back to stir the stew. "I have no doubt about that. It's different work than you're used to, though. It will take some adjustment."

Margaret glanced at the watch pinned to her shirt. "I'd better go. Pa will be done soon."

"Let me know when you'll be available to start."

"I will."

Her father was across the street on a bench when she exited the café. He saw her and waved her over. What if he suspected she was applying for the job? But no, why would he? She dashed across the street between two buggies.

"Your business is done?" If she got him talking, he would be unlikely to question her activities.

"When the buckboard is ready, we'll stop back and pick up everything. I have another mission in mind now."

The gleam in his eye was unusual. "What's that?"

"We're going to get you some dresses."

SAFE IN HIS ARMS

"D-Dresses?" Had he overheard?

"It's high time you started dressing like a woman. You were quite lovely in your mother's dress at the dance." He rose and extended his arm. "Shall we go see Sally?"

Margaret took his arm and they walked down the boardwalk until it ended, then stepped along the street to Sally's house. Sally was Lucy's aunt, and Margaret thought Lucy might look a lot like her when she was her age. The home was a neat bungalow with a large porch and flowers blooming along the brick walk. The door and shutters were painted green and so was the porch.

Sally's daughter, Fanny, answered the door. Wearing a blue dress, she looked fresh and pretty. Her dark hair was up and her eyes were bright. "Why, Margaret, how lovely to see you! Come in. Mother is in the sewing room, but I'll fetch her."

"We're here to secure her services. Pa wants me to buy some dresses."

"I should say so! You looked magnificent at the dance. Come with me."

They stepped inside the foyer. The blue-and-white-flowered wallpaper was a cheery welcome. The wood floor gleamed with polish. Fanny led them down the hall to a room off the kitchen. Fabric covered two worktables. Sally sat at a sewing machine. The needle whirred up and down as she pumped the treadle with her foot. The fabric was a soft blue that lay in lovely folds. The dress appeared to be mostly finished, and Sally was sewing lace onto the collar.

Sally glanced up. Her blue eyes peered over her glasses, then her face lit up. "Why, Paddy and Margaret. I wasn't expecting you. Fanny, you should have summoned me to the parlor."

"I offered, Mama, but Mr. O'Brien wants you to make some dresses for Margaret."

Sally rose and snatched up her tape measure. Her smile beamed out. "I've wanted to dress you for ages, dear girl. I just got in some new fabric that would be quite attractive with your hair and skin." She steered Margaret to the bolts of fabric on the far table. "This rich golden brown would look lovely on you." She flipped out a length of fabric and held it up to Margaret's face. "Exactly as I thought. And look here." She pulled a book to the edge of the table. "Have a peek at some of the styles. I think this would be attractive."

Margaret wrinkled her nose at the frilly apparition. "Perhaps some walking skirts and blouses with a vest."

"That sounds very mannish, Margaret," her father said. "I'd like to see you in something more feminine." He stabbed a thick finger at a dress. "This one. In the brown."

It had pleats on the top and deep flounces at the hem. At least it wasn't as fussy as the first one. Its sleek lines looked elegant. "All right," Margaret said. "But some serviceable skirts and blouses too."

Sally held up a length of deep aqua. It was in a shiny fabric. "And what about this for a Sunday best?"

"Very well. Isn't this going to cost a lot, Pa?"

"We aren't paupers." He scowled. "I can afford to dress you properly."

"And it's about time you did," Sally said. "She's not a ranch hand. She's your daughter and needs to look the part. You're a big man in Texas, Paddy."

"She needs to find a husband," he said. "So trick her out the best way you can."

"Don't talk about me like I'm not here," Margaret protested. "And with my height, something simple would be best."

Sally patted her hand. "You leave it to me, my dear. Let's get your measurements, and I shall get to work." She seized a pencil and paper and began to measure Margaret.

"How long will it take?" Margaret asked.

"How many dresses do you need?"

"Three," Margaret said.

"Eight," her father said. "How soon? I'll pay extra if you can get them done in a week."

"I can manage," Sally said.

Margaret turned to stare at him. "Eight? I don't need so many."

"I'm going to send you to Austin for some parties. You seemed to think Daniel isn't good enough, so we'll find someone who is."

"I said no such thing. I merely protested being auctioned off like a bull. I'd like to choose my own husband. Is that so hard to understand?" She put her hands on her hips. "I'm *not* going to Austin!"

His craggy face softened, and he tugged at his collar. "You pick him and I'll vet him, my girl. But first let's get one picked out."

"You don't have your heart set on Daniel?"

He shrugged. "He's a good man, but I'm sure there are others out there."

"And the ranch?" Her pulse beat against her ribs. Maybe he'd changed his mind about cutting her out of a share of the ranch.

Her father lifted a smug brow. "Find a husband and we'll talk."

She swallowed down her disappointment. "I don't want to leave the Triple T. I don't want to get married either."

He patted her arm. "You'll get used to the idea, Margaret. You'll soon have little ones hanging on your skirts."

She couldn't imagine such a thing. Becoming a wife would

mean more than being in charge of her own household. It would mean a change in her daily activities as well. Most husbands would expect her to take charge of the kitchen. She wasn't afraid of hard work, but she liked her life the way it was.

FIFTEEN

⤜⤛⤛⤚⤚

The aroma of fried fish mingled with that of apple dumplings. Margaret smoothed the fabric of her new skirt, a black walking skirt in soft cotton. Her blouse felt a little stiff and starchy at the collar, but it would do. Pa didn't know about her job yet. He had gone to Dallas for a few days. Her first week of work would be under her belt before she told him.

She carried two heaping plates of fish and coleslaw into the dining room. She placed them in front of two men she didn't recognize. "Here you go. I'll bring your dessert when you're finished."

One man grabbed her wrist as she turned to go. "Don't be so quick to leave us, miss. Pull up a chair. There's no one else in here right now. We could stand some conversation." He winked at the other man.

She jerked away, then paused. This job was all about meeting eligible men. He probably meant no harm. While his looks didn't appeal, there were more important things than looks. He appeared to be in his early thirties with dark hair peppered with a few strands of white at the temples. He had the handlebar mustache she despised, but with the right persuasion that might be gone. His eyes were gray and his nose was straight.

"Where are you fellows from?" she asked.

"Abilene," the man said. "Came to town looking for work. Know of any ranchers looking for help driving cattle to market?"

A cowboy, not a rancher. Still, that wasn't necessarily a bad thing. Pa would settle enough money on her to give her and any husband a start on a ranch of their own.

He grabbed her arm and yanked her onto his lap. His arm snaked around her and he puckered his lips. "How about a kiss?"

Without thinking, her hand flew out and smacked him upside the face. His head reeled back and his grip loosened. She leaped away, then stopped at a safe distance. "Keep your hands to yourself, cowboy. I'm a waitress, not a fancy woman."

The bell jingled over the door and Daniel stepped into the room. He glanced at her, then back at the man whose cheek bore a red mark the shape of a hand. "What's going on here?"

The man ducked his head and picked up his fork. "Nothing."

Daniel's lips tightened. "These men bothering you?"

"It was nothing I couldn't handle." She picked up a pot of coffee from the table and refilled the cups, then carried it back to the kitchen.

Daniel followed her. "What's going on, Margaret? I've been looking all over for you." He glanced around. "You can't be working here."

She plunked down the coffeepot and whirled around to face him. "And why can't I? I'm not competent enough, or is there some other reason you think I can't handle a job?"

He held his hands in front of him. "I meant you have more important work to do than waiting tables." He glanced at Emma, who was listening with rapt attention at the stove. "No offense, Emma."

Her lips flattened. "Margaret is doing a fine job, Mr. Cutler."

"I'm sure she is, but the ranch needs her." He drilled Margaret with a dark glance. "Does your father know about this?"

"Not yet. I'll tell him when he returns in a few days. I hadn't planned to start yet, but my clothing was ready and Emma needed the help, so I decided to work a few hours today."

"And how will you get the work done at the ranch?"

She tipped up her chin. "The ranch has you, Daniel, and my cousin. There is no shortage of hands as well."

"That's not the same and you know it. I expect your father will have something to say about this."

"He's said everything that matters—he's leaving the ranch to Lewis. Which means I must look out for myself."

He took a step nearer. "Don't do this, Margaret. You're operating on emotion now, not logic. Lewis is always going to need your help. It takes more than one person to run a ranch that large."

Heat flooded her cheeks. Emotion, indeed! "I've thought this through, and it's the only proper course of action. Women can make their own way in the world, you know. We don't have to be dependent on a man for our livelihood."

"I didn't say you did. But waiting tables isn't where your heart lies. It's with the ranch. You'll be miserable inside all day."

"I told her the same, but she's determined," Emma said.

"I can see that," he said, holding Margaret's gaze.

She picked up the pot again when the bell tinkled. "I have customers to see to. You can go out the back if you like."

"I'd like some food." He followed her. "And coffee."

She was likely to spill it all over him if he sat and watched her.

COLLEEN COBLE

But she would show him she was competent to do anything she set her mind to.

BY THE TIME Margaret's first week was over, her feet were sore, and she'd found out how hard waiting tables was. Today was her first day off in a week, and Pa would have to be told what she'd done. The rain drizzled down as she cut calves out of the herd, but she didn't mind. To her, it was a day as fine as cream gravy. She was in her element.

The poncho did little to stop the cold rain from trickling down her neck and back as she rode back to the ranch house. The rain stopped about a mile from home. A rainbow emerged from the clouds. It almost looked like the rainbow's end was at the Triple T. Such fanciful notions. It was probably because she was still so distraught at the thought of leaving it. Dusk was approaching and she wanted to be inside before dark.

Archie seemed to sense her longing to be home and broke into a trot. She leaned back in the saddle and let him go.

"Eager to get home?" Daniel asked as his horse fell into step with hers.

"I want a hot bath."

"You need some plaster on that cut too."

Did he have to remind her that Archie had thrown her? She barely felt the sting of the cut on her face, but every muscle hurt from her fall into the rocks. She could count the times she'd been thrown on one hand, and it had been humiliating that Daniel had seen this one. She shivered in her saddle, cold clear to the bone. But more than anything, she wanted to get out of Daniel's company. He made her feel things she didn't understand. It had been so much simpler before he arrived. He was such an enigma, and she didn't like puzzles. She liked black to be black and white to be white. Shades of gray were too difficult to comprehend.

"Your pa is due back today. You gonna tell him about your job tonight or wait until you go in tomorrow?"

She shot him a warning glance. "I'll tell him after dinner. Just make sure you don't say anything."

He grinned. "I'll try to stay out of the fracas."

As they neared the house, she noticed men running back and forth to the barn. "Is that the sheriff's horse?" Not that Daniel would know. He was too new. She glanced at him. "Is he here to arrest you?"

"You'd like that, wouldn't you?"

She held his gaze. "No. No, I wouldn't."

He looked away and stared at the ranch. "There's something wrong. Isn't that the doctor on the porch?"

Her fingers tightened on the reins. "Yes, you're right." She urged her horse into a run and reached the yard, where she slid to the ground and threw the reins around a post. She splashed through mud puddles to the porch. "Where's Pa?" she asked Calvin.

The ranch hand's grizzled face was white. "In his room with the doctor, Miss Margaret."

She bolted for the door, not waiting to ask what had happened. Lewis was pacing in the hall outside her father's room. He blocked her path when she started for the door.

"Let me pass," she demanded.

"Doc said everyone had to stay out here." He put his hand on her arm. "Calm down, Margaret."

"What's wrong with him?"

"He arrived about noon. Calvin found him in the back field this afternoon at one. He'd been hit on the head."

She gasped. "Someone hit him again?"

"It appears that way."

She collapsed onto his chest. "He's going to be all right, isn't he? Is he awake?"

"No, he's been unconscious since we found him, so I sent for the doctor. He's been with him only a few minutes."

Her throat burned, and she buried her face in his shirt. "Why didn't you send for me?" She lifted her head and shook him. "You had no right not to come get me!"

Lewis hugged her. "I thought you'd be here shortly."

She clutched her cousin's solid form. "He can't die, Lewis."

"He's a tough old bird. I'm sure the doctor will fix him right up."

Daniel joined them outside the door. "I heard what happened. Was the assailant caught?"

"We have no idea who did this."

Lewis's tone was aggressive, and Margaret glanced up at him. Did he think Daniel had something to do with it, or was it his knowledge about the foreman's "other" activities? Daniel had been with her, so he couldn't have had anything to do with this.

"I don't understand why anyone would want to hurt Pa." She stepped away from her cousin.

Lewis folded his arms across his chest and stared at Daniel. "You have to wonder if some other crime is going on around here and Uncle Paddy observed it."

Margaret gulped. Even if Daniel had nothing to do with this, one of his gang members could have. Pa might have seen the man in the barn and challenged him. It made sense. She hugged herself and leaned against the wall. "What's taking so long?"

Before Lewis could answer her, the door opened. His expression grave, the doctor stepped out. He blocked the doorway when she tried to move past him. "I need to talk to you, Margaret."

She plucked at his sleeve. "He's all right, isn't he?"

"I'm afraid you're going to have to be strong." He nodded at Daniel. "Get some whiskey."

Her limbs turned to lead. "Whiskey? I don't drink. Tell me what's wrong."

The doctor took her arm and moved her down the hall toward her room. "I want you to sit down first."

She stumbled as she realized how serious it was. Was Pa paralyzed? In a stupor she let the doctor lead her to her bed, where she sank onto the side. "Tell me." Lewis was looking more anxious too. The doctor knelt beside her. Daniel entered with a glass of amber liquid, which she refused.

The doctor glanced at Lewis, then back at her. "I'm afraid we've lost him, Margaret."

"Lost him?" The words meant nothing to her at first. Pa was in his bedroom. She'd caught a glimpse of him when the doctor opened the door. When Lewis's face crumpled, she understood the doctor was saying her dad was dead.

She sprang to her feet. "You're wrong!"

The doctor made a grab for her and missed as she ran for the door. She would go to him and her pa would open his eyes. They would see. Daniel blocked her passage. She stared at the compassion in his eyes and faced the truth before crumpling into his embrace.

SIXTEEN

Townspeople had thronged the house all day. The women had brought enough food to feed half the county. Daniel stayed as close to Margaret as was seemly. She was frozen in her grief, moving mechanically among the guests as she accepted condolences. She had asked for Carrie when Lucy arrived and hadn't let the baby out of her arms.

Nate and Lucy were the last to leave. As Nate gathered the children, Lucy joined Daniel where he stood by the big window in the parlor. "I'm worried about Margaret."

"I am too," he told her.

"Has she cried?"

"Just when the doctor told her." He'd replayed the way she'd clung to him like he was her only solace. He wanted to be that comfort, that protector, but he had no right.

"You need to protect her, Daniel. What if the murderer goes after her next?"

"I'll look after her, Lucy. I promise." He walked her to the door, where Margaret stood hugging the children good-bye.

"I guess you have to take Carrie," Margaret said. "She's brought me such comfort today."

Lucy put her hand on Margaret's arm. "I wish I could leave her with you. Do you want me to stay?"

Margaret's eyes widened, then she shook her head. "Nate would miss you too much. I'll be fine."

Lucy glanced at Nate, who shrugged. "Stay, Luce. I'll come fetch you and Carrie tomorrow. Do you need me to bring you anything tonight?"

"I brought plenty of things for Carrie." Lucy stood on tiptoe and planted a kiss on the corner of Nate's mouth.

He smiled and put his big hand on her shoulder. "I'll be praying for you both."

"Thanks, Nate," Margaret called after him. Her arms tightened around the baby.

Daniel walked Nate and the children out to the wagon. "Lucy will bring a lot of comfort to Margaret."

Nate lifted William and Eileen into the wagon. "Those two are tighter than bark on a birch tree. Send someone for me if you need me."

Daniel watched them disappear into the sunset, then put his hands in his pockets and let his gaze wander around the yard. Margaret was sure there had been an intruder, but what if it was one of the hands? Maybe Paddy caught someone stealing or rustling. He knew she had told her cousin what she'd overheard about his involvement with the outlaws. Lewis had been skulking around for days, but there was nothing to see.

Just before Paddy's death, Charlie had agreed to meet with Daniel, but all the turmoil had delayed the meeting once again. He had no idea what was going on with the rest of the gang, but he didn't believe any of them were involved in this. But maybe he didn't *want* to believe it. It would make him responsible too, and Paddy had been good to him. If his arrival here had caused the man's death, Daniel didn't think he could live with himself.

He saw movement over by the barn and realized a man had slipped around the corner of the building. Though his back was to the house, the shape of the man's head and shoulders seemed familiar. The man shuffled to the side. Frank. No one else had that massive head and sloping shoulders. What was he doing here? And more important, did he have anything to do with Paddy's death?

The man's appearance here didn't bode well. Daniel walked along the side of the house toward the outbuildings. The barn door was swinging. A horse neighed when he stepped into the cool dimness of the barn's interior.

He thought about calling out, but he wanted to know what Frank was doing here. He crept along the straw-strewn boards to the back of the building, from where the sounds of movement were coming. Frank rooted through a mound of hay.

"What are you doing?" Daniel demanded.

Frank yanked out his gun as he whirled to face him. The barrel of the gun jerked, then the man lowered it to his side. "You about got yourself drilled."

Daniel clenched his fingers into his palms. "I asked what you were doing here."

Frank was in his forties and had been the leader of the gang from the beginning. He and Daniel had been slightly adversarial from the moment they met. Daniel had always assumed it was because the man didn't want him hanging around Golda. Frank's method of not getting caught after a robbery was to make sure any eyewitnesses were six feet under. His violent nature was always barely covered with a veneer of congeniality.

"Looking around." Frank holstered his revolver.

"For what?" Daniel didn't like the man here on the property. Not with Margaret a few yards away.

"Rumor has it that some valuable bonds from a stagecoach heist ten years ago are somewhere around here."

"Here? That makes no sense." But even as he protested, he remembered the hole he'd found after the first barn burned. It wasn't far from the new hole Frank had started.

Frank shrugged. "Some say Paddy's boy hid it before he went off to the army. It was to be his stake for getting started when he came back."

Daniel exhaled. "Are you saying that Stephen O'Brien robbed the stage?"

"Don't know that for a fact, but it's one of the rumors I heard in town."

Had Margaret heard the rumors? Maybe that's why Stephen had headed west. Daniel had wondered why he would leave his aging father to run the ranch with only Margaret's help. The possibility explained a lot.

Frank was still staring. "I heard the bonds were worth a hundred thousand."

Daniel kept his expression impassive. The large amount of money made it even more likely the rumor was false. "I want you off the property. Someone could see you and it will tip our hand."

Frank's eyes squinted to a slit. "Tell you what. You look around. See what you can find out. Maybe we can work together and track down those bonds. I'm willing to share."

"I doubt there are any bonds," Daniel said.

"You're wanting it all for yourself, Cutler. You wouldn't have known about it if I hadn't told you. If I find out you found it and didn't share it with me, that redhead inside will pay for it."

Daniel didn't like the fact that Frank had even noticed Margaret. "She's got nothing in this. And neither do I. I don't intend to look for any bonds. I don't believe they're here."

"If you don't find them, I will."

If Daniel didn't at least agree to look for them, Frank would be back. "I'll see if I can find the bonds, but remember, I'm here for bank information. Wouldn't you say that's more important?"

"You can do both." Frank sauntered off with a smug expression.

Daniel had to wonder why Frank had picked this area of Texas. Maybe he'd come to look for the bonds all along.

THE ATTORNEY'S OFFICE was paneled in dark wood. The desk was in front of a large window that looked out onto Main Street where passersby strolled past the storefronts. Margaret sat in a comfortable leather chair with Lewis in the chair beside her. She glanced at the newspaper on the table. There was a drawing of a meteor that hit in Iowa on the front page. She shifted and sighed.

Lewis leaned over and squeezed her hand. "Don't look so scared, Margaret. Nothing will change. Even if Uncle Paddy didn't get your settlement arranged, I'll make sure you're taken care of."

She returned the pressure of his fingers. "I know, Lewis. We'll make a good team." She swallowed hard. "I just can't believe he's gone."

"I'm going to find out who did this, I swear. Uncle Paddy was a good man. He didn't deserve to be put down like a dog in his own field."

Her eyes burned. She didn't like to remember how her father had died. Had he thought of her in his last moments? The house felt empty without his large presence. The rooms echoed without his booming voice. She'd awakened last night, sure that he was standing by her bed. Until she remembered he was dead.

The door behind them opened, and Ben Mayfield entered the office. He was tall and thin to the point of emaciation, but he always wore a smile that lightened his cavernous face. "Good morning, folks." Once he was settled in his chair behind the large, polished desk, he opened a folder and adjusted his glasses. "You're here for the reading of your father's last will and testament, Miss Margaret. First, let me say I'm sorry for your loss. I thought a lot of Paddy. I shall miss him."

"Me too," Margaret choked out. She rubbed her eyes. "Go ahead. I'm prepared to hear what you have to say. Pa already told me he was leaving the ranch to Lewis."

"Indeed. Well then, I believe you'll be surprised to hear that he changed that bequest the morning of his death. The minute he got off the stage, he came to my office."

Lewis leaned forward. "What?"

Ben exhaled and extracted an envelope from the file. "He left this letter for both of you." He held it out to Margaret.

She opened it and pulled out the stiff paper inside. "It's addressed to both of us." She held it out to Lewis. "Do you want to read it first?"

He shook his head. "Read it aloud. It doesn't matter. I always thought Uncle Paddy's offer was too good to be true." His Adam's apple bobbed.

In spite of her relief, Margaret felt a pang of sympathy. Poor Lewis had never had much. This was like holding out a piece of bread to a starving child, then snatching it back. Why had her father done it?

She opened the folded paper and began to read. "'My dear Margaret and Lewis, I've pondered the best thing to do with the ranch. At one point I was convinced Lewis should receive it, and Margaret should have a settlement to establish a household elsewhere, but I've reconsidered that decision. I hope it's not too much of a disappointment to you, Lewis. I know you had high expectations.'"

She stopped and glanced at Lewis, who sat listening with an anguished expression. "I'm sorry too, Lewis. But nothing has changed. It will be you and me together running the ranch. You'll never want for anything."

"Finish the letter."

She gave him a long look, then started reading again. "'After talking with Daniel, I realized my actions were unfair to you, Margaret. You would have no guarantee of a home. Daniel pointed out that Lewis could take a wife and choose to sell the ranch to please her. I've worked too hard to see that happen. I know Margaret would never sell the ranch under any circumstances, no matter who she married. So I'm settling a generous amount on you, Lewis. I hope you will stay to help Margaret, but if you choose to leave and start a business or buy a house, you will have a substantial amount of money to begin elsewhere. I know I can trust you both to stay close and look out for one another. Paddy.'"

She was barely able to whisper the final word. He'd loved her after all. What had Daniel told him? She intended to find out at the first opportunity.

"That's it, then?" Lewis said in a low voice. "He didn't leave the ranch to the two of us, even?"

Ben shook his head. "He left you ten thousand dollars, though, Lewis. Very generous."

"It *is* generous." Lewis's voice was wooden.

Ben looked at Margaret. "Your father did leave it somewhat entailed."

"Entailed?"

"If you die without issue, the property goes to Lewis as your next of kin."

"That's as it should be." Margaret stretched her hand toward Lewis. "Don't be upset."

Lewis took her hand and squeezed it. "I'm fine. Uncle Paddy was very generous. The money will give me a good start. He did the right thing. I was just a little shocked."

Margaret sprang to her feet. "Let's get some coffee at the café and talk about this, Lewis. I don't want you to go. As far as I'm concerned, you will have an equal say in the running of the ranch. I'll make sure you're paid a fair salary."

He smiled. "You're a fair woman, Margaret. But I won't stay for coffee now. There's work to be done back at the ranch. I'd best get to it."

"Please stay, Lewis. I don't want to lose you and Pa all in the same week," she whispered. What if she offered to put his name on the deed too? They could share equally. But even as the words formed on her lips, her cousin turned and left the office.

Maybe it was just as well. Her father had foreseen the possible ramifications of leaving it to both of them. He would not want the ranch split in two, and that was always possible if they hit a wall of disagreement they couldn't get past.

So money would not be a problem for her. No one was going to force her into a loveless marriage.

SEVENTEEN

The interior of the barn was like an oven, and bright sunlight streamed through the windows. Flecks of hay stuck to Daniel's damp face. He wiped it with the back of his hand and tossed another forkful of hay to the horses. He turned when he heard a footfall. Lewis wasn't smiling as he strode across the barn floor.

"Lewis, what's wrong?"

His fists curled, Lewis stopped a few feet from Daniel. "Your plan is clear now, Cutler."

"What are you talking about?"

"You had no right to talk Uncle Paddy into changing his will." Lewis took a step forward and swung his fist.

Daniel sidestepped the punch and stepped back. "Whoa, slow down. I don't have any quarrel with you."

"Well, I have a quarrel with you!" Lewis roared, then charged at Daniel.

The pitchfork went flying out of Daniel's hand, and he landed on his back on the barn floor. Lewis grabbed him by the throat, but Daniel managed to break his grip. "Get off me!" He heaved Lewis to the side and staggered to his feet. "What's this all about?"

Lewis scrambled to his feet with his chest heaving. "Your interference stripped me of my inheritance. An inheritance I was counting on. My life is ruined, thanks to you!" He took off his hat and flung it to the ground. His eyes were wild. He started toward Daniel again.

"Paddy left the ranch to Margaret?" Daniel evaded another swing from Lewis. The man couldn't hit a door with those fists. "Calm down. I'm sure Margaret isn't going to throw you out."

Lewis stood clenching and unclenching his fists. "This changes everything."

Daniel studied his pained expression. "Only a woman would cause that expression. Have you been seeing someone, Lewis? Someone who expected you to inherit?"

He shook his head. "I—I'm just shocked my uncle would do this."

"I don't think so. Who is she?"

Lewis's shoulders slumped, the fight gone from him. "Dorothy Vaughn from Wichita Falls. Her father is an attorney and owns most of the town. He only agreed to the marriage after Uncle Paddy promised me the ranch. I don't know how to tell them what's happened. He'll make her break the engagement—I know it."

Daniel digested the news. "So you never intended to live here? You were going to steal the ranch from Margaret."

Lewis looked down. "I would have taken care of Margaret. And we were going to live here."

Daniel picked up the pitchfork that had gone flying when Lewis tackled him. "For a while, maybe. Miss Vaughn sounds like she's used to more than a ranch house and hard work."

"I would have hired servants."

"Did you tell Margaret?" Daniel could imagine how that went over. He'd been right. Lewis would have sold the ranch and left Margaret homeless.

"No. It doesn't matter now."

Lewis looked desolate, but Daniel thought there was more to the story. "If Miss Vaughn cares for you, this will change nothing. Her father is wealthy. What use would he have for your ranch?"

Lewis shrugged and turned to go. "I shall have to go see her and release her from her promise."

"I'm sure Margaret would be happy to welcome your wife to the ranch," Daniel called after him.

Lewis stopped in the barn's doorway and turned. "Dorothy deserves to be the mistress of her own house. Not the wife of a poor relative who has been relegated to a ranch hand."

Daniel had endured enough of his whining. "I doubt Margaret would ever make you feel like a poor relation."

"It would still be the truth. I wouldn't subject Dorothy to that. The ten thousand dollars Uncle Paddy left me would be a start, but her father won't count it as enough to welcome me into the family."

Daniel heard the sound of buggy wheels and saw Margaret pull the horse to a stop at the corral. "Talk to Margaret before you make any hasty decisions."

Lewis turned as Margaret came toward them. He glanced around as though he might bolt if given the opportunity. She stopped a few feet from them and glanced from him to Lewis.

"I'm leaving," Lewis said abruptly.

"To town?" she asked.

"No, I'm going back to Wichita Falls. I can't stay here."

"Leaving the ranch?" She reached toward him. "Don't do that, Lewis. You're all the family I have left. I need you. I can't do it alone."

Lewis hesitated, then shook his head. "You don't get it, Margaret. I can't take orders from a woman."

"I wasn't planning on giving you orders," she said, her voice soft. "I thought it would be a partnership."

"Would you be willing to sign over half the ranch to me?"

She bit her lip, then hesitated before shaking her head. "I can't do that."

"Because one person needs to be in charge. You," he said.

"It makes sense there would be one person with the final say."

Daniel curled his fingers into his palms at her pleading expression. She was wasting her time with Lewis. It didn't appear he was going to tell her the real story either. "Lewis is engaged. He doesn't think his wife will join him here if he isn't the owner."

"What?" She stared at her cousin. "Is this true?" When he didn't answer, she took his arm. "I would love to have another woman at the ranch. I'll make her welcome, I swear. Bring her to me."

Lewis shook off her grip. "She won't come, I tell you. We had plans to build a house, a proper home, not an overgrown cabin. She's not going to want to share the ranch house with a stranger."

"Who is this woman? I shall pay her a visit, explain to her how welcome she is. And there is plenty of money to build her a proper house. You pick out the spot, and I'll hire someone immediately."

Lewis's face reddened. "Keep your ranch and the hidden bonds! You're so selfish."

"Bonds? What are you talking about?"

"Don't play dumb. The bonds Stephen stole from the stage have to be here somewhere."

Watching her stricken face, Daniel realized she didn't know

anything about the rumor. "Do you know why Stephen ran off to join the cavalry?" he asked softly.

"H-He wanted to fight Indians. Are you saying he was a robber? Like . . . ?" She bit her lip and looked down.

"Yes," Daniel said. "Rumor has it a hundred thousand dollars' worth of bonds were buried on the property."

Her gaze bored into him, and he read the suspicion there. She thought that was why he'd come.

MARGARET YANKED OFF her bonnet and kicked her skirt off her legs. She pulled on her britches and sat in front of the dresser. Her hair was still up, and she pulled out the pins and rubbed her aching head.

Inez rapped on the door. "Señorita, you are all right?"

"Come in, Inez." Margaret's head ached so much, she found it hard to think. All the problems had come at her too fast to sort through.

The door opened, and Inez stepped inside before shutting the door behind her. "What has happened? Mr. Lewis, he leave in a great hurry. He take all his things."

Margaret stood and stretched. "My father left me the ranch." Though she was still troubled by the lies about her brother, she felt like she did at the end of calving season—tired and exultant all at once.

Inez's usual stoic expression was in place. "He leave everything to you?"

"Everything except some money he left Lewis. Pa loved me after all. I was never really sure."

Inez picked up the hairbrush and pointed to the stool until Margaret sat back down. "So Mr. Lewis leave because of this?"

Margaret's smile faded. "Yes. He was upset. I told him I would take care of him, but he was quite determined to go."

Inez said nothing as she brushed Margaret's hair. Did she think Margaret was wrong not to have shared the ranch equally with Lewis? Margaret was still uncertain of the right path. "Lewis was engaged. He didn't think his wife would want to come here with the changed circumstances. Pa didn't want the ranch split or I would have done it."

Inez's brushing slowed, then resumed. "Your papa was not always wise." A hint of pain flashed over her face, then vanished.

"You think I should split it up?" Though this was none of Inez's business, Margaret wanted to hear her thoughts.

"Is not for me to say, señorita."

"What would you do?"

"I would make sure my family had equal share."

Margaret bit her lip. She had no answer other than her father's wishes. What would Jesus have her do? She knew the answer without opening the leather cover of her Bible. Sharing was the right thing to do. "I'll send someone to the train station to try to stop him from leaving."

She rose and went to the door and called for Vincente, who promised to hurry to town to try to find Lewis.

Inez went to the dresser and pulled out Margaret's nightgown. "You want me to heat water for bath, señorita?"

"Yes, please, but not yet. I want to talk to you first." Inez would know if the rumor was true. Margaret sat back down on the stool and began to braid her hair. "I heard something about Stephen today."

"Mr. Stephen is dead. Words cannot hurt him now."

"I want to know the truth." Margaret watched Inez hang the skirt and blouse in the closet and pick up the discarded shoes. "Did Stephen go off to fight Indians because he was in trouble here?"

A flicker of dismay passed across Inez's face. "Who tell you this?"

"Lewis mentioned looking for bonds in the barn. When he wouldn't tell me what he meant, Daniel told me that Stephen supposedly robbed a stagecoach and took some bonds worth a lot of money."

Inez sighed. "It is true, señorita. Your papa thought the rumor would die off since it happened in Oklahoma. But a man came looking for Mr. Stephen. A bounty hunter, it was. Mr. Paddy, he pay the man to leave."

"I can't believe I've never heard this rumor." Surely word had gotten to Larson. "If it occurred in Oklahoma, how would Lewis have heard about it?"

"Your papa, he tell him. Lewis ask me about it."

"Pa told Lewis but never told me?" Margaret tried to keep the hurt out of her voice.

"You love your brother very much. Your papa did not want you to know."

"You're sure Pa didn't just pay the guy off to get rid of him?"

"*Sí.*" Inez looked down at the floor.

Margaret absorbed the information. She'd idolized her older brother, had thought he was a hero. Strong, faithful, law-abiding. A man above all men. "Why would he rob a stagecoach?"

"My Vincente, he hear big fight between Stephen and your papa. Very bad." Inez shook her head. "Mr. Paddy ask Stephen why he do such thing when he had only to ask for what was needed."

"What did Stephen say?"

"He say that he hate ranching. He want to do something else with life. Your papa say he must help with ranch. He yell back that he is man. He can do what he wants."

"That doesn't quite sound like an admission. Why didn't I hear this argument?" She tried to remember the events before Stephen's departure.

"You gone when it happen. On trip with your aunt to Austin."

Margaret nodded, the memory sharpening. "I was gone for two weeks. When I returned, Stephen announced he'd enlisted and would be leaving. Pa didn't say much to him. We had a big dinner, and he left the next day."

"Sí."

"But I don't understand one thing. If he robbed the stage, why would he hide the bonds? Why would he leave if he had plenty of money? That makes no sense." She shook her head. "I don't think he robbed that stage. Knowing Stephen, I suspect he was hurt that Pa would assume he was guilty. I think he waited around for an apology, and when it didn't come, he left."

Inez said nothing. She straightened the items on Margaret's stand, then went toward the door. When Margaret was alone, she pulled the sheet to her chin and resolved to get to the truth.

EIGHTEEN

The house was quiet with everyone in bed. Daniel should be there himself, but he sat in the kitchen with the kerosene lamp casting flickers of shadows on the walls. A sense of danger had fallen over him ever since Paddy's death. Daniel was certain it wasn't an accident. There had been no accidental fall.

A piano key plunked and the sound echoed into the kitchen. Someone else was up. Carrying the light, he went down the hall to the parlor. The lamp atop the piano illuminated Vincente's face. He was about thirty-five with black hair and eyes that seemed to take in everything. He ran the house with his mother, which had seemed an unusual arrangement to Daniel, but it worked for the household.

He stopped playing when he saw Daniel. "I hope I did not wake you."

"I was in the kitchen. Where did you learn to play like that?"

"Mrs. O'Brien taught me when I was a boy. She was very kind to me."

"You came with your mother when she first started working here?"

The man nodded. "I have lived here for most of my life."

So the fellow had been here when Stephen left. "I'm disturbed by Paddy's death, as I'm sure everyone is. Did he have any enemies?"

"You believe it was not an accident?"

"Don't you? Someone hit him on the head."

Vincente's hands fell away from the piano. "I had not heard that. I had hoped that he fell and hit his head."

"I wonder if someone has been searching for the stolen bonds."

Vincente smiled. "You speak of the stagecoach robbery."

Daniel couldn't figure the man out. He played the piano, worked quietly beating rugs and cooking in the kitchen, and Daniel had seen him soothing pregnant mares in the barn. Inez had raised a strong and interesting man.

"What did you hear about the robbery?"

"Are you here to look for the bonds?" the man countered. "I believe the treasure is a myth."

"I only heard about it a few days ago. I'm simply curious if the rumor could have anything to do with Paddy's death."

Vincente placed his fingers on the ivories again and played a few notes. "We have seen drifters now and again who ask about the bonds. I have seen them in some of the caves and along the river. They have found nothing. I do not believe there is anything to find."

"Because Stephen took them with him, or because he didn't have anything to do with the robbery?"

The music grew louder. "Stephen was innocent of the accusations."

"You're sure?"

"I am certain. He was not that kind of man."

"How do you know?" Daniel didn't mean to sound surprised, but it slipped out.

"We were childhood playmates and friends as adults." Vincente's hands stilled. "The members of this family have always treated me with respect and friendship. We abandoned the employer-employee relationship long ago. If it was ever there." He stared at Daniel. "You yourself should have seen that by now. You and the rest of the workers eat at the table with the family."

"True enough." Daniel had not worked at a ranch before, so he'd had no idea if that was usual behavior. Evidently it was not.

"Paddy was very good to me. Paid for my schooling and allowed his wife to teach me the piano. I will miss him."

"About Stephen?"

Vincente roused from his reverie. "Stephen was not even in Oklahoma when the theft happened."

"Where was he?"

"Enlisting in the cavalry without his father's knowledge."

"Does Margaret know any of this?"

Vincente shook his head. "Not before today. Margaret questioned my mother before bed."

"If there's no treasure hidden on the property, then why was Paddy killed?"

"I do not know. If he had any enemies, I am unaware of them." Vincente rose from the stool. "Did you know Lewis left?"

"I knew he'd planned to leave."

"Margaret asked me to find him, but no one in town had seen him."

Daniel frowned, uneasy. "He never made it to town?"

Vincente shrugged. "I do not know. But he was not at the stagecoach station."

MARGARET WIPED DUST from her face and swatted a fly with her hat. It had been a long morning in the saddle, and she was ready for water and some food. She dismounted beside the Red River and tied Archie to a bush, then knelt by the water. She splashed it on her face and wiped her skin with a handkerchief. She stood and pulled out her lunch, a roast beef sandwich.

Her lagging energy surged when she saw Daniel riding her way. He'd been on the other side of the pasture for most of the day. Not that she'd watched for his broad shoulders, of course. She had too much work to worry about what he was doing.

She shielded her face with her hand and waited until he dismounted. "Is there a problem?"

"Nope." He walked to the river and splashed water on his face. "Just needed a break like you. You've been avoiding me for two days. It's time you aired your grievances."

"I have no grievances." She took a bite of her sandwich so she didn't have to say more.

He pulled a handkerchief from his back pocket and wiped his face. "I didn't come to look for some stolen bonds. When Lewis mentioned it, it was the first time I'd heard the story."

She wished she could believe him. Oh, how she wished things were different! If only he were the kind of man he appeared to be—honest, hardworking, kind.

"What are you thinking?" His gaze searched hers.

She looked away. "Did you bring your lunch? I can share my sandwich if you didn't."

"I brought it." He grabbed a sandwich from his saddlebag. "Let's sit under the cottonwood."

She should make an excuse, but heaven help her, she wanted to sit and listen to his deep voice. The air was ten degrees cooler in the shade, and there was a patch of grass around a rock near the water. She settled on it and took a bite.

"Any word from Lewis?" he asked.

She shook her head. "No one in town has seen him."

"Maybe he headed for the train station instead."

"The trip would have been much farther. Unless he wanted the time to think about what to say to his fiancée and her father."

Daniel dropped onto the grass beside her. "I talked to Vincente about your brother."

"This is not your business! You just told me you didn't come here for the bonds."

"I didn't. But I was curious about the rumor and wanted to find out if there was any truth to it."

"So you could get the bonds too?"

"*Too*? What does that mean?"

She tossed the rest of her food to the birds. "Nothing."

He stared a moment, then shrugged. "I'm trying to find out what happened to your father, Margaret. There's something going on at the Triple T. First your father was assaulted, the barn burned, then your pa ends up dead. Now your cousin is missing. We have to figure out what's going on."

"Why do you care?"

He leaned over close enough to tuck a dangling lock of hair behind her ear. "I'd do most anything to keep you safe."

She should look away from his intent gaze, but she found it impossible. She wet her lips, but no words came to mind. Had anyone ever looked at her like he did? It was like he saw past her skin to her thoughts and feelings.

She finally managed to look away. "You think it has something to do with the missing bonds?"

"I did. Not since talking to Vincente. He says your brother wasn't even in Oklahoma when the stagecoach robbery took place. He was signing up for the war."

She peeked at him to make sure he wasn't upset she'd steered him away from talking about anything personal. "He's sure?"

"So he says. I believe him. He seemed close to Stephen."

"He was. They were like brothers. Inez brought him here when he was a baby."

"Vincente says a bounty hunter showed up from Oklahoma, and your pa paid him off and sent him on his way."

"Well, someone knows. Otherwise, you wouldn't have heard the rumor. Where *did* you hear about it anyway?" He was frowning at something past her shoulder. She turned to look too. "What's wrong?"

He jumped up. "Is that Lewis's horse?"

She followed him toward a familiar bay mare. The horse was still saddled. "Lewis?" she called. He had to be around here somewhere. He wouldn't just let his horse wander by itself. A bird sang in answer to her call, but she didn't see Lewis.

Daniel grabbed the horse's reins and tied them to a shrub. "Look here." He held out his hand, smeared with red.

"He must be hurt. Lewis!" She shouted as loudly as she could and began to run along the river.

Maybe the horse had thrown him and he'd been bleeding

when he tried to remount. Vincente hadn't found Lewis in town. Maybe he never made it there. She was about to turn and hike across the pasture when something red caught her eye where the river started to bend. She rushed toward the splash of color, but Daniel passed her and reached it first. His body blocked her view, but she saw him stiffen.

She reached him and was almost afraid to look at what he held in his hand. "What is it?"

He turned and held out a red shirt. "Does this belong to Lewis?"

The shirt was familiar. "Yes."

His face was grave. "Why don't you sit down while I look around."

"I'll help you. I'm not squeamish." Her words were brave, but her stomach churned. She didn't want to find Lewis's body. "He might have taken it off."

"Sure." Daniel's words lacked conviction.

He would think her a weak-willed female who couldn't face facts. Lewis wouldn't take his shirt off. He was fair-skinned and would be burned by the heat of the summer sun in a few minutes. And they'd found blood.

She hiked her chin. "Comanche?"

"Unlikely. More likely that an outlaw accosted him."

And left him for dead. Lewis had to be here somewhere. "You take the pasture. I'll walk along the river."

His warm fingers closed around her arm. "Stay within shouting distance. And take your gun."

At least he wasn't trying to force her to stay back. This was her land. If someone had come onto her property and shot her cousin, it was her responsibility. She nodded and walked back to her horse to get her rifle. He did the same and tugged his Winchester free from the saddle.

"Be careful."

"I will." Her heart warmed at the concern in his voice.

She walked along the river, following its curves and jogs. There was a fork just ahead, and she wasn't sure which way she should go. The decision was made for her when she reached the spot because on the right side she saw a saddlebag half submerged in the muddy water.

"Daniel, here!" She pulled the waterlogged leather from the river and flipped it open. The only item remaining in it was a photograph damaged by the water. It was of Lewis with a young woman. She was pretty, with full lips and bright eyes.

Daniel reached her. "What is it?"

She held it wordlessly out to him. Her eyes burned, and she swallowed down the lump in her throat.

"He would never leave this," Daniel said.

"No. Let's keep looking. He has to be here somewhere." She had to find her cousin. He was all the family she had left. *Please let him be alive, Lord.* Maybe the robbers had taken his money and left him. He was probably lying out here praying for someone to find him. And she *would* find him.

Calling his name, she ran down the river until her lungs burned and she had to bend over and gasp for air. There was no more sign of Lewis or his belongings. She crossed the river at the shallowest spot. The muddy water soaked her britches to the knees. Perspiration trickled down her neck, and she paused to wipe it away, then trudged back to where she'd left Archie. He'd pulled his lead loose but stood munching on grass.

When she met up with Daniel, the sun was low on the

horizon. She read the discouragement in his shoulders and mouth.

"I didn't find him either." He held up a boot. "I found this, though."

"It's Lewis's."

She wouldn't cry. She wouldn't. But she found herself sobbing against Daniel's rough shirt. She was alone in the world now.

NINETEEN

⚘

Darkness was falling, and the sheriff's office was nearly deserted. Daniel stood close to Margaret in front of Sheriff Borland's desk and wished he could ease the stricken expression from her face. He'd comforted her as much as he dared, but it wasn't enough.

The sheriff put a beefy hand on Margaret's shoulder. "It's been an upsetting week, Miss Margaret. You should go home and rest. I'll send a couple of deputies out to look around, if that's all right with you."

"Of course."

Daniel had never seen her so dispirited. He took her elbow. "How about some food? We missed dinner at the ranch."

"I don't think I could eat anything."

"Let's give it a try." He guided her out of the sheriff's office. Twilight gave the town a golden, misty glow.

A buckboard rattled past, and he stepped between Margaret and the street to shelter her as much as possible from the dust. A few people strolling the boardwalk expressed their condolences about Paddy, but she made no mention of her missing cousin.

Daniel was sure he was dead. Coyotes had probably made short work of the body, though he had said nothing of it to her. He didn't have to. She'd lived here all her life. She knew the harsh realities.

They reached the café, but she stopped. "I'm just not up to socializing, Daniel. I'm sorry. Let's go back to the ranch. Vincente will warm me up a plate of food."

"Whatever you say." He turned toward the livery.

His attention was arrested by a group of men standing outside the saloon. Richard stood talking with Frank. One other man stood in the shadows behind Richard. Daniel's gut clenched. Was it Charlie? He thought it might be. He dared not indicate he'd seen them or knew them. If Frank spoke to him, it would bring up more questions from Margaret than he wanted to answer.

"Let's go the long way." He steered her down a side street.

She stopped and stared up at him. "Who were those men, Daniel?"

He should have known she wouldn't miss his reaction. Those eyes noticed everything. "Some men I knew from a long time ago."

Her long stride kept up with him. "Why did you avoid them?"

"That life isn't part of who I am now." He willed her to believe him. She suspected he was more than he seemed and had even mentioned she thought he was a robber. If she found out the entire truth about his past, she would throw him off the ranch. He couldn't risk that. Not now when he needed to be here to protect her.

Her expression softened. "I guess we all make mistakes." She glanced behind them. "What does it all mean, Daniel? First Pa is killed and now Lewis. We don't have any enemies. At least I don't know of any."

"I wish I knew. I thought it might have something to do with that stagecoach robbery, but there's nothing to that rumor."

"What if someone believed it, though? And came here determined to find the bonds?"

"But why kill your father and Lewis? Who would benefit by Lewis's death? He was on his way out of the area."

Her shoulders drooped, and she rubbed her forehead. "It's all so confusing. Surely there is some link we're missing."

"I think you're right, but it's going to take some time to figure out. I want to get you home. I don't like this street."

He led her along the unlit street and wished there had been another route. The lane was too dark, too close. They exited a block away from the back side of the livery. It was dark here too, but a warm glow of lamplight came from the window of the livery. He picked up the pace and practically propelled Margaret to the safety of other people. They mounted their horses and headed toward the ranch.

It took only ten minutes for him to realize they were being followed.

"I'm tired, how about you?" He thought his voice sounded casual enough not to scare her. "How about we pick up the pace?"

"I'm not sure I can." Margaret sounded weary. "But you go on ahead. I'll be there shortly. I wouldn't mind a little time by myself anyway."

"There's no way I'd leave you alone out here."

Her head jerked around at his clipped tone. "Is everything all right?" Her expression uneasy, she glanced behind them.

He forced a smile. "I'm not sure it's safe for anyone to go out alone. Not until we know what happened to Lewis and your pa."

"Oh, all right. Let's go." Her horse broke into a canter, then into a dead run. Her hair came loose from its pins and tumbled down her back in the moonlight.

He leaned forward over his horse's mane and followed her. Glancing back, he saw the shadows he'd noticed were keeping pace with them. Whoever they were, they didn't mean to be left behind. Something whizzed by his ear. A bullet!

"Someone's shooting at us!" He pointed toward a pile of rocks about fifty yards ahead. "Take cover!"

Margaret reached the rocks moments before him. She practically fell from the saddle, then dove behind the shelter of the boulders. He yanked his rifle free from the saddle, then leaped after her. A bullet sparked the rock by his face as he landed in the dirt.

"I should have grabbed my rifle too," she panted in his ear.

Their horses took off toward the ranch. It was just over the hill, so if he could drive off their attackers, they could hike the rest of the way. Resting his rifle on the rock, he waited for the next flash of a gun, then pulled the trigger. The rifle kicked against his shoulder. There was a shout of pain, then quiet. He listened and heard nothing but the wind.

"I think they're leaving," Margaret said.

He heard it too—the clatter of hooves. When he rose a few minutes later, they were alone. "Let's get out of here."

INEZ HAD WARMED some soup for them, and she brought it to Margaret as she sat huddled under a blanket in the parlor.

"I don't know why I'm so cold," she said. "It's warm outside."

"Shock." Daniel took the soup from Inez and placed the bowl in Margaret's hands.

She let the warmth soak into her fingers for a moment, then sipped the broth. Shudders had wracked her body when they stumbled into the house after the attackers left. "Whoever they were, they meant to kill us."

Daniel nodded. "If I hadn't wounded one of them, they wouldn't have left." He moved over to sit by her on the sofa.

His body heat and the soup warmed her, and after a few minutes she let loose of her grip on the blanket. "I'm better now." She suspected the sudden warmth in her cheeks had something to do with his nearness. No man had ever affected her like Daniel.

She inched away a bit. "What would they have to gain by killing us?"

He stretched his arm across the back of the sofa. "If we knew that, we'd know who was behind it. And I'm not convinced whoever it was meant to hurt you."

"You think you were the target?"

"I think Calvin would like to see me dead and out of the way. He was not in the bunkhouse the night your father was attacked in the corral. I don't trust him."

"I'll mention your suspicions to the sheriff. Maybe he can get to the truth," Margaret said.

She could almost imagine he was embracing her with his arm near her head. For a moment she let herself dream that they were married and sitting here together discussing the events of the day. But it was only a dream. A husband like Daniel would be too good to be true.

She sighed and let her head drop back a bit. The heat of his arm against the back of her neck told her she was nearly resting her hair on his skin. If only he weren't an outlaw. If only she could trust him. If only she knew why he was really here. Her eyes drifted shut and she felt lethargic. Then she was drifting to sleep in such a comfortable position.

When she awoke, the light from the sputtering lamp was dim. It was nearly out of oil. She was stretched out on the sofa with her head on something unyielding. The blanket was pulled up around her chin and smelled of fresh air from being laundered and hung out to dry. She felt deliciously comfortable. She squinted in the faint light and looked up into Daniel's face. Her head was pillowed on his muscular thigh. A slight sound escaped his lips. Not really a snore but deep, even breathing.

With his eyes closed, she could stare at him all she wanted. Her gaze traced the firm line of his lips. She'd seen a picture once of the statue *David* by Michelangelo. The statue's wide forehead and aquiline nose reminded her of Daniel's strength. There was a bit of stubble on his strong jaw. Her fingers itched to touch his thick and unruly brown hair. A smile curved her lips when he shuffled and sighed. His ears were neat and tight against his head. The column of his neck was strong and muscular like his chest.

His eyes opened, and she found herself unable to look away. Though he'd caught her staring, he didn't seem to mind. Had he looked at her while she slept? He'd shuffled her head to his leg and covered her with the blanket.

"You're awake." He made no effort to move away.

"What time is it?"

"I don't know. It was about midnight the last time I looked."

She barely breathed as his hand moved from his thigh to her face. His thumb rubbed her cheek as his fingers cupped her jawline. Was that tenderness in his face? Her gulp was audible as she swallowed.

"You're so beautiful," he whispered. "You don't even realize how beautiful."

A denial was on her lips, but she couldn't force any words past her tight throat. She wanted to be beautiful for just a moment if it kept that expression on his face. She could dream that things were different.

His thumb moved as he rasped it over her lower lip. His eyes darkened, then his other hand cupped the back of her head. When he bent his head and lifted her slightly, she closed her eyes and accepted the kiss he offered. The masculine scent of him was heady and intoxicating. She forgot the fact that she didn't trust him and embraced the passion he offered in his firm lips. Forgetting all propriety, she wrapped her arms around his neck and kissed him back. A surge of heat went through her and she lost herself in his embrace.

He pulled her onto his lap in a seated position. Her fingers wound into the thick curls at the nape of his neck. She didn't want to ever let him go. The blood pulsed to her head and all that mattered was how she felt right now, this moment, in his arms. There was such a strong sense of belonging, as if he were the missing piece she'd been looking for all her life. Her doubts meant nothing in these seconds. All fear dissolved and she yielded to her feelings for this man.

Until sanity returned. She stiffened and sighed. There could be no future with him. He must have sensed the way she regained her senses, her logic. He pulled away, but only a few inches. His breath still whispered across her face, and it took all the strength she had not to pull him close for another kiss.

His eyes were quizzical and a little hurt when she scooted off his lap. "W-We should get to bed. Chores will come early."

He stood. "Can we talk about what just happened?"

"No."

"We'll have to sooner or later, Margaret. I have things to say to you."

She fled to her bedroom before she was tempted to let him whisper sweet words in her ear. She wasn't strong enough to resist them.

TWENTY

〜◦〜

D aniel hadn't slept much. He kept trying to follow the trail between Paddy's death and Lewis's disappearance. And he kept replaying the kiss over and over in his mind. He had no doubts that he wanted Margaret in his life forever. The trick would be convincing her. He could tell her the truth about why he was here, but she was such a literal, truthful woman that he feared she might accidentally give him away. The kiss had revealed the depth of feeling she had for him, whether she was ready to admit it or not. Life would never be the same for him after last night.

"Good morning," he said, entering the kitchen. The enticing aroma of pancakes and maple syrup made his mouth water, and the ranch hands merely grunted as they shoveled food into their mouths.

Margaret didn't look at him as she flipped the pancakes. "Morning."

So it was going to be like that today. "Why are you cooking this morning?"

"Vincente was a little under the weather. A bad cold, Inez

said. She was sneezing too, so I told her to go back to bed." She put a plate of pancakes on the table. "Have a seat."

He slid into the chair and pulled the plate of food closer to him. "Looks good."

She put the last plate on the table and sat in the chair next to him, the only one left. She inched away and he had a perverse desire to scoot close enough that their shoulders touched. He swallowed a swig of coffee to fortify him for the day ahead. The two of them would be cleaning out the barn today. The proximity would be torture when all he wanted to do was repeat last night.

The other ranch workers didn't say much as they ate. Their chairs scraped on the floor as they got up and gathered their things for the day's work. Daniel tried to decide what to say to Margaret, but the right words wouldn't come.

It was going to be a long day.

She pushed her plate away and got up. "Calvin, when you get supplies in town, would you ask the sheriff to pay me a visit? I want to tell him about the attack yesterday." Could he really have wanted to hurt her father?

"I can do that." Calvin had been staring at Margaret with a longing expression.

She glanced at Daniel. "Ready to clean the barn?"

"Just about." He swallowed down the last of his coffee, then followed her to the front porch.

Dawn was pinking the sky when they stepped outside. The air was fresh and clean with the scent of dew. She said nothing as she led the way to the barn. Cattle moved in the pasture to the west of the buildings. Chickens pecked in the dirt, and a rooster crowed somewhere. He jogged past her to shove open the barn door.

She brushed past him. "Thanks, but I could have done it. I don't want anyone coddling me."

She was as prickly as a sticker bush this morning. He opened his mouth to force a discussion about last night, then closed it. Best wait until he could be honest with her.

He grabbed a pitchfork. "Where do you want me to start?"

"The horse stalls in the back. I'll work in the pigpens."

Just as well they were in separate areas of the barn. It was hot, smelly work, but he made quick inroads as he forked the manure into a wheelbarrow and emptied it in next year's garden plot. He took a break at midmorning and went to the springhouse to fetch a pail of cold water. When he carried it to Margaret, she thanked him without looking at him.

"Would you quit looking at me like that?" she said when she handed back the tin cup.

She was so adorable he couldn't help the smile that sprang to his lips. "Like what? Like I'd like to kiss you again? It's true."

Her cheeks flooded with pink, but she glanced over his shoulder. "The sheriff is here."

"That won't save you forever." His heart lightened when she couldn't hold back a slight smile.

He followed her out to meet the sheriff. Daniel watched her as she stood there with the glow of the sun on her cheeks. The dungarees and tucked-in shirt didn't hide her curves. She was all woman and all heart. He had to be patient. When this was all over, he could woo her properly. Once the full truth was out.

He joined Margaret as Sheriff Borland dismounted. "Sheriff, you're out early."

"I heard someone shot at the two of you."

"Calvin must have gone straight to your office," Daniel said.

"He did. And I'm concerned. I stopped to look around at the ambush position and found plenty of shells. Looked like two men. Found some blood too."

"I winged one of them. He was still in his saddle when they rode off, though."

"So I should be on the lookout for a wounded man. Any idea where you hit him?"

Daniel shook his head. "I heard him yell but it was too dark to see. They left right after that."

The sheriff glanced at Margaret. "Any idea who the men might be?"

"Daniel has a theory that one of them might be Calvin. He had a grudge against Pa for hiring Daniel, and h-he's a little sweet on me."

The sheriff looked grim. "I'll have a talk with him."

"Thanks," she said.

"And I'll ask Doc to keep an eye out. If the man is wounded, he'll need some care." He stared hard at Margaret. "You mind my words, Miss Margaret. I don't want you out wandering the property alone. Not even here in the barn." He held up his hand when she frowned. "Someone seems to be after your family. First your pa, then Lewis. I don't want you to be next." He glanced at Daniel. "See to it."

"I will."

"Let's talk to Calvin now." The sheriff walked toward the barn and motioned for Calvin to join them.

Calvin's expression was wary as they approached. "I didn't see nothin'. And I've got work to do."

Margaret didn't smile. "You made no secret that you were mad at Pa and that you hated Daniel. Where were you yesterday?"

"Rounding up strays on the other side of the river."

Daniel didn't like the arrogant twist to the man's mouth. "By yourself? Can anyone vouch for you?"

Calvin balled his fists. "You'd like to pin this on me, wouldn't you?"

Before Daniel could answer, the man launched himself in the air. His fist smashed into Daniel's mouth. Pain exploded in Daniel's head and he tasted blood on his lip. Without thinking, he grabbed Calvin and bore him to the ground.

The sheriff grabbed Daniel and pulled the two apart. "That's enough."

Calvin jumped to his feet and dusted off his pants. He glared at Daniel but said nothing.

Margaret stepped between them. "I want you gone, Calvin. I can't trust you. Pack your things and don't come back."

Calvin's face worked. "I've worked for you fifteen years. You got no cause to fire me. I'm a good worker."

"My decision is final. Get off my land."

He practically snarled, then jammed his hat on his head and stalked off.

Borland watched him go, then mounted his horse. "I'll let you know if I find out any new information. I'm heading to the river now to look for evidence of who killed Lewis."

"If he's dead," Margaret said.

"Yes." Borland's voice held no conviction.

When the sheriff was out of earshot, Margaret flipped her braid over her shoulder. "I don't need someone to look after me."

"Everyone needs someone to have his back. I've got your back and you've got mine. So no heroic feats to impress someone with your bravery. You don't need to do anything for me to love you."

Had he just said that? He quickly turned toward the barn and grabbed his pitchfork on the way back inside. There was no way he was ready to talk about his feelings. Not until this was over.

MARGARET REPLAYED DANIEL'S words over and over in her head. Could he possibly love her? She didn't want to think about it. The world was full of women who believed the lies men told them. Weak women who refused to see past a handsome face. She wasn't going to be one of those women.

Unless he could change. Was it possible? She mulled over the idea. Following Jesus was all about change, and Daniel's spirituality seemed genuine, strange as it was. Maybe she could help him start a new life. Leave crime behind.

The next morning Margaret was still full of resolve to save Daniel from himself. She didn't know why she hadn't thought of it sooner. He just needed a little help to extricate himself from his life of crime. She did her chores and lurked around to see what Daniel was up to, but he spent the entire day branding calves and working in the barn just like most every other day. The entire week went by without any deviation from his normal schedule.

On Thursday word came of another bank robbery, this one in Clarendon. Was Daniel involved? Margaret hoped it wasn't so, but she hadn't been able to tail him every minute. He'd looked tired yesterday, so maybe he had been up all night running with his gang. She wished she could be sure. She had to watch him more closely.

By Saturday Margaret was about ready to give up. When did he sneak away to do what he came here to do? After supper she played checkers with him in the parlor for a while, then went to her bedroom. Maybe she needed to shadow him at night. She'd tried a couple of nights ago, but she had fallen asleep before she saw anything suspicious. Her bedroom window looked out on the bunkhouse, but so far that had been no advantage. There was so much work to be done on the ranch that she was exhausted by bedtime.

If Daniel was involved in the robberies, how did he find the energy? She had to admit he was no slacker during the workday. Tonight she was determined to find out. She put on some britches and sat in the chair by the window with the lamp unlit. The night dragged by and her lids grew heavy. She finally slept, then awoke with a start. The moon shone in through the curtains, and she peered outside to see what had disturbed her. Only the sound of crickets reached her ears. Maybe she should just go to bed. No one was stirring tonight.

Then a shadow flitted by her window, and she drew back, her throat tight. Daniel's unmistakably tall figure joined another man at a dark corner of the barn. Their whispers didn't reach her open window, though. She had to hear what they were saying.

She tiptoed down the hall and let herself noiselessly out the kitchen door. Sneaking around the edge of the house, she sidled up to the bunkhouse until she was close enough to overhear. She hoped he wasn't up to anything criminal. Against all odds, the more she got to know him, the less convinced she was that he was a thief.

"We're ready to move in tomorrow," the man's voice said. It was the same man she'd heard through her window once before. "You ready to act?"

"I reckon."

"You don't sound convinced. We've come too far to back out now. You getting cold feet?"

"I just don't want anyone hurt, least of all Charlie." Daniel's voice was low.

"If everyone does what they're told, no one will get hurt. I know you want your baby brother out of the way first, but this job is more important than what you want."

"And if they don't do what they're told?"

"Then they'll suffer the consequences. Don't tell me you're getting soft after all these years. I want to make them pay, and you'd better not get in the way. I've gone out on a limb for you all I'm going to."

"I know, Richard, and I appreciate it. Not many friends would do what you've done for me. I won't let you down."

"You'd better not," Richard growled. He clapped Daniel on the back.

"What time do I meet you tomorrow?"

"Midnight. I'll be at the cottonwood tree at the road that leads to the river."

"I'll be there," Daniel said.

So will I. She would save Daniel from himself, and save his little brother, Charlie, too, if she could. She tiptoed back to the house and went to her room. She had to carefully plan what she should do. The sheriff could help her, but the thought of betraying Daniel made her wince. Maybe she was wrong about what was going on, but what did that man Richard mean about making them pay? That didn't really sound like robbery. It sounded worse.

She prayed Daniel wasn't planning on murdering someone. This was such a hopeless muddle. He didn't seem like the kind of man who could do the things he seemed to be doing. If only she could be sure. If she had the courage to act, tomorrow would reveal it all. She resolved to find that courage somewhere. Tomorrow she would do what had to be done even if it hurt her.

TWENTY-ONE

❦

M oonlight glimmered through the trees as the minutes ticked by. In the distance a coyote yipped. Margaret wrapped her coat tighter around her body and pressed farther into the shadows of her hiding place. Where was he? Her ears strained to hear soft footfalls, but so far the only disturbance in the area had been the frogs.

Her breath fogged the air. This morning the temperature had finally taken a plunge and ushered in an almost winter cool-ness. Margaret longed for the warm temperatures of a few days ago. But at least the cold had quieted the sound of the crickets. She would be able to hear better.

A noise came through the trees. Someone cleared his throat, then she heard a rustle in the leaves. She peered around the trunk and saw the familiar set of Daniel's shoulders as he rode his horse into the clearing. Sucking in her breath, she barely moved. Moments later another rider joined Daniel. They talked for a moment, but she was too far away to hear the conversation. Then they both turned their horses' heads and left the clearing.

She was going to lose them. Margaret bounded to her feet

and made her way to where she'd tethered Archie. She mounted and followed Daniel and the other man. Careful to stay well back, she nearly lost them at the turnoff to Miller's Canyon. At the last second she realized they'd taken the turn. So the crooks were holed up in the canyon.

She shivered, more from excitement than from the cold. It felt good to be doing something instead of just waiting in fear to see what Daniel was planning. Tightening her jaw, she squinted through the gloom.

A figure leapt from behind a rock, and Archie reared. Caught off balance, Margaret struggled to stay seated in the saddle, then a hand caught the reins and jerked her horse's head down. The man's eyes glittered in the moonlight behind the mask he wore. Terror held her motionless, and then her shock-induced inertia faded and she placed the pointed toe of her boot squarely in his chin. Leaning down, she jerked the reins out of his hand.

With a muttered oath, he fell onto his backside. Margaret didn't wait to see if he was hurt. She dug her heels into her horse's flank and raced away over tumbled rocks, sage, and cactus. The wind caught and tugged at her hair, and her breath came fast in her chest. He would be right behind her—with his cohorts. Bending low over her horse's neck, she urged him to go faster.

She galloped over a hill and into a small valley. A series of campfires dotted the area. She pulled on the reins and slowed her horse to a walk. She listened but could hear no sounds of pursuit. Maybe she'd lost him. A nearby stand of trees looked safe. She dismounted and led her horse into the dark recesses of the grove and tethered him to a limb. She took out her rifle and stepped into the clearing again and crept toward the flickering firelight.

Raucous laughter spilled from the men clustered around the

fire. She searched their faces but saw no sign of Daniel. Maybe these weren't the bank robbers at all. Her gaze traveled from face to face. Who else would be hidden in this valley? They were much too rough-looking to be mere cowboys. They all wore six-shooters slung low on their hips, and the reek from their whiskey bottles made her wrinkle her nose. Cowboys would already be asleep after an arduous day of work. These men showed no signs of any inclination for sleep as they played poker and drank straight from their bottles.

"Well, well, what do we have here?"

Margaret spun around at the harsh growl behind her. A burly man of about forty had a revolver pointed at her. His expression was cold as his gaze swept over her, then his eyes widened as he realized she was a woman. A leer tugged at his mouth.

Her heart sank. This wasn't going to end well.

CHARLIE TOSSED HIS cards into the pile. "I'm done." He was ready for bed since Golda had retreated to her tent.

"A woman! Hey, fellers, see what I just caught." Frank had a woman roughly by the arm as he dragged her toward the clustered men.

Charlie shot to his feet. "Is the law with her?" He squinted in the firelight, and his gut clenched when he saw her red hair. "Hey, she's the O'Brien gal."

The woman's eyes widened when she saw him and recognition swept over her face. Her eyes pleaded with him. She must know who he was. Her eyes signaled *Help me.*

He shuttered his gaze and stepped back. What could he do?

COLLEEN COBLE

The men were all older than he was and had more authority. What was she doing out here? Was Daniel somewhere close too?

"Let go of me!" She struggled to get loose from Frank's grasp.

Charlie glanced around at the other men. They all wore expressions of eager anticipation, and he knew her arrival had provided them a break from boredom and routine. What would they do with her? Dread congealed in his stomach as he watched her try to break free.

But no matter how she struggled, Frank's grip remained tight. He dragged her closer to the nearest campfire, then shoved her to the ground. With hard hands, he bound her wrists together in front of her.

"Now you just explain what you're doing skulking around our camp in the middle of the night." Frank crossed sinewy arms across his chest and glared down at her.

She stared at Charlie again. "Could I have some water?"

Frank jerked his head at Charlie, and he handed her a tin cup filled with water. She took it in both bound hands and drank greedily. Handing it back to him, she kept looking at him, but he looked at the ground. If she appealed to him directly, they'd both be sunk.

"Now answer my question," Frank said.

"I was looking for a friend."

"A friend. At this hour? Do your people know you're out here?"

The glance she threw toward Charlie was full of desperation, but he glared at her so she knew not to ask him for anything.

"No," she said, when Frank shoved her with his foot.

"At least you're telling the truth. For now. Who is this 'friend' you're looking for? And why here? You're a far piece from home."

"Hey, Munster, we got company."

Frank swung around at the interruption. "Charlie, go see what's going on."

Charlie was glad to escape her stare. He jogged toward the disturbance, but he was even less pleased to see Daniel with some of the other gang members. "Daniel." He nodded coldly.

Daniel made as if to hug him, but Charlie stepped back, and Daniel's arms fell to his sides. "You'd better talk to Frank."

"That's why I'm here." Daniel strode toward the group with his head held high.

Charlie watched his confident stride falter when he got near enough to see Margaret. A widening of his eyes was the only indication he gave that he knew her. Charlie bit his lip. There were few options available for him to help his brother. And for the first time, he realized he might have to make a choice between his friends and Daniel.

Daniel stopped in front of Margaret. "What's she doing here?"

"We thought maybe you could provide the answer to that," Munster said smoothly. "She tells us she's been looking for a friend. Maybe you're that friend and have led her right to our camp."

Daniel laughed. "We're acquainted. What are you going to do with her?"

"I haven't decided. We could hold her for ransom. Her old man was one of the wealthiest cattle barons in the Red River Valley. I reckon she owns the ranch now. Her attorney would authorize a ransom, I bet. Plus, I've a mind to make her tell me where those bonds are."

"I told you—there are no bonds. I looked and they aren't there." Daniel still didn't look at her. "Let me talk to her before you decide anything."

Munster sniffed. "I suppose. You always were the smarts of the outfit, Cutler. You've been gone so long, I was beginning to think you'd turned legal." Munster picked his teeth with a piece of straw.

Daniel laughed. "You must have been eating locoweed. I want my share of that haul you just took."

"Hey, you had no part in that operation. That money's ours!"

"And how are you going to get out of here? You're boxed up tighter than a calf on branding day. You need me to figure out how to get you out of here alive so we can finish the big job."

Munster chewed on the straw. "You got a point. Okay, we'll cut you a share if you can get us out. You got a plan?"

Daniel smiled. "Don't I always?" He jerked his head toward her. "Got anyplace where I can talk with her?"

Munster grinned. "There's an old shack through those trees there if you want some privacy. Here, take a lantern." He handed Daniel a battered kerosene lamp.

Daniel took it, then set it on the ground while he removed Margaret's bonds. He picked up the lantern again and took Margaret's arm.

Frank winked at Daniel as he led Margaret away, and Charlie turned away. He didn't know what his brother's game was, but he didn't want it to mess up his life here.

WHY HAD SHE ever come up with this harebrained scheme? She must have been crazy. Margaret followed Daniel toward the grove of trees to a ramshackle cabin with part of the roof missing. Daniel pushed her inside and stepped in behind her. Even in the dim glow of the lamplight, she could see the stiff set of his shoulders and the icy glint in his eyes.

He shut the door and seized her by the arms. "Margaret, what do you think you're doing here? You've made my job even harder."

Margaret glared at him. "I was trying to save you. I thought if I discovered where they were holed up, the sheriff could arrest them and you'd be able to put your past behind you. I can see I was mistaken that you might want to do that."

"Do you ever think before you act?" He sighed.

"It was a good plan. I know this land better than anyone."

"But you don't know these men and how bad they are."

Margaret watched him until his gaze met hers again. "Let me go. You can say I escaped. They won't do anything to you—you're their leader."

Daniel's lips thinned. "Is that what you think? You still have no discernment, Margaret. I care for you, but you refuse to see it. I don't know why I bother." He took off his hat and ran a hand through his thick brown curls. "I don't know how I'm going to get us out of this mess."

She pushed away the initial joy his words of affection had brought. It was just more of his deceit. "I thought you had that all planned. Ransom and all that."

He snorted. "You really think Frank will follow through with that plan? More likely he'll take the money and still kill you. Frank isn't known for mercy." He chewed on his lip. "You'll have to agree to marry me, Margaret."

"What?" Surely she hadn't heard him correctly.

"It's the only way I can keep you safe. If the men think you belong to me, they will leave you alone."

Margaret couldn't breathe. She had to get out of here. She bolted for the door, but Daniel caught her by the arm.

"I'm sorry the idea is so distasteful," he said grimly.

But what had appalled her the most was that the idea was far from distasteful. The thought of being married to Daniel nearly made her knees buckle from the sweetness of that hope. There seemed no way to reconcile this tender man who looked at her with pleading eyes with the rough man outside who spoke so casually of robbing banks, death, and ransom. Which one was the real Daniel Cutler? And what did he really want of her?

"I won't lie to them," he said. "God wouldn't like it. Will you agree to marry me, Margaret? I'll tell them you've said yes and that they must leave you alone."

"What about my life on the Triple T? Do you expect me to follow you around the countryside while you rob every bank in Texas?" She shuddered.

Daniel grew still. "Can't you trust me just a little bit, Margaret? Things aren't always what they seem. That's all I can tell you."

"Things aren't always what they seem?" She studied his face, unsure of what he meant. His firm jaw and dark eyes gave away nothing. It was hard to let go and believe when the evidence before her was so condemning. Maybe he really did want to find a way to get out of this way of life. If so, she must do all she could to help him accomplish that.

What a strange thief he was. He would rob a bank, but he wouldn't lie to his fellow bandits. He could expound on Scripture with the best of preachers, but he donned a mask and broke every commandment. In spite of her questions, she couldn't help but want to trust him.

He must have seen the struggle going on in her heart, for he leaned forward and brushed his fingers against her cheek. "It will be all right, Margaret. I won't let you down. I love you, and I think you love me too, even if you won't admit it yet."

She hardened her heart against his sweet words. What did a bandit know of love? And the thought of giving him that power over her made her tremble. And she saw no way to resolve the conflict between the two sides of this man.

He grinned. "Does the thought of marriage to me fill you with such joy you can't speak?"

A smile tugged at the corner of her mouth, but she quickly squelched it. His charm was too easy to believe. She had to remember that. "Let's just say we're engaged."

"You want a way to back out, is that it?"

She nodded.

He sighed and ran a hand through his hair. "You're a stubborn woman, Margaret O'Brien." He attempted to embrace her, but when she resisted, he released her. "Our time will come. I'll be patient for now, but you'll see you can trust me." He turned from her and paced across the floor. "I have to be careful how I proceed," he muttered. "So much is riding on the next few days."

She didn't understand any of this. Why had she ever gotten involved with this mess? "What about your brother?"

His restless pacing stilled. "Charlie? What about him?" His tone was casual, too casual.

"How does he figure in all this?"

"Charlie is why I'm here."

"What do you mean?"

"Nothing, forget it. It's safer that way." He picked up the lantern and took her hand. "They'll be wondering what's taking so long. Come with me and try to act happy."

It wouldn't be a total act. Part of her thrilled at the thought that she could have a future with Daniel. That part ignored the truth all around her that spoke of Daniel's lack of concern for the

law and other people. But the rational part of her head knew that only heartache lay in wait for her. It couldn't be otherwise. In spite of Daniel's calm assurance that he would work things out, Margaret saw no possible way to resolve the problem. Either the robbers would kill them both or the posse would.

Once she threw in her lot with Daniel, no one would believe she had no idea who he really was or what his plans were. She forced a smile to her lips. Her name would be worthless among the people whose opinion she valued.

She glanced up into the night sky as he led her back to the campfire. *What should I do, Lord?* God couldn't possibly be in favor of a match between her and a bank robber, in spite of Daniel's profession of Christianity.

Just thinking about it gave her a headache. All she wanted was to find some hole to crawl into and sleep. She'd pull a blanket over her head and forget all about this for a few blessed hours. "You'll have to take care of this, Lord. I don't know what to do," she muttered under her breath.

"Did you say something?" Daniel asked softly.

She shook her head. "I was talking to God."

"Good idea. We need all the help we can get. Smile, we're almost there," Daniel whispered.

Smiling was the last thing she felt like doing, but she tried.

"Can't you do better than that? You look like an orphaned calf. Try to look excited at the thought of being Mrs. Cutler."

Mrs. Cutler. The thought sent a bolt of electricity tingling along her nerves. Margaret Cutler. She tried it on for size and found she could get used to that name. If she lived long enough. She lifted her head and smiled at him.

He blinked, and the light in his eyes brightened. "That's

more like it." He took her arm, and they stepped into the light of the campfire. Some of the men had gone to bed, but Frank and Charlie still sat on logs near the fire. The fire was still blazing high and shooting sparks into the cool air.

Frank got to his feet as they neared. "She don't look like you roughed her up too bad." He chortled. "You find out why she came out here?"

"Looking for me."

The smugness in Daniel's voice made Margaret want to kick him, but instead she smiled sweetly and said nothing.

Frank narrowed his eyes. "I figured that much. Why is the question."

"She loves me," Daniel said. "You ever heard the word before, Frank? Even a reprobate like you must realize there're some fates a man can't run from. I'm going to marry this gal."

"Marry? You?" Frank burst into guffaws. His laughter trailed away when Daniel just stood there with a pleasant smile on his face. "What about the ransom?"

"We don't need a ransom. We'll make plenty on this next haul."

"You sure you ain't blackmailing her into a wedding? Maybe that's the ransom you're wanting. That way you get control of the ranch too. Smart move." Frank nodded approvingly.

Margaret's chest tightened. Maybe that's what all his talk of love was about. His love of money and her ranch. It made perfect sense.

TWENTY-TWO

The next morning Daniel directed a glance in Margaret's direction. He made sure his expression betrayed none of his worry. They were both lucky her confident air had allayed any suspicions Frank and his gang might have had. A good night's sleep had given her more backbone and gumption.

The men had clamored for breakfast, and she offered to fix some flapjacks. Now he watched her as she worked over the cooking fire making stew. Even under duress she had kept her cool. A glow warmed his belly as he watched her cook. He'd never met a braver woman.

His grin faded. Or one more stubborn. She was convinced she knew what he was all about, and nothing swayed her opinion. Still, that stubbornness could be turned to good use. Once she loved a man, she would stand and fight at his side. Unlike his mother, who stayed in her room and was more a piece of the furniture than a true wife. He'd always sworn he would never want a wife without fire.

What had possessed Margaret to follow him out here? When he saw her in the hands of these outlaws, he'd wanted to throttle her. That impulse had quickly been followed by a rush of pleasure that she cared enough about him to follow him. For all her pro-tests, Daniel knew she felt something for him. He just had to help her discover what it was.

She hadn't answered him when he told her he loved her, but he'd seen the struggle in her face. Once she understood why he was with this gang, maybe she would be able to face her feelings. All he could do was hope and pray that would be the case.

Her face glowed from the heat of the fire. The night had brought colder temperatures, and even this morning, frost still limned the grass. Charlie had brought her a blanket to pull around her shoulders. Her long red braid hung over one shoulder, and she looked a little bedraggled and distraught.

"I want out of here." She bent over the cook pot with her back toward him. "I want to get on my horse and get home. Surely they'll let me go now that they think I'm going to marry you."

Daniel pressed his fingers against the hand she had on his arm. "You don't understand all that's going on here, Margaret. Please, just stay quiet and let me do what I have to do."

Bafflement darkened her eyes and she sighed. "I don't have much choice."

He went toward the group of men sitting around the camp-fire. This operation was going to be tricky. Frank was no dummy. If he smelled a rat, he'd dump both their bodies in a ravine.

Daniel hunkered down beside Charlie and picked up a stick. He poked the fire and sparks flew into the air, leaving a tang of wood smoke and burning leaves. He could almost feel Margaret's gaze boring a hole in his back, but he forced himself to focus on the job at hand.

"Let's talk about the heist at the Larson bank. What do you think about using explosives, Cutler?"

The sharp look in Frank's eyes reminded Daniel of a ferret. Frank was wily and dangerous, like a rabid fox. The knowledge sharpened Daniel's attention. "Might be all right if you use the right kind. We wouldn't want to get blown up along with the vault door."

Frank nodded. "When you joined us a year ago, you said you were an expert with nitroglycerin. I think we might be able to get our hands on some. You game to try it?"

"I'd rather not use orphan elixir," Daniel said, referring to the mining synonym for nitroglycerin. "Dynamite would be better, provided it's not old. I can use nitro if you're set on it, but it takes longer to get the right amount set. Dynamite would be quicker and easier. But the noise will bring the whole town running. You sure you want that?"

Frank nodded. "Guess you know what you're talking about."

"What was this—a test?"

Frank grinned. "You got it. I wanted to know if you were the expert you claimed to be. Guess you'll do." Picking up a stick, he drew lines in the dirt. "I figure we hit the bank next week. The last time was just a trial run to test the bank security. The back door is here." He poked the stick in the dirt. "A big deposit is expected on Wednesday, and we'll hit the bank on Thursday before they can ship it out again. The security will be beefed up, but they won't be expecting us to hit it again so soon. Pretty crafty, huh?" He gave a self-satisfied smirk.

Cutler nodded. It was pretty smart. No one ever said Frank was stupid. "How you figuring on getting past the guards?"

Frank's grin widened. "That's where you and your girlfriend come in. She's known in the community and so are you. You escort her in to make a withdrawal about closing time when the place is almost empty. You pull your gun and tie up the guards and the tellers. We'll be waiting around back. When you open the back door for us, we get the manager to open the vault and make a little larger withdrawal than they were expecting." He gave a hearty laugh.

His laughter grated on Daniel's ears. "Good plan. But what if the manager won't cooperate?"

"Then we blow the door with dynamite. I've got plenty of power to handle the yokels in town."

"These few men?" Daniel gave a sweeping gesture with his hand.

"Oh no, these are just the start. Kid Loco and his gang are throwing in with us."

Daniel bit back his dismay. Kid Loco was a notorious gun-fighter who shot first and asked questions later. He hated Daniel, and the coming encounter would not be pleasant.

Frank grinned again. "I know you two have a history. The Kid has already been warned to leave you be."

The Kid never listened to advice. If he'd been told to leave Daniel alone, that would be enough to make him try to pick a fight. "If you think he'll listen, I reckon you don't know him as well as you think you do." This could ruin the entire plan. A year of hard work was about to pay off mightily, and he would have to think carefully about how to get around the Kid.

Frank narrowed his eyes. "If he wants his share, he'll do whatever I tell him."

"He may take yours along with his. He's a loose cannon."

"Yeah, well, he says the same thing about you. You must have some really bad blood between you. Bet it's over a woman."

Frank's guess would be right. Daniel's jaw tightened at the thought of Kid Loco and what he was capable of. Daniel didn't want him anywhere near Margaret. But they were in the thick of this now, and Daniel didn't see any easy way out. Not without putting Charlie in jeopardy.

A buckboard clattered around the curve, and several of the men sprang to their feet, brandishing their guns. Golda drove recklessly, her golden hair flying behind her. Daniel's heart sank when she got out of the buckboard. Margaret was not going to like this one bit. He gave an uneasy glance back to where she still stirred the stew.

"It's just Golda," Frank said. "Put those peashooters away before you hurt someone."

The men put away their guns and sat back down as Golda sauntered toward them. Her hair rippled down her back in the sunlight, and her lithe body swayed as though to an inner tune, a tune that proclaimed her the most beautiful woman in the world. She walked and acted as though every man should turn and look. And Daniel had to admit she wouldn't be far wrong about that. For sheer beauty, few women could compete. Unfortunately, she was as corrupt as her brother, Frank.

Eyes as blue as the sky fastened on Daniel, and she gave a slow smile. "Why, it's our runaway come home. I've been wondering when you'd show your face again." She gave a becoming pout. "Though I should slap you for leaving without saying good-bye."

She came closer, and her overpowering perfume wafted toward Daniel. He took a step back. How was he going to explain this to Margaret?

MARGARET WATCHED A beautiful blond woman get out of a buckboard and walk toward the group of men around the campfire. She looked vaguely familiar, and Margaret realized she was the small blond woman in the mercantile who had laughed at her choice of material. The woman's pristine appearance made Margaret feel like a drudge. Her own hair hung in bedraggled wisps around her face from the heat. Dirt and soot marred her shirt. She brushed at her shirt ineffectively and tried to pat her hair into place.

The woman sauntered up to Daniel and put her hand on his arm. With her head thrown back, she smiled into Daniel's face. A shaft of sunlight illuminated her beauty even more, and Margaret's heart sank to her dusty boots. She gave a sniff. What did she care? Let the woman have him. He was no great catch anyway. But Margaret's heart gave a painful throb at the thought that he might prefer that woman to her.

The woman's throaty laughter floated on the spring air, and Margaret tossed down the ladle. He'd said they were engaged, and an engaged man didn't allow some other woman to touch his cheek the way that hussy was doing. Margaret straightened her shoulders and marched toward the group. It was about time she made her position known.

The woman's head swiveled at her approach. Her eyes narrowed as she took in Margaret's appearance. "What's the redhead doing here?"

Margaret didn't wait for anyone else to introduce her. She stepped forward and took Daniel's unencumbered arm. "I'm Daniel's fiancée, Margaret O'Brien."

The woman's eyes widened, and her hand fell away from Daniel's other arm. "Fiancée?" Her blue eyes flashed, and she glared at Daniel. "What's this nonsense?"

Frank laughed. "Miss O'Brien, this is my sister, Golda. I'd say you've put her nose out of joint. She had pegged Cutler here as her personal property."

Personal property. Margaret had a notion that Daniel would never be anyone's personal property. He was too much of a man to be owned by any woman, even a beautiful one like Golda.

Golda bared her teeth at her brother, then flew at Frank and slapped his face. His brows drew together, and he drew back his hand. He hit her across the face, and she fell to the ground. Staring up at her brother, the beautiful face twisted into an ugly mask of petulance and anger.

Before anyone could help her to her feet, she jumped up and flew at her brother again. "I hate you!" Her nails raked his face, then she grabbed a handful of hair and gave it a vicious tug.

He held her at arm's length and laughed in her face, which seemed only to inflame her. "Not woman enough to keep him, are you?"

She spat in his face and he shoved her away. She attacked him again and he grabbed her by the shoulders. "Behave yourself, Golda." Frank shook his sister, and the fight finally seemed to leave her. Her shoulders slumped, and she pulled out of her brother's grip.

Tears shimmered in her eyes, and Margaret almost gasped at how beautiful she looked when she showed her vulnerability. Petite and dainty, she made Margaret feel like a bumbling bull in a sheep pen. She tightened her grip on Daniel's arm.

Golda turned her blue-eyed gaze on Daniel. "How could you do this to me?" she whispered.

"Oh, knock it off, Golda." Frank's tone was impatient. "Cutler never made you no promises. Just because you got shut out by another filly is no reason to carry on like a madwoman."

Golda's full lips trembled, and Margaret almost felt sorry for her. In spite of her beauty, she was a bit childlike in her willfulness. It was as though she'd had her favorite doll taken by a neighbor child. Margaret slanted a glance into Daniel's face. His gaze was on her, not on Golda, and she took heart at that.

She warmed at the concern in his glance.

There seemed to be only approval in his gaze. She tore her gaze from his and glanced back at Golda. The young woman was examining Margaret in great detail.

"Why on earth would you choose her over me, Daniel?" Contempt curled Golda's lip. "She isn't even feminine. Why, look at the size of her feet and hands. And redheads freckle in the sun. You need a woman to grace your home with style and elegance, not one who is more like a man than a woman. You want softness, not someone like this."

"You don't know me well enough to know what I want," Daniel said. "I don't want to hurt you, Golda, but this is really none of your business. If you can't see Margaret's beauty, you're blind. She's good and kind as well as beautiful."

Golda sniffed and flounced away. Margaret savored the words he'd said about her. Praise wasn't something she'd heard much growing up, and the compliments fell on her heart like rain on a dry riverbed.

The men settled back around the fire. "That stew about ready?" Frank asked. "We're starved."

"It's ready." Margaret turned to go back to her pot.

"I'll help you," Daniel said.

Frank guffawed. "She's got you roped and tied already, Cutler."

Daniel didn't answer. He just slipped his hand under Margaret's elbow and escorted her back across the hard ground. "I'm sorry."

"For what? For dallying with a beautiful woman?"

His lips pressed together. "I reckon I deserve that. I was young when I met her, and she made no secret of the fact that she wanted me. I lost my head. When she asked me to help her and Frank rob a bank, it seemed a lark. Or else I was so infatuated, I couldn't think."

"Were you helping her when your mother wanted you to take her to the doctor?" When he winced, she knew she'd guessed the truth.

"Is that when you woke up?"

"Yeah. When my mother died, I realized what I'd become. I walked away from Golda and her brother, but it was hard."

"Golda seemed hurt."

He shrugged. "Golda is like a child who sees a toy and decides it belongs to her regardless of reality. I just happened to be that toy this time. She'll get over it."

"You break that young woman's heart, then say she'll get over it?" Margaret shouldn't be goading Daniel like this. She knew he was telling her the truth. Golda was exactly as he described. But she wanted to hear him say he loved her again. That she was beautiful.

"Brokenhearted?" He huffed and then shook his head. "She'll have her sights set on some other sap by tomorrow morning. She only loves herself." He gripped Margaret's arm and pulled her toward him. "You're more woman than ten Goldas. I like that you're tall. I like your gorgeous hair and green eyes. And you've also got more heart and guts than any woman I've ever met. I don't want some lifeless doll who plays parlor games and invites people to tea. I want a real woman, and you're that woman, Margaret. You're the only woman I want."

Her breath caught in her throat as his lips found hers. She clung to him for a long moment, then pulled away with a sob. "Don't break my heart, Daniel." She regretted the words the instant they escaped her mouth. Now he knew her heart was involved.

He didn't let her loose. "You can trust me, Margaret. I won't let you down."

She gave up the struggle and nestled her head on his shoulder. "You'll never be able to put the past behind you. The law will be looking for you until you're caught." The thought was a knife in her heart.

He gave her a little shake and released her. "I'll make things work out. You'll see. Just try to put your doubts aside until this is over."

That was asking the impossible. She could think only of her doubts. And this fiasco with Golda hadn't helped much. She just wanted to go back to bed and sleep a few more hours. The short night of four hours' sleep had left her with a fuzzy head. Maybe with a fresh day she could figure it out. She turned her back on him and ladled the stew onto tin plates.

Daniel carried them to the men spaced around the camp. The aroma of burned coffee mingled with that of the stew, and Margaret realized she was hungry herself. She hadn't eaten all day yesterday. Her stomach had been too on edge from nerves as she waited to follow Daniel. Surely her men were looking for her by now. Two of them were good trackers. Maybe they would be able to lead Sheriff Borland to this camp. She didn't know whether to pray for deliverance or hope they couldn't find her. She had to figure out a way to help Daniel out of this mess.

Margaret cleaned the empty pot, using sand to scrub the baked-on parts until it was spotless. Daniel had disappeared, no doubt to finish plotting the robbery. At least she had a few hours away from his distracting presence.

She should be in church right now. But she could worship God right here. She left the camp behind and went down a track to a meadow along the banks of the Red River, just beyond the sound of the men laughing and playing cards.

Sitting on a rock, she listened to the gurgling water and silently prayed for wisdom, strength, and help.

"Want some company?"

She turned at the sound of Daniel's voice. Then she looked back at the water and heard him move through the brush. He settled beside her on the rock. "I bet the sheriff is looking for you. And your ranch hands."

"I'm sure they are. They can't run the ranch by themselves."

"You think that's the only reason they're searching for you?" Daniel's voice was gentle.

Did she think that? She considered it, then shook her head. "I'm sure most of them like me." Margaret picked up a rock and tossed it into the stream. Birds scattered from the trees at the sound.

Daniel slipped his arm around her and she stiffened. "You're admired by everyone who knows you, Margaret. You just don't see it."

She turned and gazed into his eyes. Why did he make her feel so safe, so accepted? More so than in any other person's presence, except maybe for Lucy. It made no sense for her to be drawn to someone like him.

His smile warmed her heart and she relaxed ever so slightly, allowing herself to lean against him. "Why do you talk like this to me?" she whispered. "I don't want to be hurt."

"I wouldn't hurt you, Margaret." His gaze never wavered from hers. He leaned forward and pressed his lips to hers.

Margaret closed her eyes and breathed in the male scent of him mingled with the soap from his morning shave. She reached up and touched his cheek. He pulled her closer. She tore her mouth from his but didn't jerk out of his embrace. Instead, she laid her head on his shoulder. She couldn't think when he was this close.

"What if I manage to escape?" The idea had been nagging at her. "They trust me a little, I think. I could lead the sheriff here to stop them."

"Honey, they are only pretending to trust you. The minute you left sight of the camp, the lookout would grab you. I don't know what they'd do to you."

His uneasy tone told her more than his words. But she knew this land. If she could slip away, she knew a dozen places to hide and many trails to take to town. "Would they punish you if I got away?"

He shook his head. "They need me. But don't even try, Margaret. I've got a plan."

They both jumped when they heard Frank calling for Daniel.

"I'd better go," he said reluctantly. "While you're out here, ask God what to do. He'll show you." He pressed a kiss against the top of her head and released her.

With a sore heart, she watched him walk away. God didn't seem to be answering her question about Daniel. Could that be an answer in itself? She rubbed her head and went back to the camp.

TWENTY-THREE

ll day long Margaret prepared meals and endured angry glances from Golda, though she didn't know what beef the woman had against her. The best Margaret could do was ignore the other woman and try to stay out of the way of the men.

As soon as it was dark, Margaret shook her bedding out to make sure no critters had crawled in, then spread it out again and slipped inside. She found it hard to fall asleep in spite of her exhaustion. The men laughed and played cards far into the night, and the clink of whiskey bottles and the sound of their harsh laughter woke her every time her eyelids drooped. It seemed a long time since she'd gone to bed when the men's voices changed. They no longer merely played cards but had begun to discuss the upcoming robbery. The breeze carried their words to her ears.

She stifled a gasp when she realized what they planned. The Larson bank—the bank where her money was stored—was the next target. Her father had just deposited the money from the spring sale before he died. She had to find a way to get out of here and warn the sheriff. Otherwise, she would lose all she owned to these misfits. So would her friends. There were so many of them. How was she to escape when they watched her so closely?

Daniel had assured her that it would turn out well, but she'd seen the uncertainty in his eyes when he talked. While she didn't know what his plan was, she suspected he didn't care as much about saving the town bank as she did.

She gulped as she thought about everyone's reaction to her disappearance. Daniel was missing as well. Would her friends think they had eloped? She felt sick. If they thought she had run off to marry Daniel, they might not even be looking for her. It was very likely that was exactly what they would think. Everyone had seen the way he courted her at the dance. She sucked in a deep breath. It was up to her to get herself out of this mess. If she could get away, she could warn the town and save her friends' savings.

According to the conversation Margaret had overheard, she only had a few days to get away and get help. "Help me, Lord," Margaret whispered. She would need his strength to do what she had to do.

MARGARET STRETCHED OUT the aching muscles in her back. If she hadn't known better, she would have sworn she was lying on lumps of coal all night. Her eyes felt leaden from lack of sleep, and it wasn't only because of the hard ground. Her heart ached at what she knew she had to do today, and moping around about it wouldn't change the facts. She had to escape and warn the town, even if it meant leaving Daniel behind.

After their late night, the men still snored in their blankets. The camp was silent except for their occasional snorts and the horses huffing in the makeshift corral. Margaret rose and tiptoed out of the camp in the direction of the Red River. From here she could hear the sound of the water rushing over rocks and tree roots. She wished she could bathe, but there was no privacy for that.

Crouching by the river, she splashed water on her face and arms and washed away the worst of the dust. Her hair was another matter. She had no comb or brush, nothing to bring her hair to some semblance of order. Using her fingers, she worked the knots out until her hair was as smooth as she could make it. It lay down her back in a heavy curtain, and she began to part it into sections to braid it again.

"Don't."

She whirled at Daniel's deep voice and almost tumbled into the river. He caught her arm and steadied her.

"I thought you were all sleeping," she whispered.

"The rest of the men are. I thought you'd be here." His eyes caressed her face.

She felt herself flush and stepped away. Running her fingers through her hair again, she began to braid it.

"I wish you'd leave it down. It's so beautiful. I've never seen hair like that. It's the color of red maple leaves in the autumn." He reached out and wound a strand around a finger.

The touch of his hand in her hair made her mouth go dry. She tugged the lock away from him and braided it in with the rest. "It's too messy to leave loose. I must look a sight."

"A beautiful one."

She caught his hand. "They're all sleeping, Daniel. We could slip away and warn the town. Get the sheriff."

"I can't leave my brother behind. He's the reason I'm here. Give me some time to fix this, Margaret. Two days."

"In two days they'll have the money from the bank."

"Is that what you care about? The money?" A muscle twitched in his jaw. "There's so much you don't know."

"Then tell me! I don't understand anything. And yes, I do care about the money. It's not just my money, but the money from the entire county is there."

His hand went from her hand to cup her cheek. His eyes were earnest. "You talk of being a believer, but you can't seem to trust anyone, not even God. You cling to your wealth as your security and carry the baggage of being unworthy, even though God loves you and has forgiven you. You should have listened a little closer to that sermon in church a couple of weeks back." He opened his mouth as though to say more, then shook his head and turned away again. His tall form disappeared among the trees as he headed farther out from camp.

She raised her hand to stop him, then let it drop. Was he right? With horror, she realized she *did* cling to her status as a wealthy ranch owner for her identity. And she trusted very few people. Her eyes burned. How did she let go of all the baggage she carried?

She made herself as neat as she could without a comb or clean clothes, then walked back to the camp. The men still snored beside the smoldering coals, their breath pluming in the cold morning air.

Frank was the only one awake. "Take some breakfast to Golda. She needs to get up."

Margaret nodded and dished up overcooked eggs from the skillet, then went to the tent where Golda had disappeared to the night before.

She scratched at the tent opening. "Miss Munster? I have some breakfast for you."

Only silence greeted her at first. Finally, she heard, "Give me a minute, will ya?"

Golda flung back the tent opening. Her hair fanned over her

shoulders and down her back like molten gold. "I don't remember ordering breakfast." Her hostile blue eyes raked over Margaret. "Daniel will take one look at you this morning and run the other way."

Margaret winced, then relaxed. That's not how Daniel had acted. "Frank told me to bring your breakfast. He said you needed to get up."

Golda rolled her eyes but stepped back to allow Margaret entry. Margaret blinked as her eyes adjusted to the darkened interior of the tent. As her vision focused, she saw clothing and possessions strewn around the tent as though a fitful child had taken everything from her closet and heaped it on the floor. There was barely room to stand without stepping on a lovely dress or two.

Golda kicked a dress out of the way and settled on an upended bucket. "I need my beauty sleep more than those disgusting eggs."

"You're already the most beautiful woman I've ever seen," Margaret blurted out.

Golda raised an eyebrow, but a pleased smile spread over her face. Then her smile faded. "I know what you're trying to do. I'm not stupid. You won't get on my good side that easily. I want you out of here." Her eyes narrowed. "I can tell you don't fit in here. Wouldn't you like to go home and sleep in a bed until this is over?"

Would the woman really help her? Margaret studied Golda's cunning expression. There was likely some plan being hatched behind that beautiful face, but Margaret could easily overpower her if they got out of sight of the camp. "Well, this is the busy time of year at the ranch. It would be good to get home."

"How about the two of us slip away, then? I'll give you a horse and you can head for home."

"What about Frank and the others? Won't they be angry?"

"You're just in the way and a distraction right now. I can handle my brother."

Did Golda think she could attract Daniel if there was no competition? Staring into the woman's beautiful face, Margaret thought it likely. "Let me talk to Daniel about it and make sure he's in favor of the idea."

"You're one of *those*, then. You let your man dictate to you."

"Daniel doesn't dictate." Margaret bristled at the thought.

Golda's slim shoulders shrugged. "Looks like it to me."

The woman was trying to goad her into something, but Margaret didn't trust her.

While the thought of getting help was appealing, she wasn't sure what Golda had planned. Margaret wasn't going to rush into anything without thought. "I'll think about it and let you know."

"You're a very stupid woman." Golda's eyes flashed, and she pushed Margaret out the doorway, then yanked the opening closed.

Margaret stood staring at the closed tent flap. Her heart beat in her chest as though it wanted to get out with the same desperation as she longed to escape the camp. She turned and bumped into a broad chest. Strong hands reached out and gripped her shoulders. She knew those hands. Staring into Daniel's face, she felt a funny hitch in her chest as emotion swamped her.

She loved him.

The shock of that realization nearly brought her to her knees. This wasn't attraction or her head being turned by his compliments. This was love, pure and simple. Why hadn't she seen it sooner? Something inside her recognized the man behind those dark eyes.

Who would have thought she would have so little sense?

That she—who prided herself on her common sense and straight-forward approach to life—would lose her heart to a bank robber? He'd asked her to trust him. He'd said that not everything was as it appeared. But the evidence kept piling up against him. She longed to let go of her distrust.

Trust. Such a small word, yet so hard for her.

"I was just looking for you," he said. "I'm sorry I rushed away. I think it's time we had a talk. I keep telling you to trust me, but I don't give you any reason to do that. God showed me how wrong that was."

God again. How could a bank robber talk about God the way he did? As though God was a best friend Daniel consulted all the time. It made no sense to her. His relationship with God made her envious.

A man on horseback rode into camp. Daniel glanced over his shoulder, then grabbed Margaret's arm. "Come with me." He steered her toward the woods at the other end of the camp.

Margaret's pulse quickened. Maybe she would finally under-stand why they were here—why Daniel was friends with these men. They had almost reached the edge of the woods when Frank's voice reached them.

"Hey, Cutler, come 'ere. Our plans just got moved up."

Daniel grew very still. Margaret could feel the coiled tension in his arm. He released her and stepped away. "Be right there," he called. He bent his head and whispered in her ear, "Don't wander far. Things may call for quick action. Wait for me by the river. I'll try to be as fast as I can."

Margaret nodded numbly. There would never be time for them to sort out all this mess.

TWENTY-FOUR

D aniel kept his face impassive as he strode toward Frank. He resisted the impulse to turn and look back at Margaret. This interruption had come at the worst possible time. She would think he was putting her off again.

He reached the camp. The gang leader's red face spoke of his anger and agitation. "What's up?"

Frank was frowning as he paced in front of the fire. "I've just found out the money is going to be transferred out tomorrow. We have to get it today at closing time. Can you and your lady friend be ready? I've got the dynamite."

"Sure." Daniel's stomach clenched. He had to get Margaret out of danger. This job wasn't as important to him as she was. But how did he whisk her out of harm's way with all the members of the gang watching every move they made? There had to be a way. He had to get Charlie as well. The tasks seemed overwhelming with the time frame even shorter.

Munster pointed to the west. "Your brother's on lookout. Go get him, and we'll ride within the hour."

Within the hour. He needed more time. His thoughts whirled, but he saw no easy way out, so he nodded. "I'll get him."

Maybe he'd be able to talk to Charlie alone. There hadn't been any opportunity to do that since he'd arrived. Richard had kept in the background as well, and only a nod from him had confirmed to Daniel that all the plans were still on target. If he could get to Richard, maybe they could come up with an alternate plan.

Why did Margaret have to show up? It would take everything in him to keep her safe. He clambered over rocks and boulders as he made his way to the top of the lookout hill. A rifle across his knees, Charlie sat with his back to the camp. His hat was pulled low to shield his face from the sun, but in spite of his tough stance, Daniel saw the little boy he'd always loved.

"Frank sent me to get you."

At the sound of Daniel's voice, Charlie grabbed his rifle and spun around. "Oh, it's you." Relief lightened his freckled, sunburned face.

"The job has been moved up. We ride today."

Charlie licked his lips, and his youthful face looked suddenly old and worn. "Munster sure we can handle it?"

"You having second thoughts?" If Charlie was uncertain, it would make Daniel's job easier.

Charlie shrugged. "Nah, I can handle it."

His brother's swaggering bravado touched Daniel's heart. All of nineteen, Charlie's desperate desire to make a name for himself—even if it was a bad one—had brought him here. Daniel touched Charlie on the shoulder. "You got time to come to the river with me? Margaret is waiting there, and I need to talk to both of you."

"My relief is coming now." Charlie nodded toward Sheppard,

a surly man of about fifty, who was climbing the steep hill toward them. "I thought you said Frank sent you to get me."

"He did, but we have a few minutes. We need to talk."

"What about? And why are you even here, Daniel?"

"I have a lot to tell you. Meet me at the river." Daniel went back down the hill toward the river. His heart sped up at the thought of the coming revelations he had to make to Margaret and Charlie. He prayed they would understand.

MARGARET SAT ON a rock and let the good sunshine bake onto her arms. The cool morning had quickly given way to a hot spring day. Dark clouds gathered in the southwest, their tops reaching toward the heavens in dark masses. The coming storm would blow this warmth away, so she'd better enjoy it while she could. A movement caught her eye. Golda came toward her along the path from camp. She kept looking furtively back over her shoulder.

"I thought I'd find you here," she said, huffing from the exertion of the walk. "You ready to go?"

"What?" Margaret's heart plummeted. Daniel wanted to talk to her, to explain things. He was on his way here right now. "I told you I needed to talk to Daniel about it."

"It has to be right now while Frank is occupied with the coming job. I have horses waiting by Thunder Creek."

Margaret pulled away from Golda's grip. "I don't think so."

Golda pulled a small pistol from the pocket of her dress. "I want you out of here. Now. So you'll come with me, or I'll shoot you where you stand. I'll tell Frank you jumped me and he'll believe it."

Margaret was sure he would. Her thoughts raced, but she could see it wouldn't take much for Golda to pull the trigger. One false move and that tiny gun would put a hole right through her.

Golda didn't wait for an answer. She motioned with the gun. "Move."

Margaret allowed Golda to prod her toward the path. If only Daniel hadn't been called away. What would he think when he got to the river and didn't find her? Would he suspect something had happened to her?

She and Golda made their way along the path to a small tributary that fed into the river. Two horses munched on grass beneath the tree where they were tethered. Neither was Archie.

"My horse isn't here."

"These will get us where we're going." Golda made her mount, then led the way along a path sprinkled with wildflowers.

They came to a crossroad, and Golda turned her gelding's head to the fork that went to the right. Margaret wasn't familiar with the area but knew the path didn't go in the direction of home. She pulled the horse's head up short and stopped in the middle of the path.

"This isn't the right way." She tensed, ready to urge her horse away from the gun Golda still held.

The other woman grinned, but the smile didn't reach her hard blue eyes. "Oh, it's the right path, all right." Golda laughed, and the sound was full of mockery.

She whistled, and three riders came from behind an outcropping of rocks. Margaret was surrounded before she realized what was happening. One man grabbed her reins, and the other two flanked her mare on each side.

"What's going on?" Margaret struggled to free herself. Tension rippled through her body.

"You said your ranch was worth a lot of money. It must be if Daniel is willing to marry you," Golda sneered. "You didn't think I would let you waltz out of camp without making sure I got a piece of that, did you? If Daniel wanted you with the ranch, he'll want me with a large chunk of cash from it." She fished in her saddlebag. "You're going to write a note to your attorney and tell him you're being held for ransom by Daniel Cutler. If he doesn't pay fifty thousand dollars in two days, he'll never see you again."

"I won't do it!" Margaret tried to wrench the reins from the henchman's grasp, but he growled at her and swatted her across the face. She fell from the saddle to the ground, her face burning. She raised a hand to her throbbing cheek.

"You'll do what you're told, or we'll kill you here and now," the man told her.

Margaret rubbed her cheek. "Why blame Daniel?"

"I don't want there to be any chance that he can go running back to the Triple T. He shows his face at the ranch after this, he'll be shot."

"Not if I tell him the real story." As soon as the words were out of her mouth, she realized the truth. Once they had the money, she was expendable. Her heart squeezed in her chest, and her mouth went dry. She was in the clutches of a madwoman.

Golda dismounted, then pulled a paper and pencil from the saddlebag. She handed them to Margaret. "Write what I tell you."

Margaret stared at her implacable face. *Help me, Lord.* "I won't. If you shoot me, you'll lose Daniel. And your brother will be furious you ruined his plans."

Golda's eyes narrowed. She grabbed Margaret's hair and gave

it a vicious yank. "I could give you to the men for a little while. You'd soon change your tune."

"I won't." Margaret put all the conviction in her voice that she could muster. "You don't know me, Golda. There's nothing you can do that will make me agree. I could never hurt someone I love."

The blond woman screeched and flew at Margaret. Her fingers were hooked into claws, but Margaret was bigger and stronger. She fielded the blows at first, then Golda's long nails raked Margaret's arm. Margaret grabbed Golda's arms and wrestled her onto her back, then sat on her and pinned her hands to the ground.

"You'll die for laying a hand on me! Wait until Frank hears what you've done," Golda panted. "I'll kill you!" She bucked and squirmed, but Margaret held her fast. "Help me, you idiots!"

Margaret had forgotten about the men. She glanced to the right and saw the man who had struck her dismounting. She rolled off Golda and sprang for her horse. She'd put her boot in the stirrup when a hard hand yanked on her braid, and she went tumbling onto her back. The man hauled her to her feet and a massive fist descended on her. When the blow struck, the pain was immense, then her vision faded to black.

TWENTY-FIVE

❦

The storm clouds still continued to gather overhead and flocks of birds circled above Daniel's head, but he barely noticed as he hurried toward the river. He had to see Margaret and explain. Once the truth was out, he could relax. Just looking forward to that moment eased the tension from his shoulders.

As he approached the rock where he had expected to find her, he stopped and looked around. There was no sign of her, but maybe she had gotten tired of waiting. He had taken longer than he'd expected. Munster would be looking for them both, and there was no time to waste. He ran back toward camp, slowing to a walk just before entering the clearing where the camp was located. He didn't dare let anyone see his agitation. He skirted the edge of the clearing but saw no sign of Margaret. Maybe she was waiting in a different spot at the river.

He plunged into the trees and hurried back to the Red River. But fifteen minutes later he had to admit defeat. Margaret was missing. He found Charlie waiting by the big rock.

"Where you been?" his brother asked.

"Looking for Margaret." Daniel's stomach churned, but he was unable to put his finger on why he was so uneasy.

"I saw her with Golda heading away from camp." Charlie's eyes were troubled. "I was surprised Golda was having anything to do with her."

Daniel's unease mushroomed to full-fledged panic. Golda was pure evil, even more so than her brother. Whatever she was up to, it couldn't be good.

"Show me!" Daniel hauled Charlie to his feet and shoved him toward the camp. "I'll grab the horses and meet you at the base of Lookout Hill. Don't tell anyone where we're going."

"I reckon I don't know anything to tell," Charlie said.

Daniel didn't either, but he felt sick inside to think that Margaret was in jeopardy because of him. He had to find them. He slipped into the remuda of horses and found his gelding and Charlie's mare. The horses were all saddled in preparation for the ride to the bank. Frank would be after them the minute he discovered the horses were gone. The problems were multiplying faster than a pet rabbit, and he didn't know what to do about it.

He led the horses to the meeting place where Charlie waited, and they both mounted. "Show me where you saw them."

Charlie led the way down the rocky path, and Daniel concentrated on finding the trail left by Golda and Margaret. He finally found it and saw where they veered off the track away from Larson. His last hopes that Golda wasn't up to something sinister ebbed away.

"You going to tell me what this is all about?" Charlie asked.

"Not now. We have to focus on finding Margaret."

"You really love her, don't you?"

"Sure do. I didn't know I could feel this way about a woman."

Daniel didn't want to talk about it. A terrible fear and foreboding gripped him that his obsession with his own plans was going to lead to Margaret's death. He couldn't live with that. Hardening his jaw, he vowed he would not let anything happen to her. He prayed silently as they hurried along the trail.

"Frank is going to be on our trail like a duck on a June bug," Charlie said after a few moments. "The rest of the gang is all ready to go rob the bank. We're going to miss out on all the fun."

"Frank won't go without us. Me and Margaret are key players in his little plan." Only after he said the words did Daniel realize how dry and critical his words were. Charlie caught his tone, for his head came up sharply and he stared at Daniel.

"You don't like Frank much, do you?" Charlie asked. "You were part of his gang long before I was. Why did you leave?"

"It's complicated. But I need to tell you something." Daniel inhaled and squared his shoulders. "Ma asked me to take her to the doctor the day before she died. I put her off because Golda and Frank needed me to stand lookout with the horses."

Charlie went white. "Y-You left her when she needed you?"

Daniel nodded. "When she died, I realized what I'd become, Charlie. Sin leads you in little steps until you're far from home."

Charlie's eyes were wet. "You killed Ma." He clenched his fists.

"The doctor said he couldn't have prevented it, but that doesn't mean much. I was still guilty. I'll never get over it, Charlie. Never."

Charlie rubbed his eyes with the back of his hand. "I should shoot you where you sit."

Before Daniel could respond, the trail turned toward a small butte. "Wait here," Daniel told his brother. He dismounted and handed his reins to Charlie. "I'll check it out. Maybe they're holed up there."

Crouching behind rocks and scrubby bushes, Daniel crept forward. Soon the sound of voices drifted to his ears. He paused and listened. Golda's voice. He couldn't make out the words, but the mockery in her tone was hard to miss. He retraced his steps to where his brother waited.

"They're just ahead," he told Charlie. "Leave the horses here and take your rifle." Daniel grabbed his own Winchester from the saddle and led the way back to where Golda held Margaret captive.

Lying on their bellies, Charlie and Daniel peered from behind a rock at the camp. Golda had been joined by Kid Loco and two other men. A series of caves sprinkled the rocks behind the group. Daniel scanned the area for Margaret and finally spotted her lying near the mouth of one of the caves. Her eyes were closed in her white face, and for one heart-stopping moment, he feared he was too late. Then she opened her eyes and sat up. When he saw her holding her head, he realized part of the red wasn't her hair but blood.

A cold rage settled in his bones, and he nearly rushed into the camp with guns blazing, but an inner voice counseled caution. Charlie nudged him, and Daniel saw the lookout Golda and her gang had posted. The man was about thirty feet from their hideaway, and he hadn't spotted them yet. Daniel motioned for Charlie to circle around the other way so they could rush the lookout from both sides.

Charlie crept along the rocks. When his brother was in place, Daniel crawled closer. Picking up a rock, he aimed it at the man's head. The rock zinged through the air with precision and hit the lookout in the forehead. He went down without a whimper.

Daniel scrabbled to the man's prone form and took his revolver, then Daniel tied him up and gagged him with a bandana. That should keep him quiet. One down and two more men to go.

He and Charlie slithered down the slope toward the camp. Kid Loco and Marty Nelson, one of the Kid's cohorts, were arguing with Golda. As Daniel got nearer, he was finally able to hear what they were saying.

Kid Loco's hard voice carried well on the rising wind from the approaching storm. "I say we kill her now and get it over with. We can seal her in one of these caves, and no one will be the wiser. We're going to kill her anyway."

"We may need her. Until her lawyer delivers that money, she's collateral," Golda told him.

"Who says you make the decisions around here?" Kid Loco sneered. "What's to keep me from killing her right now?"

"You don't want to do that, Kid." Golda's voice was heavy with menace. "I don't like people to cross me."

Kid Loco held up a hand. "I was just joshing you, Golda. We're partners. I don't double-cross partners."

"You'd better not." Golda's voice turned silky, but there was still a trace of warning in her tone.

Daniel had heard that expression in her voice before, and Kid Loco had better beware. She was a black widow spider, and she couldn't be trusted. If she didn't do it herself, she would have her brother see that he paid for any slur on her.

"Marty, you take the ransom note into town. Get directions to the ranch and get it delivered. I'll stay here and watch over the prisoner," Kid Loco said.

"What if the lawyer realizes it's a forgery? The letter, I mean," Marty asked.

"We'll figure that out if it happens. Little snit should have done what she was told." Golda glared at Margaret. "She's going to pay for it."

"She don't look like she'll give you much trouble." Marty picked at his teeth with a piece of straw, then took the paper Golda held out to him and sauntered to his horse. "I'll be back in a few hours. You staying here?"

"Yeah, the caves should give us some shelter from the storm that's brewing," Kid Loco said.

Marty rode off, and Daniel let out the breath he'd been holding. Another down. The odds were much better now, but Kid Loco was still no man to fool with. His reputation with the gun had reached as far as California. The notches on his belt numbered twenty-two the last time Daniel had heard. Still, if he and Charlie could get the draw on him before the Kid knew they were here, they had a chance.

He motioned for Charlie to follow him. They crept still closer.

"You reckon Cutler is looking for her yet?" Kid Loco asked.

"He'll find me," Margaret said, raising her head.

Warmth spread through Daniel at the certainty in her tone. There was actually faith and trust in her voice. Maybe he was getting through to her. He crept a bit closer.

Golda gave an unladylike snort. "Why would he bother finding you? He's probably on his way to rob the bank right now. He has more important things on his mind than searching for you."

Daniel clenched his fists, and his gaze lingered on Margaret. He longed to get her to safety. She rose and brushed the dust from her britches. *Stay back.* He willed her to hear his silent warning and remain in the relative safety of the cave, but she walked slowly forward until she faced Golda.

"You're not going to get away with this, Golda. God is in control."

Golda burst into gales of laughter. "Oh, she's *religious*, Kid." She spat the words as if they left a bad taste in her mouth. "Even more than I realized."

A rush of joy at Margaret's words rose in Daniel's chest. Maybe she was learning to walk closer to the Lord through this experience. The next step was for her to accept his unconditional love. Maybe then she could accept Daniel's own love for her. His heart throbbed with hope.

"Laugh all you want," Margaret said. "But I won't let you hurt Daniel." She walked toward the horses.

"Where do you think you're going?"

"Home. And if you intend to stop me, you'll have to kill me now. I won't let you rob us."

"That can be arranged," Kid Loco growled. He drew his revolver.

"Oh, please stop showing off," Golda said with an impatient wave of her hand. "Margaret knows she's not going anywhere. Tie her up, Kid."

But Margaret darted to the horse and threw herself atop its back before Kid Loco could react. He took aim at her back, and Daniel made his move. His rifle came up almost of its own volition. He fired, and the bullet slammed into the Kid's wrist. The gunfighter dropped his gun with a yowl. The surprise on his face was worth everything Daniel had endured this day. If he'd had time, Daniel would have laughed at the snarl Kid gave when he recognized him.

"Cover me!" Daniel told Charlie. He leaped forward into the clearing. Margaret was astride the horse and heading down the path away from him.

"Margaret, wait!" Daniel ran forward and kicked the gun away from Kid Loco. Charlie ran to help him and stood guard over the gunfighter.

Kid looked up at Daniel and drew back his lip in a snarl. "You're a dead man, Cutler."

"Nice to see you too, Kid." Daniel turned, then stepped back as Golda screamed and rushed at him.

She raked her nails over his face. "What's wrong with me?" she panted. Her face was wild with insane jealousy, and she went at his eyes with her nails. "You choose that red-haired Amazon over a real woman?"

Daniel caught her hands and stopped her from inflicting any more damage, though he could feel the blood already beginning to trickle down his face. He grabbed the rope that had been intended for Margaret and tied Golda's hands together, then pushed her down beside Kid Loco. Then he tied the Kid as well.

Margaret must have heard his shout, for she came cantering back toward them. "Daniel!" She waved and dismounted. He caught her as she ran into his arms. With her in his embrace, all the world seemed right again. He buried his face in her hair. Never again would he let her be put in this kind of danger. If anything had happened to her, he wouldn't have been able to live with himself.

She patted his face. "You came," she murmured. "I knew you would."

"Sorry I was late," he whispered against her hair. He held her close and breathed in the scent of her hair. She fit against his heart as if she were made just for him. As far as he was concerned, God had done just that.

TWENTY-SIX

⌒⟡⌒

Margaret had thought she was dreaming when she heard Daniel's voice. Nestled against his chest, she knew how much she loved him. She was content to trust now, even though she didn't see how the future could be clear for them. Daniel was likely to go to prison for what he'd done in the past, but if that happened, she would wait for him.

But she wouldn't think about that now. Now the only reality she wanted was the sense of his strong arms around her and the sound of his heart against her ear. She branded into her memory the sensation of being cradled against his chest. It might be all she had to remember when this episode in her life was over.

"Very touching." A harsh voice broke into their reunion.

Margaret jerked around to find herself and Daniel staring down the barrel of a gun. Frank was at the other end of it, and behind him clustered the rest of the gang. Daniel's arms tightened around her. Frank's eyes promised retribution, and she shuddered. *God, help us.*

"Would someone mind explaining what's going on?" Frank

growled. "Golda, I'm disappointed you let them tie you up. I thought you had more gumption than that."

Golda jumped to her feet. "They planned to hold me for ransom to get all of the bank money instead of just their fair share." She walked to her brother, then turned her back to him. "Untie me."

"You got yourself into this mess, you get yourself out."

Margaret drew away from Daniel. "She's lying." She touched her head. "Look at me. I'm bleeding. Your sister has already sent a ransom demand to my attorney. She and her men were going to kill me."

Frank scowled at her. "You think I'd believe you over my own sister?"

"Think, Frank," Daniel said. "She's jealous of Margaret. You warned me that she'd be upset and she was. You know your sister better than anyone. She was double-crossing you."

Frank frowned and stared at his sister. "That true, Golda? You trying to make money while my back was turned?" He jerked his head at one of the men. "Untie her and the Kid. It don't matter what she was planning. All that matters is that she's blood. We're all together now, and we'll do it my way."

The man hurried to obey, and Margaret's stomach plummeted at the thoughtful glance Frank turned on Daniel and her. What would he do with them? They were heavily outnumbered, and Daniel's revolver had been taken away. Charlie's too.

Golda rubbed her wrists. Kid Loco retrieved his gun and stalked toward Daniel with the weapon in his left hand. He kept his injured wrist against his stomach. "You're a dead man," he snarled.

Frank held up his hand. "This can all wait. We've got a bank to rob, or the bulk of that money will be gone tomorrow. There'll be time for revenge when we're out of here." He shoved Margaret toward the horse.

"Don't touch her!" Daniel started toward him with his fists clenched, but Kid Loco slammed the butt of his revolver in Daniel's stomach. Daniel doubled over and gasped.

Margaret jerked her arm out of Frank's grasp and went to Daniel. "Don't fight them now," she whispered. "We'll figure out a way to get out of this."

"I still need you both," Frank said. "You're going to get me in that bank. After that, we'll let Kid use you for target practice. No one messes with the Munster family. You're both going to wish you'd never been born."

He made them mount their horses, and they turned toward Larson. As they rode along, Margaret glanced at Daniel. "Why does the Kid hate you so much?" she whispered.

"It's a long story," Daniel said.

"It's a long ride."

He sighed. "It's not something I'm proud of. The gang had just robbed a bank in Houston, and we were holed up in a cabin outside Fort Worth. The Kid was in town, and he was flirting with my cousin Sarah. Sarah had no idea who or what he was, but I knew. I thought I shouldn't get involved, though, so I didn't say anything. One of his cronies took a liking to her too, and there was a gunfight. A stray bullet killed her. She was only nineteen."

He fell silent, and Margaret could feel his pain.

"That was before I began to trust God, and I went looking for Kid Loco and the other man. I killed the other man in a fair gunfight and captured Kid. I turned him in to the sheriff. The sheriff locked him up, but the Kid escaped two days later. He's never forgiven me for turning him in. He intends to get revenge someday."

Daniel had killed a man. Margaret swallowed hard. The knowledge hurt even though he'd admitted as much once. What else had he done? Bank robbery, killings—yet he spoke of God. Glancing at him from the corner of her eye, she realized that God had forgiven him. It shone out of everything Daniel did and said. She was content to wait and see why he'd come back to this group, but she suspected it was something honorable.

She didn't understand, but she desperately wanted to. She loved him.

DANIEL FLEXED HIS muscles against the ropes that bound him, but all he succeeded in doing was to rub even more skin from his raw wrists. This was his fault, and he had to get them out of here.

Rivulets of perspiration trickled down his face. The heat and humidity had built through the day, and the towering clouds had not yet brought the relief of a rainstorm. So many people were counting on him, and he'd let them all down. He glanced around the shack where they were confined. About three feet away, Margaret wrestled with the ropes on her wrists as well. Her green eyes stared out of her white face, and she bit her lip as she fought against her bonds.

Frank had confined them here while he checked out the town. He wanted to make sure there weren't too many people around before they made their move. Guards were posted just outside the open door.

The desperation on her face renewed Daniel's urgency to free himself. Gritting his teeth, he ignored the pain and struggled to wrest his wrists from the ropes. There—they gave just a bit. The guards didn't seem to be looking, so he inched closer to Margaret.

She stopped her struggling and stared up into his face. "I'm scared, Daniel. What's going to happen?"

"We're going to get free. I'm going to scoot around when the guards aren't looking. See if you can untie me." He wiggled around until his hands touched hers.

Her hands moved up to his wrists. "You're bleeding," she gasped.

He heard the concern in her voice, and guilt wracked him. What had he gotten her into? Before he came along, she had lived a safe and happy life with her father. Because of him, she was in deadly danger. "I'm sorry. I never meant to put you in jeopardy. I promised to protect you, and I've failed."

She turned her head, and the whisper of her breath touched his neck. "I'm not sorry."

An ache of love built in his chest. His thoughts blurred as he tried to sort out what she meant. "You're not sorry?"

"I'm not sorry I spent this time with you. I want the chance to get to know you better," she said. "We'll get out of here. Will Charlie help us?"

"I think so. If I could just talk to him in private, make him understand what I'm doing here."

"What are you doing here?" Her fingers continued to fumble with the knots, but so far they remained as tight as before.

"That's what I was going to tell you." He lowered his voice even further. If Frank found out the truth, he would string them up at the first tree he found. "I'm a Texas Ranger now, not a bank robber. Another ranger, Richard, helped me after I was shot. He led me to Christ. He convinced me that if God could forgive Paul in the Bible, he could forgive me. I turned my back on crime and joined the Rangers with Richard's help. He was the short, gray-haired man who was part of the gang when we were first brought here."

"But why didn't you go to prison?"

"Richard again. I hadn't actually stolen anything yet. I was outside with the horses, and he persuaded the Rangers that I could be more useful as one of them. He infiltrated the gang, and we were both sent to apprehend them. I'm not sure what's happened to him."

Her eyes brightened. "You're not a robber?"

He gave a slight shake of his head. "The Rangers wanted to move in and arrest the gang two months ago, but I persuaded them to let me get Charlie out before he actually broke the law. So far, all he'd done was to join them. They haven't let him participate in the smaller robberies they've done so far. After this one, I won't have any choice but to arrest my own brother. I can't let that happen." The thought of his brother behind bars made his voice tremble, and he cleared his throat.

"A Ranger," Margaret breathed. Her nails dug into Daniel's arm.

He gasped a bit. "What's wrong?"

She exhaled softly. "A Ranger is almost worse than being a bank robber, at least as far as Pa's concerned. If he were alive, he would never sanction me being with you." Her fingers plucked desperately at the rope, and the bonds began to loosen.

"What are you talking about?" One wrist broke loose, and he furtively slipped his other out of the ropes, then flexed his fingers.

"A Texas Ranger killed my uncle." Her voice was hoarse with fatigue. "After that, Pa always hated them worse than scorpions, and that's saying something."

"I don't want to marry your pa. I want to marry you. And I think he'd agree if he were alive. He liked me." *Marry.* He'd just said he wanted to marry her.

She exhaled. "Marry me?"

He quickly untied her. "We'll talk about this when we get out of here." He had to stay focused on the problem at hand. He'd handle the Ranger issue when the time came.

Movement at the door of the shack made him freeze. Charlie poked his head inside.

His brother carried a tin cup and two plates of beans. "I brought you some supper." He set the plates on the dirt floor. "I'll have to untie you so you can eat, but don't try anything. I'd have to shoot you, and after what you told me about Ma, I'm ready to do it." His voice quavered and he blinked rapidly.

Daniel couldn't let Charlie see that the ropes were loose. Not yet. "You wouldn't shoot me, and you know it, Charlie."

"I would if I had to." Charlie's words were almost too low for Daniel to hear.

Daniel knew better. "Let's get out of here, Charlie. Pa needs you back on the ranch. He asked me to bring you home."

Charlie sucked in his breath, and his gaze darted to Daniel's. "*Pa* asked you to bring me back?"

The hope in his voice almost broke Daniel's heart. It held all the emotion of Charlie's lonely growing-up years as the nearly forgotten son. And Daniel was to blame for some of it. He was the big, strong son and Charlie was built more like their mother. Small-boned and short with her passive nature. It rankled their dad, as did their mother's babying. Daniel should have stepped in, helped Charlie become a man instead of their mother's lapdog.

"And there's more, Charlie." This news would be hard for him to take. It was still hard for Daniel to grasp. "Pa's dying. He wants you home to make his peace with you."

Daniel heard Margaret gasp at the same time as Charlie's face crumpled. He visibly struggled to maintain his composure, swallowing hard and shaking his head. Tears streamed down Charlie's face, and he buried his face in his hands. "Not Pa," he choked.

Daniel wanted to put his arms around his brother, but he didn't know if Charlie would allow it. He glanced at Margaret. She was staring at Charlie with tears in her eyes. She rose and went to Charlie and put her arms around him. He buried his face against her shoulder.

"We'll go through this together," she said soothingly as she patted his back.

Charlie's sobs tore at Daniel's insides. He clenched his fists at his sides and wished there was some way to take the pain for his brother.

Charlie's sobs finally subsided, and he raised his head. His glance dropped to Daniel's hands. "You're untied. Frank will have a fit."

"Let's get out of here, Charlie," Daniel said. "You don't belong with this gang. I realize you were trying to hurt Pa and me, but put away childish thoughts like that. Now is the time for us to hang together as a family. I feel responsible for you being here, Charlie. That's the other reason I'm here. I can't live with myself if you go down this path where I led you."

Charlie stared at him for a long moment. "But Frank and the rest are my friends. They care about me. They took me in when no one else cared anything about me."

"Pa and I are your family. Margaret now too. You think Frank wouldn't hesitate to shoot you if you disappointed him?"

"There's Golda," Charlie said.

"Open your eyes, brother! She's using you even more than her brother. You know it's true."

Charlie's face worked. He finally nodded. "Okay, Daniel. I don't know how we'll manage it, but okay. Frank will be back any minute. We'd better hurry with whatever we do." He wiped his eyes with his sleeve. "I'll try to keep anyone from coming in here."

"We'll need a diversion to get past all of them," Margaret said. "I'll provide one."

"I reckon that won't happen. You stay put right where you are," Daniel said. "I've put you in enough danger already."

"The rest of your Rangers aren't here. I'm all you've got."

Charlie gasped. "Rangers? What's this?"

Margaret dropped her gaze and turned away to let Daniel explain.

He sighed. "I'm a Texas Ranger, Charlie, sent to bring in the gang. I want you out of the way before you do something that's against the law and I have to bring you in too."

"A Ranger," Charlie breathed. "When we were kids, you always said you wanted to be a lawman. Does Pa know?"

Daniel nodded. "I went home nine months ago and confessed everything. He knows it all, my bad past and the good God has done in my life."

"God?" Charlie's eyes went wide. "You never had time for religion before, Daniel. Pa neither. What did he say about that?"

"When a man's dying, his perspective can change. Pa is a believer now too. That's why he sent me after you. He wants you to forgive him."

Charlie's eyes welled with tears again. "He said that?"

"That and more." Daniel put his hand on Charlie's shoulder.

"But there will be time later for explanations. We have to get out of here."

Charlie slowly backed up. He shook his head. "But I can't let you arrest my friends."

"They're not your friends, Charlie. Real friends wouldn't want to kill your only brother. They're just using you. Any willing gunman would do for them."

"That's not true," Charlie snapped. "They care about me."

"Hey, Charlie, you hand-feeding them?" a voice called from out by the cooking fire. "Get out here and clean up this mess."

"See what I mean?" Daniel whispered urgently. "You're just a servant to them. Think about Pa, Charlie, about what it would do to him if you went to prison or were hung."

Charlie blinked rapidly, then uttered an inarticulate cry and rushed from the shack. Margaret went to Daniel and buried her face against his chest. "We're in trouble, aren't we?"

"I don't think he'll betray us." Daniel cradled her closer. The scent of her hair and the feel of her in his arms soothed him. He kissed the top of her head. If he could only keep her close and protect her all the days of their lives. But first he had to get them out of here.

"We'll wait fifteen minutes, then we'll act. With or without Charlie." Daniel's eyes burned at the thought of leaving his brother behind. But he had a responsibility to Margaret and to his job. He had no choice.

She nodded and lifted her head. He bent and pressed his lips to hers. Her soft kiss gave him courage and hope. "Right is on our side," he whispered. "Things may look dark now, but God has it all under control."

She smiled tremulously. "No wonder all the talk of God didn't fit. You're a knight on a quest, not an evil man. No wonder you kept my head spinning."

"Here I thought I kept your head spinning with my kisses." He grinned.

Her face turned scarlet and she started to draw back, but he clutched her closer. "You make my head spin, so it's only fair if I do the same to you."

She nestled against his chest again, and he rested his chin on top of her head. At least she wasn't fighting him right now. He should enjoy this while it lasted, but there was no time. "This is not getting us out of here."

"No." She drew back and looked into his eyes. "You really want to marry me?"

"Are you trying to back out now?" His lips curved in a smile. A dimple played at the corner of that delectable mouth of hers, and it just made him want to kiss her again.

"Only if you want free. I know I'm no catch."

"I'm going to convince you differently yet. And you couldn't get rid of me with a horse whip." He released her reluctantly. He had to think, and he couldn't do that with her so near.

He stepped away from her and peered through the gloom. "We need to come up with a diversion. Got any ideas?"

CHARLIE GATHERED THE dirty dishes and carried them to the creek. What was he supposed to do with everything Daniel had told him? There was a ring of truth about it, but Frank and his men had welcomed him as one of them. A man didn't turn his back on his friends.

Frank looked up when he brought back the clean dishes. "When you're done with that, check my horse. I think he's got a stone in his right shoe. And make sure our provisions are ready."

Charlie stared at him a minute. Had Frank ever talked to him as an equal, or had he always ordered him around like a servant? Frank had never once asked his opinion about anything. Charlie studied the cruel twist to the man's mouth. He had a choice to make today, and he'd better make the right one. His brother's life was at stake. Did he want to have the regrets Daniel clearly had about their father?

"What are you standing around for? You're gaping like a lunatic," Frank snapped. "Do what I told you."

Charlie ducked his head and walked toward the remuda. When he was out of Frank's sight, he doubled back toward the shack.

The wind was beginning to pick up again as the towering clouds moved closer. They were going to get wet for sure. He ducked into the shack, but it was empty. A hollow sensation settled in his midsection. Daniel hadn't trusted him to come back. And why should he? When Charlie had been asked to choose between his family and the gang, he'd waffled.

He stepped back into the stinging sand. Where would they have gone? He spied a thicket a few feet behind the shack. Maybe there. Once he was sure no one was around, he jogged over to the vegetation where he saw a boot. They were hiding, but they'd never get away undetected without a diversion. He pulled out his pocketknife and made his way back to the remuda where he cut the horses free, then slapped one on the rump. They all took off as he melted back into the trees.

Men shouted and ran after the horses. When Charlie got back to the thicket, his brother and Margaret crawled out from their hiding place.

She brushed the bits of thorns and twigs from her skirt. "How do we get any mounts now? I can't leave Archie here."

"We may have to use the old shank's mare and hoof it on our own two feet," Daniel said. "We'll collect Archie later. Let's go."

Margaret gave a low, warbling whistle. It sounded almost like a bird. "Archie will come when he hears me. What about Charlie?"

At least they hadn't totally given up on him. He stepped from behind a tree. "I'm here."

They both whirled at Charlie's voice. "You came," Daniel said.

Charlie swallowed hard, and his eyes burned. "I'm going with you. I can't let Pa die thinking I'm a criminal."

"I'm proud of you, boy," Daniel said.

"I'm not a boy any longer, Daniel. Not anymore."

Daniel nodded and clapped Charlie on the shoulder. "You're right. You're a man, Charlie. One Pa and I are both going to enjoy getting to know. Let's go."

Daniel led them down a path toward Jacksboro. Charlie wasn't sure what his brother had in mind, but with each step they were getting away, so he didn't care. All he wanted was to get home before Pa died.

Margaret looked around anxiously as they walked the path. "I was sure Archie would hear me." She whistled again, but there was no neigh from her horse. Frowning, she allowed Daniel to lead her on. After several minutes she stopped short. "This isn't the way to Larson."

Daniel shook his head. "We're not going to Larson. We're going to get the rest of the Rangers at the fort."

She tipped up her chin. "I'm going to Larson. We have to warn the sheriff before those men get my money."

"My men will handle the robbers. It's not a long ride to Larson from the fort."

"But they may hit the bank first. Larson is closer. I'm going there." She wheeled around and hurried toward the fork in the trail.

Daniel grabbed her arm. "No, it's not safe, Margaret. We need help."

Charlie opened his mouth to agree with his brother, but when he saw the determination in Margaret's green eyes, he knew it was useless to argue. "She's not cottoning to your idea, Daniel."

Daniel sighed. "All right, we'll go to Larson. But you'll do exactly as I tell you. Our future kids are counting on us to survive."

TWENTY-SEVEN

ur kids. The way Daniel said those words—as if it were a foregone conclusion that they would marry and have children—brought a tide of emotion roiling in Margaret's stomach. She'd never thought to marry, let alone have children. Not since Nate married Lucy, anyway. Margaret trudged along the path at the fastest clip she could manage and tried not to think about what Daniel had said.

In her mind's eye, she saw little boys with Daniel's dark eyes. Maybe a little girl or two with her red hair. But no, she wouldn't wish this mess of a mop on any child of hers. Better to have Daniel's dark curls. She smiled at the thought of dark ringlets on a cherubic face.

"What's so funny?" Daniel's face shone with perspiration, and his breath came fast from the exertion of jogging toward town. Charlie had gone on ahead a few yards.

Heat burned her cheeks. Wouldn't he just love to know she was thinking about children? He would smile that self-assured grin of his as if he knew it was going to happen. She wiped the smile from her face. "Nothing."

His gaze swept over her face, but he didn't argue with her. A grin tugged at his mouth, but there was no way he could know what she'd been thinking. At least she prayed that was so. Surely she wasn't that transparent.

They paused under a juniper tree. "Storm's almost on us. I need to catch my breath." Daniel sank to the ground and lay there with his hands laced behind his head. Charlie doubled back toward them, then leaned against a rock and closed his eyes. His face was red with exertion.

The wind had steadily built for the past hour, and the roiling clouds had turned to a blackish green that foreshadowed a bad storm. "There's no time to rest." Margaret bent over and caught her breath. Every muscle ached, and a blister on her foot felt as though it had broken open. If only she could have a good cry. There were all kinds of pent-up emotions just begging to be let out.

"You're about to drop." Daniel patted the ground beside him. "Sit and rest. Tell me more about why your father hated Texas Rangers."

Margaret glanced at the sky. "We really should be moving along. That storm is imminent."

"We all need a rest or we won't make it at all."

Margaret sat beside him on the lush green carpet of grass and wildflowers. She plucked a bluebell and buried her nose in the flower.

"Quit lollygagging and tell me." He studied her face. "It can't be that bad."

"It's worse. You're lucky he's gone on to heaven because he would have shot you."

Daniel grinned. "So what's the story?"

Margaret's eyes darkened. "My uncle was out rounding up cattle for the fall trail drive ten years ago. He had a fire going and was branding the few strays we'd missed marking in the spring. A Ranger came through looking for rustlers. He took one look at my uncle's branding operation and jumped to the conclusion that my uncle was a cattle thief. When the Ranger tried to arrest him, my uncle drew his revolver and the Ranger shot him."

"Sounds like it was as much your uncle's fault as the Ranger's. Why didn't he explain who he was?"

"He was always a bit of a hothead. No one knows for sure why he pulled the gun, but when it was all over, my uncle was dead, and Pa vowed vengeance on all Texas Rangers. He wrote letters and tried to get the man in trouble, but nothing was ever done." Margaret shivered at the remembrance of those dark days.

"He was Lewis's father?"

She nodded. "So Pa always tried to make it up to Lewis since my uncle was working here when it happened."

"I'll see what I can find out." Daniel stood and held out a hand to her. "We'd better get on the way again."

Margaret gave him her hand, and he tugged her to her feet. He pulled her into his arms and she rested there a moment, feeling safe and protected. Little by little, she was trusting God to work things out according to his will. That knowledge brought her comfort she'd never expected.

A SENSE OF urgency pushed Margaret on, though her feet throbbed and weariness slowed her steps. At this rate it would take two days to reach Larson. She paused and wiped the perspiration from her brow. "You have any idea where we are?"

Daniel grinned, his teeth gleaming in his dirt-streaked face. "You're the native. I'm just a transplant. Nothing looks familiar?"

She shook her head. "I'm lost. This is probably Stanton land, though. If I could get my bearings, we might be better off to make for Nate's ranch house and borrow horses."

He nodded toward a lone cottonwood. "Think you could climb that tree, Charlie?"

"Sure." His brother took off at a trot.

"I'll have to do it," Margaret said. "I know the area, and neither one of you does." She followed Charlie and Daniel to the tree. She hadn't climbed trees in years, but surely it wasn't something a person forgot. She'd practically lived in the oak outside her bedroom window when she was growing up.

From that oak tree she had dreamed her girlish dreams of her hero riding over the hills to sweep her away to some enchanted existence far from the red dirt of northern Texas. She would dress in stylish clothes that minimized her size, and when she came back to visit, the other girls would stare with envy. They would all want to be her friends instead of giggling behind her back.

Instead, she had learned to love the land as the husband she thought she would never have. And the men of the area had given her their respect. The reminder of how many other ranchers were depending on her strengthened her resolve as she stared up through the branches. She had to get to town in time to save the money everyone had worked for all year.

"Give me a leg up," she told Daniel.

He laced his fingers together and offered them to her. She

put her foot in his big hands, and he lifted her as she reached up to grasp the lowest branch. The rough bark bit into her hands, but she gripped it firmly anyway. It was a good thing she was wearing britches. She swung her leg over the branch and scooted firmly onto it, then stood and climbed higher. Through the leafy canopy she could see for miles in all directions. Staring at the landscape, she searched for a familiar landmark. There. That formation of three rocks. In an instant Margaret knew where she was. On the other side of that formation was a track that would lead to the Stanton homestead.

"Got it!" she crowed. "I'd know this land anywhere." She scrambled down the tree limbs. Pausing at the last branch, she gauged the distance to the ground, then jumped. Instead of landing smoothly on the grass, her ankle twisted and she fell. Pain seized her ankle and refused to let go.

Daniel whipped around at her muffled groan. Concern shone from his dark brown eyes, and he knelt beside her. "You should have let me help you."

Burning pain encased her ankle and left her gasping for breath. She groaned softly. This was no simple injury but something that would take time to heal. "You'll have to go on without me. Just beyond the rock formation is a track that will take you to Nate and Lucy's. You'll be there in half an hour or less."

"I'm not leaving you here." Daniel's warm fingers probed the tender flesh and she winced.

"You have to. I'll be fine." Bracing herself against the pain, she shook her head. "I'm sorry."

"You've been amazing." Daniel's voice vibrated with emotion.

Margaret searched his gaze through a haze of agony. Her ankle felt like it was being squeezed flat. "Hurry," she panted.

Daniel folded her into his arms. "I'll pray," she whispered. "Go now."

His heart beat steadily under her ear, a comforting sound of constancy and steadfastness. Daniel was someone she could trust—she felt that in her bones. But there was always that niggling doubt in the back of her mind. She couldn't bear for him to regret wanting her. She sucked in a breath. She was done with worrying about it. It was time to trust God with that too.

Daniel's gentle fingers brushed the curls back from her face. "I'm not leaving you." He kissed her forehead. "We'll go on together or not at all. I'll help you."

"I could go for help," Charlie said.

Daniel pressed his lips together. "I'd rather we stayed together."

"Don't you trust me?" Charlie's voice was hurt.

Margaret drew back a bit from Daniel's grasp. "Let him go. I'm not going to be able to walk that far, even with help."

"I'll carry you."

"You're not carrying me two miles!" The thought made Margaret pull even farther away.

"You can trust me," Charlie broke in. "I won't run off or go back to the gang. I'm through with that."

"I trust you," Daniel said. "I'm just worried about the gang catching up to you."

"I can take care of myself."

"I reckon we don't have a choice," Daniel said. "But be alert. Munster and Golda won't give up easily. Get back here as quick as you can."

"Don't fuss like Ma. I'll be fine." Charlie tightened the gun holster around his hips, then strode off in the direction of the Stanton ranch.

Margaret sighed. "I feel so helpless. There should be something I can do."

Daniel sat beside her and slipped his arm around her shoulders. "We can sit here while you tell me what a wonderful husband I'm going to be. We can decide how many kids we want and make some plans for our future."

Kids was such a lovely word. She nearly groaned at the thought of what Pa would say about it all if he were here. The Bible said to honor your parents. Pa would roll over in his grave if she married a Ranger. But he wasn't here, so did it matter?

"What's wrong?" Daniel tried to draw her back against his chest, but she resisted. "What did I say?"

She leaned away from him and wrapped her arms around herself. "Just thinking about Pa. I think he's okay with you being a Ranger. Heaven would have wiped away his resentment."

Daniel leaned forward and tipped her chin up. She refused to meet his gaze and tried to turn away her head, but his hard fingers refused to allow it. "I thought that's what it was when you went all prickly again. Sometimes talking to you is like walking through a field of cowpats. I'm afraid of putting a foot in the wrong place."

Her lips twitched at his words, and she laughed. "The things you say. You see me in ways I don't think anyone else does."

He wound a long curl around his finger. "That's the way it's supposed to be. You're still fussing about your pa?"

She shook her head. "It was just a fleeting thought. Everyone at the ranch is probably worried sick, and Munster and his gang are likely riding to Larson right now. What if we're too late?"

"I have faith in God's provision in this situation. Think of all the ways he's been faithful in these past weeks, Margaret. He'll be faithful in this too. You are safe in his arms." He buried his face in her hair. "He brought us together."

"He did, didn't he? I was quite terrible."

"Not terrible, just challenging. And worth every misstep. We belong together. Can't you feel that in your bones?"

She knew he was right. God had performed miracle after miracle for them. She still hadn't said the words *I love you*, and she was still afraid to admit to the extent of her feelings. "It's hard to know God's will about things. What if it's *my* will I'm sensing and not his?"

"You know. In your heart you know." He pulled away and folded his arms across his chest. "I'm sure it's his will that we be together, that we be married. Aren't you?"

"You haven't really asked me," she said teasingly.

He embraced her. "So I haven't asked you, eh? I can remedy that." A sound reached their ears.

"Someone's coming," he whispered.

Her heart hammering, she held her breath as he stood and peered through the brush that hid them. "It's Charlie and Nate."

She closed her eyes at the relief in his voice. Trying to get to her feet, she winced at the pain in her ankle.

He must have heard her soft inhalation, for he turned and came toward her. "Let me help you." He swept her up into his arms.

Margaret gasped and clasped her arms around his neck. "Put me down! I'm too heavy for you to be toting around like a feed sack."

"You don't weigh anything," he scoffed. Striding to meet Nate and Charlie, he carried her as he would a child.

She felt light and free in his arms. Staring into his face, she watched to see signs of overexertion, but he carried her easily. His muscles bulged beneath his shirt, and she couldn't help the thrill of admiration at his strength and compassion. He was the kind of man who would make a woman feel safe and protected. She was glad she was that woman.

TWENTY-EIGHT

❦

Daniel wanted to keep walking with Margaret in his arms. Just walk into the sunset all the way home to Austin where he could show her off to his father, who would immediately love her too. He would teach her that she was beloved by both him and God. Her hands clasped him at the back of his neck, and she felt warm and pliable against his chest. They belonged together, and he would do all in his power to be worthy of her.

Nate waved. "The cavalry is here." The horse behind him jerked his head and snorted at Daniel's appearance.

Daniel grinned and stopped in front of him. "I don't see any blue coat."

"My blue shirt will have to do." Nate stared at Margaret and his smile faded. "What have you gotten yourself into now, missy? You've got Lucy in a tizzy, and the baby is screaming her head off. It was all I could do to keep Lucy from coming with me. I had to remind her that her first priority was Carrie."

Daniel frowned. Why did everyone make remarks that made Margaret feel even more inadequate and foolish? One look at her set face, and he knew Nate's words had hurt her. He tightened his arms around her, then reluctantly put her down. Focus—that's what he needed. There would be time enough to sort this out when the Munster gang was behind bars.

Margaret's face was pale, but she bit her lip and leaned against him for support as she smiled at Nate. "You know I hate boredom, Nate." She limped toward the horse Nate had brought for her.

She never let anyone know she was hurt. Holding her head high, she trod through life with determination and grit. Daniel was fortunate she revealed her inner hurt and feelings to him. With God's help, he would make sure he never betrayed that trust.

Daniel put his arm around her waist to help her. When she came alongside the horse, he lifted her into the saddle and she grabbed the reins. "Let's get to town," she said. "There's no time to waste. We have no way of knowing whether or not Munster is hitting the bank even now. We have to stop them."

"I promised Lucy we'd stop by the house so she could take a look at your ankle. It was the only way I could get her to stay behind," Nate said.

"There's no time!" Margaret protested.

"We have to make time. I promised her. We'll be going right past there, and we'll just stop for five minutes." Nate tossed the reins of the other horse to Daniel, then turned and started back the way they'd come.

Daniel mounted up and fell into place behind Charlie. His brother had been quiet, and Daniel wanted to talk to him, to reassure him that they would work things out. Margaret led the way and kept them at a fast clip. Her tense shoulders gave Daniel a sense of urgency as well. The gang planned to hit the bank at five.

They didn't have Daniel to handle the dynamite, but he doubted they'd give up when they knew how much money was in there. Margaret would never forgive herself if she failed and the robbery took place.

By the time the Stanton ranch came into view, Margaret was swaying in the saddle. When they stopped in front of the house, Daniel quickly dismounted and rushed to help her down. She practically fell into his arms.

"I'm sorry," she gasped. "I'm not usually such a weakling."

"You've been through a lot." He lifted her into his arms and carried her to the house.

Lucy met them at the door. "Lay her on the sofa." Her blue eyes were dark with worry.

Finally, someone who cared about Margaret. Holding her protectively, Daniel carried her to the sofa and gently laid her down. "You're going to be fine." He pressed his lips against her forehead. "I know you're worried, but I'll head on into town and take care of things there. You let Lucy take care of you. I'll get back as quick as I can."

Her green eyes darkened and she shook her head. "I'm going with you. Don't leave without me."

"You're not going anywhere." Lucy pushed Daniel out of the way. "Look at you—you can barely hold your head up. There's no way you're getting back on that horse."

"You've got the baby to worry about, and you don't need to be fussing over me. I'm fine. I'll check in with the doctor when this is all over." Margaret attempted to rise, then fell back against the sofa.

Before Daniel could insist she stay put, shots rang out. Charlie burst through the door.

"We've got trouble! Frank and the gang have the house surrounded. They barely missed me."

He held out his hat, and Daniel saw a bullet had punched a hole clean through the crown. "You got any extra rifles?" Daniel asked Nate.

Nate was already rushing to the gun cabinet. He handed two rifles to Daniel and two to Charlie before taking another two for himself. He grabbed a bag of bullets, then ran toward the window. Just as he reached it, the glass shattered and bullets rained through the opening.

Nate dropped to the floor. "Stay down!"

"Give me a rifle," Margaret muttered. She struggled up from the sofa and limped to the gun cabinet.

"Get down! We'll take care of this!" Daniel rushed toward her as a bullet whizzed through the air and narrowly missed her.

"Thank God that didn't hit you." He quickly led her back to the sofa.

"We can't let them win," she whispered.

"They won't. Let Lucy look at your ankle. I'll handle Munster and the gang."

"I'll take care of her. Go!" Lucy pushed away his hands.

He relinquished his position by Margaret's side and crawled on his belly to a window. A quick thrust with the butt of his rifle broke the glass. He poked his rifle through the hole and fired.

All around them the bullets flew as the gang moved closer. Daniel, Nate, and Charlie were hopelessly outnumbered. He couldn't bear the thought of Margaret back in Golda's clutches. He was sure Golda was out there somewhere. Kid Loco too.

As he mindlessly fired, then reloaded and fired again, he gradually became aware that the air had taken on an even more oppressive feel. The sky was a strange greenish tint. Then a rumble rattled through the parlor. His ears popped, and debris began to fly.

"It's a twister!" Charlie screamed.

Even as his brother shouted, Daniel saw the tail of the storm begin to descend almost directly over the barn. Other tails began to spin and dance away from the main one, then converged and split again. Sharp pieces of sand bit into his face as the tornado sucked the air from the house. Windows blew out, and he heard men outside shout and curse. The storm whirled around them, and the main tail began to approach the house.

Nate leaped to his feet. "Get to the cellar! Lucy, get the baby and I'll get Eileen. Daniel, grab little William."

Daniel turned and struggled through air that had suddenly turned as heavy as molasses. He fought to get to Margaret and William. If he was going to die, Daniel wanted to be looking into Margaret's face.

Then the storm bore down on them in all its fury.

TWENTY-NINE

〜

All too often Margaret had seen the black demon drop from the sky to ravage a home, a town, a friend. Now a twisting snake full of fury with the sting of death in its tail was right on top of her. She lurched to her feet as the debris flew. Strangely, she found her terror fading as she concentrated on making sure everyone she loved was safe.

Daniel grabbed her hand, and she barely felt the pain of her twisted ankle—though in the back of her mind she knew she would pay later—as they hurried toward the kitchen as fast as her swollen ankle would allow. Pressure built in her ears as the storm loomed closer.

At the door to the kitchen, Daniel scooped up William without breaking his stride. "I've got William," he called to Nate as they rushed on.

Nate hollered for Jed as he escorted Eileen, Lucy, and the baby to safety. Charlie put a hand against Margaret's back and urged her to go faster.

"Jed's in the barn!" Lucy screamed. "There's a cellar there but he may not think to get to it."

Margaret's stomach churned. The tornado was directly over the barn. Boards flew across the yard as the twister ravaged the outbuildings. Daniel dropped Margaret's hand. Time seemed to stand still, though she knew it was only seconds that he stared into her eyes.

"I'm going for the boy. I love you, Margaret. I'll try to get Jed into the cellar." Daniel passed William over to her, then bent and pressed his lips to hers for one brief moment. Then he was gone.

She blinked. He was gone so quickly she hadn't been able to tell him she loved him. *Dear God, keep him safe.* Her throat was so tight she could not have spoken if she'd tried. Eileen's face was white with terror, and Margaret smiled encouragingly as they rushed toward the cellar.

She seemed to run in slow motion. Time had run out. The serpent had found them and was preparing to gobble them up. The roof lifted above her head. Her ears popped. Margaret screamed and dived toward the heavy wooden kitchen table, tucking William's head against her shoulder. She heard Nate shout, then Eileen, Lucy, and the baby were huddled under the table with them. Charlie dived under the table as well.

"Nate!" Lucy screamed.

Lucy fought to go to her husband, but Margaret grabbed her arm. "No, Lucy, you have to keep the baby safe."

Lucy sobbed and buried her face against the newborn. Clutching William tightly, Margaret strained to see through the swirling dust and debris, but there was no sign of Nate. And Daniel was out in this as well. Crushing fear for the men bore down on her, and she choked as she fought to keep from wailing with Lucy. The storm would be over soon, and they would find their men. Margaret clung to that hope.

"Please, God," she whispered. In that moment she knew that all the things she'd thought so important didn't matter at all. The ranch, what people thought of her. They were dross that God was using the storm to burn away. Facing eternity, she saw the things that were really important—trust in God and a love that loved her even when she was unlovable. There were two who had that love for her: God and Daniel.

"Save us all, Lord. Bring Daniel, Nate, and Jed through this safely. Put your hands of protection around them. You're stronger than any storm."

"Oh yes, please help them, Lord," Lucy echoed. Her sobs could barely be heard above the screaming of the wind.

The storm seemed endless, a maelstrom that time didn't touch. Crouching beneath the table with her heart beating in her ears and the shriek of the wind raging through the house, Margaret prayed with an intensity she'd never felt before. And in that fury, she gradually became aware that God was with them. It was as though he held them in a safe little bubble, a world the tornado couldn't touch.

She glanced over at Lucy's wide eyes.

"You feel it too?" Lucy whispered.

Margaret nodded. Awe kept her tongue-tied.

Then as suddenly as the storm had started, it was over. The wind faltered, then died. The swirling sand came to rest again on the earth. The bubble around them burst, and the world felt familiar again. The rain started then. With the roof gone, there was no escape from the cold, stinging chill as the last of the wind blew the rain under the table onto them.

Eileen gave a hitching sob. "Is it gone?"

Margaret pulled her onto her lap with William, then rocked

both children a bit. "Yes, sweetheart, it's all over." Margaret crawled from beneath the table to find it was the only thing left in the kitchen. Her feet rested on a bare wooden floor. The dry sink was gone, as were the chairs, the ice chest, the canned goods, and all the utensils. The storm had picked up everything. Everything but the table and the people. A miracle straight from God's hand.

Lucy stood next to her and shook out bits of debris from the baby blanket. Miraculously, the baby wasn't crying. She had her thumb corked in her mouth and stared with blue-eyed wonder at her mother. Her tiny face grimaced as the cold rain hit it.

Margaret set William on the floor, but the little boy clung to her skirts with tight fists. "I want Jed," he wailed. "And where's Papa?"

Margaret patted him on the head. "I'll go find them." She turned to Lucy. "You keep him with you." Margaret didn't want the little boy to come until she knew what had happened to the men. Nate had been in the kitchen just minutes ago. She limped to the parlor. The rain pelted down and left the floor slick. It ran in rivulets down her face and soaked her clothing.

The parlor was empty except for a heap of debris against the one remaining wall. Then part of the debris moved, and she heard a groan. A hand reached out from the rubble, and Nate's face appeared. He was covered in mud, but he was alive.

"Lucy, it's Nate!" She ran toward him, but Lucy reached her husband first. She thrust the baby into Margaret's arms, then knelt beside her husband. Tossing the debris to one side, she finished uncovering him. A huge bruise covered half his forehead, and there was a lump on his head.

Margaret took comfort from the small bundle in her arms and prayed she would find Daniel safe as well.

Lucy gave a cry and fell onto his chest. "Oh, Nate, you're alive!"

As she sobbed, Nate's arms circled her, and he patted her back. "Don't take on so, Luce. We'll rebuild everything."

"I'm just so happy you're all right!"

"I don't know about all right, but I'm alive." He grinned and tried to sit up. Grimacing, he put a hand to his chest. "Feels like I might have a busted rib or two. Where're Jed and Daniel?"

Margaret handed the baby back to her mother. "I was just going to look for them."

"I'll go with you." Nate started to get up, then fell back with a groan. "Give me a minute."

"You stay here. Charlie will come with me in case any of the gang is left, though I suspect they ran off." Her mouth dry with dread, Margaret limped to the edge of what used to be the house and stepped down into the yard. "You check out the side yard," she told Charlie. He nodded and she saw the fear and misery in his face. He moved to the side yard and she headed toward the barn.

The rain tapered off to a light mist, and she was thankful for that. Light-headed from all she'd been through, she staggered, then clutched the nearby well pump for support. Spots danced in her vision, but she blinked fiercely. She had to find Daniel.

Her vision cleared and she started toward the barn. Puddles had formed, and she stepped around them as she hobbled along. The tornado had torn away chunks of the yard. Where there had once been roses and lilac bushes, there were now gaping, muddy holes. The winds had scoured the bark from the giant oak tree that stood in the yard. Most of its branches were ripped away as well. With dread, Margaret turned her attention toward what was left of the barn.

It had no roof, and two of the sides were gone. The door hung haphazardly to one side, attached only by one hinge. Her heart in her mouth, Margaret approached the barn. "Daniel? Jed?"

Only the creak of the door answered her. Hope was beginning to fade. There was no guarantee Daniel had even made it to the barn. He would have been exposed to the full fury of the tornado. She blinked back the tears that burned her eyes. No, she wouldn't believe that. Still calling his name, she entered the barn.

Like the house, most of the insides had been lifted away. Only a few stray wisps of straw lay scattered over the floor. Several pieces of straw had been embedded in the wood of the barn door by the force of the wind.

The floor creaked and she whirled. "Daniel?" The words died in her mouth.

"You're just who we've been looking for." Frank grabbed her arm.

Before Margaret could react, she heard a screech. She jerked her head toward the sound and flinched back at the sight of Golda. Her immaculate blond hair now in wet strings around her face, she rushed toward Margaret with her hands curved into claws. "This is all your fault!"

Frank stepped into her path, and with a casual backhanded motion, he felled his sister with one blow. "There's time for killing her later. If we hurry, we can still get that money before it is sent on." He grabbed Margaret again as she turned to flee.

His calloused fingers bit into the tender flesh of her forearm, and she winced. Margaret jerked her arm out of his grasp, then backed away from him. "I'm not going anywhere with you."

"Yes, you are." Golda slowly stood. Her mouth twisted in a sneer. "Unless you want a world of hurt to come down on your friends. And with a new baby, that wouldn't be nice at all." She pointed toward the house. "There's a gun trained on that pretty blond lady right now. You come along without a fight, and no one will be hurt."

The spunk went out of Margaret. With the walls of the house gone, the Stantons had no protection, and Nate was too hurt to defend them. But she wasn't going anywhere until she knew what had happened to Daniel. "Where's Daniel? Do you have him too?"

"He's dead." Golda smiled as she said the words.

Margaret closed her eyes against the cruel satisfaction she saw in the other woman's eyes. "You don't know that," she whispered.

Golda's smile deepened as she held out a bloody shirt. "Recognize this?"

Margaret recognized it all right. It was the shirt Daniel had been wearing. Blood soaked it with crimson. No one could bleed that much and live. Her knees went weak, and she would have fallen except for Golda's cruel grip on her arm.

"None of that." Golda propelled Margaret toward the back of the barn. Several of the gang waited with a buggy outside. Margaret moved through a fog of pain. She wanted to cry and scream a denial to the wind, but all she could do was numbly obey. Daniel couldn't be dead. She clung to hope, but it was fading like the morning mist.

Riding to town through the mud-soaked track, she was barely aware of the throb in her ankle. The pain in her heart far overshadowed it. They stopped just outside Larson. Golda rooted around inside her valise. Drawing out a comb, she handed it to Margaret.

"Here, make yourself presentable. There's not much we can do about your attire. You're far too large for any of *my* clothing." Golda's gaze raked Margaret's figure, and she gave a disdainful sniff.

Even Golda's contempt failed to hurt any longer. Margaret had left that baggage far behind while the tornado shrieked its fury. Nothing could penetrate the misery that choked all other emotions from her heart. What did it matter if she lost her money or even lost the ranch because of today? It didn't matter that the sky would be blue again or the birds would sing. The world was a darker place without Daniel. He made her laugh, and he made her believe in herself.

Why, Lord? The question kept pounding itself over and over in her brain. Why would God take Daniel? He had so much to give to those who met him. A sparkling sense of humor, caring and compassion, a real faith that showed itself in everything he said and did. All these traits made Daniel a special person, one whom God could use mightily. It made no sense to take him now.

She slowly loosened her braid and ran her fingers through her tangled hair. Working the comb down the tangles lock by lock, she groomed it until it was smooth, then neatly braided it again. They'd stopped beside a stream, so she splashed water on her face and arms to remove the worst of the dirt.

"That's good enough. The bank will be closing in fifteen minutes." Frank pulled her roughly to her feet and pushed her toward the buggy. "You and Golda are going to go into the bank. You get the tellers and the manager locked up, then open the back door for the rest of us. Don't try anything. Golda won't hesitate to shoot you."

MARGARET STEPPED OUT of the buggy and looked around downtown Larson. Rain had left the debris-littered streets a muddy quagmire. The large window in the front of the bank was streaked with mud and water. The storm had lifted a few shingles, but there was no major damage. She saw no one out whom she could ask for help.

Golda got out of the buggy behind her. "Remember what Frank said. Don't give me an excuse to shoot you."

"I didn't think you needed an excuse."

"I don't. So don't try my patience." Golda shoved her in the small of the back. "Smile and act like nothing is wrong. If we get enough money, maybe I'll let you live."

Margaret knew better than to believe her. Death was in every line of Golda's face. Margaret approached the bank door with a sense of dread beginning to penetrate her grief. She tried to smile, but her lips trembled and tears felt close. How could she smile when her heart was breaking? Right now she felt like she would never smile again. *"Safe in his arms."* She reminded herself of what Daniel had said. Live or die, she belonged to God.

She pushed open the door and limped inside.

Orville Parker pushed his spectacles up on his nose. His thinning hair lay in a carefully contrived placement. His mouth dropped open when he saw her. "Miss Margaret, the whole county is looking for you!"

Margaret had always liked Orville. He had a caring way about him, and she wished she could tell him to run. She nodded to him. "Good afternoon, Mr. Parker. I've come to withdraw some funds."

He frowned. "What are you talking about, Miss Margaret? Where you been? Everyone has been worried half to death. Have you let everyone know you're all right? Have you been to the sheriff's office?"

"This is getting us nowhere." Golda drew the gun from her valise. "I want all of you to back up slowly. Mr. Parker, you open the safe."

"The safe?" Orville blinked slowly and shook his head. "Not again!"

"You heard me, mister." Golda motioned with the gun, and the tellers backed away. "Margaret, open the back door."

"You're in this with her? My, my," Orville said with a worried frown.

"It was her idea," Golda sneered.

Margaret wanted to tell him the truth, but Golda would shoot her if Margaret opened her mouth. She had to find a way to stop her.

"Quit dawdling and go open the door!" Golda shouted at Margaret. "And while she's gone, you get that safe open."

"My, my." Orville hurried to the safe and knelt in front of it. He licked his fingers and applied them to the tumblers.

Margaret limped toward the back room. She would be out of Golda's sight when she stepped into the back room, but the other woman would come looking for her if she didn't hear the back door open immediately. Margaret's gaze darted around the room as she stepped inside. What could she use for a weapon? She had to make sure no one else got hurt.

The back room held empty cash sacks, coin rolls, and other small items. Nothing that was any defense against the gun in Golda's hand.

"What's taking so long?" Golda shouted. "Don't make me come back there!"

What if she waited until Golda came to check on her? She could hide behind the door and jump her when she stepped into the room. It was a lame plan, but it was the only one Margaret had. Then she spied a large feed sack. Maybe she could pull that over Golda's head when she came through the door.

Margaret snatched it up, then slid behind the door. She watched through the crack in the doorway.

Golda shouted at her again as she backed slowly toward the back room. "I'm warning you, Margaret. Get that door open and get back in here now!" She kept the gun trained on the bank employees. She got to the back room and braced her back against the door that Margaret hid behind. Her gaze darted between the men in the bank and the dingy back room.

"You can't hide from me," Golda snarled. She took another step into the room and finally she was clear of the door.

With a silent prayer for help, Margaret lunged out from behind the door and brought the feed sack down over Golda's head.

The other woman screeched and clawed at the rough burlap that covered her face. The hand holding the gun waved wildly in the air, and she tried to crack Margaret over the head with it before Margaret wrestled the gun away. Although Margaret was bigger and stronger, Golda fought like a caged cougar, and it was all Margaret could do to subdue her.

Orville ran to help her. He grabbed a rope from the back room wall and quickly trussed up Golda, then snatched the sack off of her head. "Great work, Miss Margaret," he panted. "I knew you wouldn't have any part of stealing from the townspeople."

It was all over. The strength ran out of her legs, and she sagged against the door. All she wanted to do was find a quiet spot to grieve and remember Daniel.

Golda spat in her face. "You're dead," she snarled. "When my brother catches up to you, you'll wish you'd never been born."

"He can't hurt me more than I already hurt."

The other woman smiled. "Too bad Daniel didn't suffer more. He was already pretty far gone by the time we found him. His last words were of you. Does that make you feel better?"

Margaret clenched her fists so tightly that her nails bit into her palms. The pain was more than she could bear. He died not knowing she loved him. She wished she could relive the last twenty-four hours. In fact, she wished she could relive the last few weeks again. But that wasn't possible. She would have to live with the regrets the rest of her life.

She swallowed hard and squared her shoulders. She was Paddy O'Brien's daughter, and she'd been raised to take whatever life dished out. The fact that it had turned out badly was not unusual. She'd grown to expect it all her life.

"I have a plan," she told Orville. Now it was time to show those men they'd picked the wrong woman to mess with. She would finish the job Daniel had come here to do.

THIRTY

G olda drummed her fingers angrily against the top of a desk in the bank manager's office. "Frank is too smart to fall for your little tricks."

Margaret saw through her bravado. Golda's face was a sickly color beneath the rouge she wore, and her blue eyes were haunted. Margaret found it in her heart to pity the woman. Maybe Golda had never known any other way of life, but in prison she would realize the things she'd done had consequences.

Margaret looked at Golda. She seemed to have everything it would take to be a success in the world. Beauty, brains, guts. But she'd used it all for the wrong purposes. As Margaret stared at the woman, she realized that it wasn't looks or any other physical attribute that mattered. God had given her his love, and she'd despised it by longing for more. Right then and there she resolved to thank God every day for what he had given her instead of focusing on what she thought were shortcomings.

She took a deep breath. How free she felt to know that God saw her as special. She would strive to always remember and thank him for the way he'd made her. First the baggage of caring too much for her worldly possessions had dropped away, and now the sense of blaming God for how he had created her was gone too. She would go on from here, grieving over Daniel but rejoicing in the fact that God was with her. And she would see Daniel again. He couldn't come to her, but she could go to him someday. She would never stop loving him, not for a moment.

She tied Golda's hands behind her back, then left her with one of the tellers. Margaret took Golda's gun, then went to the back room and tiptoed toward the door. She pressed her ear against it and tried to determine whether Frank and the rest of the gang had run or if they just thought things were taking longer than expected.

At first there was only silence, then she heard low voices and some shuffling movements. Good. They still lingered by the door. But not for long. She had to move quickly.

She motioned to Orville. "Can you open the vault and transfer the money somewhere else?" She seized a fistful of money bags from the desk. "I'll stuff these, and you can put them in the safe in place of the real money." Looking around, she spied a pile of newspapers by the door. "We can use newspaper. Those folded stacks are heavy."

Orville grinned. "That just might work. We've got a temporary safe in my office where I can lock the money." He hurried from the room.

Margaret began to stuff the bags with the stacks of newspaper. There was a slight tap on the back door.

"Golda, you in there?" The whispered hiss belonged to Frank.

Margaret jumped, and her heart galloped in her chest. They would have to make their move soon, or Frank would get suspicious and escape. She couldn't allow that. He had to pay for Daniel's death.

A few minutes later she had the bags stuffed. She carried them quickly to the vault and helped Orville load them inside the small room. She felt claustrophobic in the windowless vault and breathed a sigh when she finally escaped to the sunshine-filled main room.

"I think we're ready," she said. "Is the sheriff around?"

Orville nodded. "I saw him and his men take up their positions in the hotel across the street."

She nearly gasped at the pain of his words. Reinforcements were here, but they were too late for Daniel. The sting of tears nearly broke her concentration, but she fiercely willed herself to go on, to finish Daniel's mission.

"I'll let Frank inside now." Her palms were sweaty, and she felt light-headed. Frank would kill her if he got wind of the trap. He wouldn't go peacefully to jail. She took a deep breath and walked to the back room. Was he gone? She and Golda had been inside twenty minutes, far longer than Frank had anticipated.

She rushed to the door and fumbled with the lock. She threw open the door and peeked out. No one was around. Her heart in her mouth, she stepped outside. "Frank?" she whispered.

He stepped from the shadows and grabbed her arm. "You pullin' a double cross?"

She gasped and jerked away. "The safe is open. Golda had a little change of plan. She couldn't wait to see how much was there. You'd better hurry. She took a bunch of sacks out through the front. I think she got more than her share."

Frank scowled. "She wouldn't dare." He drew his revolver and rushed inside. The rest of the gang followed him.

Praying it would work, Margaret followed him.

Frank ran through the storeroom and into the vault room. He

saw the open vault and rushed inside. The other men crowded in behind him, and they all snatched up moneybags.

"She's robbed us!" Frank shouted. "There should be more than this."

He started toward the vault exit, but Orville stepped from behind his hiding place and slammed the vault door shut. Margaret sagged against the counter. Giddy with relief, she closed her eyes. Not a shot fired, and the thieves were all safely locked up.

The front door burst open, and six men rushed into the room. The Rangers were here. Then Margaret's eyes widened, and she gasped at a tall figure limping through the door behind the others. Daniel? He must have gone to get the Rangers. She closed her eyes, then opened them again. Her mouth went dry and her heart thumped painfully in her chest with almost overwhelming hope.

Tears blurred her vision. "Thank you, God, thank you." Daniel hadn't seen her yet.

Daniel stared around the room. "Where is she?" he growled.

A tide of warmth rushed over Margaret. She could see the love he had for her in his tightly clenched fists and the fierce tone of his voice. Daniel would never let anyone hurt her as long as he lived. The knowledge made her feel cherished in a way she'd never known. She wanted to rush to him, but there were too many other men in the way.

"I'm here, Daniel," she said, her tone brisk. This love she bore for him was too new and precious to be displayed in front of the whole town.

He started toward her, but the sheriff came through the bank door with his pistol drawn. He skidded to a halt and looked around. "Where are the bandits?"

Margaret gestured to the bank vault. "Waiting to be taken into custody."

"We'll take charge of them," a man said.

Margaret recognized the voice as the man Daniel had talked with several times. The other Ranger, Richard.

Margaret remained frozen in place as Daniel explained to Sheriff Borland who he was and what he was doing in the area. She longed to run to Daniel and throw her arms around him, but shyness held her in place. Now that she knew the full power of the feelings she held for him, she found herself looking at him with new eyes.

His face was a bit pale and his shoulder was bleeding, but he was alive. Alive! Joy bubbled in Margaret's heart like a freshwater spring. It was all she could do to stay where she was.

"You've done good work here," the sheriff said. "But it looks like you could use Doc's services. Margaret, you'd better help your young man down the street before he falls over."

Only then did Margaret's stiff muscles obey. She moved to Daniel's side and slipped her hand around his arm. "It's this way."

DANIEL FOUGHT THE disappointment that raged inside. He'd hoped that Margaret would show some sign she'd worried about him, that she cared. She had just looked at him with wide green eyes and practically ignored him.

He knew she loved him, so why did speaking the words seem so hard for her? Hearing the words was important to him. How did he break through that wall she had around her? It seemed an impossible task. If the events of the last few days hadn't done it, he didn't know what would. Maybe nothing.

Margaret limped beside him with her cold fingers on his arm. He wasn't sure if she was helping him or if he was helping her. They were both pretty war torn and road weary. At least they were both going to live.

They walked around the corner of the bank and headed down Main Street. Margaret stumbled, and he slipped an arm around her waist. She stopped and stared up at him. Were those tears in her eyes?

"I thought you were dead," she whispered. "And Jed—is he all right?"

"He's fine. I was searching for you and found him under a wheelbarrow in the barn. Scared and a little scratched up but all right." Daniel examined her face. There was something going on in that beautiful head, but he couldn't quite decipher the expression in her eyes.

"What happened to you? Golda told me you were dead. She showed me a bloodstained shirt."

"The wind blew me through the air, and I landed by the end of the porch. I crawled under it before the tornado could carry me off completely. A branch stabbed me in the head, and I bled like a beheaded rooster. I reckon I passed out. When I came to, the storm was over and Nate was hollering for me and Jed. I crawled out from under the porch and tossed the shirt in the weeds. I found one of Nate's in a tree and borrowed it. Then I went looking for you. When I couldn't find you, I figured Frank had to have taken you."

"Thank God. I—I thought you'd died w-with-out . . ." She stopped and buried her face in her hands.

Sobs shook her, and the sound of her crying broke his heart. He pulled her into his arms. Her arms came up and wrapped around his neck in a tight grip that was almost painful. "I'm fine. A little beat up, but it would take more than a tornado to make me leave you."

She only wailed more and burrowed harder against his chest. "Hey, this shirt may not take any more watering," he said gently. "Don't take on so."

"I thought you died without knowing I love you," came the muffled reply against his chest.

A budding joy exploded in his chest. She'd finally said the words. He gripped her shoulders and pulled her back from his chest so he could look in her face. Though her eyes were red and swollen from her weeping, Margaret's face shone with love.

"You love me," he whispered. "It's about time you admitted it. I knew the truth long ago. It was sure hard waiting for you to realize it."

Her lips trembled. "Don't ever leave me." She reached up and touched his face.

"A mad bull couldn't drag me away." He smiled. "You ready to hear that marriage proposal?"

She looked down at her muddy shirt and britches, then back up at him. "Looking like this?"

"You've never been more beautiful. I love you." He went to one knee. "Margaret O'Brien, would you do me the honor of marrying me?"

Her cheeks flamed but she didn't look away. "I'd be honored to have your name."

"That's a yes?"

She seized his hands and pulled. "Come kiss me, and I'll tell you then."

Grinning, he obliged. Daniel couldn't believe his luck. No, it wasn't luck. This love was God's gracious gift, and Daniel would thank him for it the rest of his life. She kissed him back, and for the first time, he could feel her whole heart in that kiss.

She wrapped her arms around his neck, and he forgot all they'd been through and where he was. They belonged together. For always.

He broke the kiss. "Let's get home." *Home.* Was there a more wonderful word in the vocabulary? This was home to him now.

Her eyes shining, she nodded. "I'll rest here until you get back."

He went to hire a horse and buggy while she waited on a bench. He drove the buggy to where she waited, then helped her up onto the seat. The landscape was dark as the buggy rumbled toward home. The stars beamed down from overhead, and he pointed out a few constellations to her. "It's a new moon again."

She snuggled against him. "Very appropriate."

With Margaret beside him, he was determined not to let anyone stand in their way now.

THIRTY-ONE

‿◡‿

S
till in her mud-caked clothes, Margaret lay in her bed. She wasn't sure she'd ever see her room again.

Inez bustled around the room tsking about the state of her clothes. Margaret gave her instructions about preparing the guest rooms for Lucy's family who would stay with them until their house was rebuilt.

Daniel sat on the edge of her bed. He smoothed her hair away from her forehead. "I'm going back to town while you get some rest. Archie found his way home, by the way."

"Oh good! I was afraid I'd lost him." Her fatigue fell away and she sat up. "Why are you going to town?"

"After we got home, I got to thinking. Frank never mentioned killing your pa or shooting at us. If the gang didn't target you and your pa, then who did? I want the sheriff to ask him and his cohorts about that."

She frowned. "You're right. What reason would they have to hurt Pa?" She studied his worried face. "You think the murderer is still out there?"

He hesitated. "I wonder if it was Calvin."

She thought about it, then nodded. "He had a grudge against Pa for sure. It's possible."

"I want to make sure we're safe here before we start planning the wedding. Stay inside and away from the windows until I get back. If we had one of those newfangled telephones, I could stay with you and make sure you're safe."

Her cheeks heated when he held her gaze and smiled. "Inez and Vincente will watch out for me."

"I know they will." He leaned down and gave her a lingering kiss. "I love you."

"I—I love you too." She stumbled over the unfamiliar words a little.

He rose and shut the door behind him. Her eyes drifted closed. She didn't know how long she slept, but she awakened at the sound of a voice. Was Daniel back already? Her door was cracked open a bit, so she sat up.

The room was dark except for the glow of the lamp. Inez was sitting beside her on a hardback chair. "You are awake." She rose to touch Margaret's forehead. "No fever. Miss Lucy and her family arrived with some of their salvaged belongings. They're all abed."

The door opened, and Vincente entered with a teapot and a teacup on a tray. He paused when he saw his mother. "I thought perhaps you were resting, Mamá."

"I could not rest when Margaret was unwell."

He put the tea down and lifted the pot to pour it. "Of course not."

Inez patted Margaret's head. "You are like a daughter to me."

The teapot clattered against the cup, and Vincente smiled. "Rest, Mamá. I will look after Margaret."

His mother studied his set face. "Very well. I am tired. Call me if you need me." She patted Margaret's hand. "You sleep." The room was silent when she hurried out and closed the door behind her.

Vincente set the tea on the stand and stirred sugar into it. "It's hot." He held out the cup.

Margaret looked at him curiously. "Are you all right, Vincente? You're pale." She spied a trickle of blood on his arm. "You're hurt."

"It is nothing. Here, drink your tea."

"In a moment," she said. "Let me see your arm."

"I am fine. Here is your tea."

Margaret wrapped her fingers around the warm cup and lifted it to her lips. Vincente's face was red, and perspiration trickled down his face as he watched her. A strange agitation came off him in waves.

Her lips touched the rim of the cup, and she smelled a familiar blend. "Mm, Earl Grey." She took a big gulp. There was a strange aftertaste. Laudanum?

He stared at her, then his eyes widened and his face went white. "Don't drink it!" He knocked the cup from her hand, then sank to the chair beside the bed and covered his face with his hands. "I can't do it."

Margaret stared at him, her gaze lingering on his injury. The blood on his arm and his strange behavior . . . One of the men who had attacked her and Daniel had been shot. Surely Vincente hadn't been the one. But staring at his injury, it looked very much like a gunshot wound.

"Vincente?" she whispered.

"You are my sister. I cannot harm you."

Sister? "W-What are you saying? Sister?"

He lifted his head and held her gaze. "Yes."

His mother and her father. Margaret swallowed hard. "Did my mother know?"

"My mother said she did not."

She shoved the tea-stained sheets off of her. A numbing warmth began to spread through her, but he'd likely stopped her from drinking a deadly amount. If she wanted to live, she had to stay alert.

Vincente stood and paced the floor. "It was necessary if I was to have what is rightfully mine."

Margaret swung her legs to the side of the bed. "But why wouldn't Pa leave the ranch to you? He wanted a son. When Stephen was killed, there was no one else but me. It would have been logical to acknowledge you and give you the ranch."

"So it would seem," Vincente said.

"Did you talk to him about it?"

Vincente shook his head. "We never spoke of our relationship. He corresponded through my mother only. As far as he was concerned, I was an employee."

How could her father have done such a thing? It was beginning to be difficult to think. "That's cruel."

"I agree."

The door creaked, and a familiar figure stepped into the glow of the lamp with a gun in his hand. She gasped. "Lewis? You're alive!" Her elation faded when she realized he was pointing his gun at her.

"Enough of this tender reunion. Our deal is off, Vincente. I knew you didn't have the guts to do what had to be done. Since you can't do it, I'll do it myself. We've come too far to lose it all now."

Deal. She tried to think past the growing numbness in her brain. These two men were the ones who had attacked her and

Daniel. They tried to kill them. And . . . "You killed Pa. How could you? He'd been so kind to you."

Lewis shrugged. "It was an accident. We argued and I shoved him. He hit his head on the sharp edge of the rake. I didn't want him to die, but I wanted him to do the right thing."

"And leaving me homeless was the right thing to do?" She didn't know this man with the cold eyes.

"You would have had a home with me."

"I loved you like a brother, Lewis. And Pa loved you. How could you do this?"

His eyes hardened even more. "You loved me so much you were willing to deed me half the ranch, weren't you?"

She needed a weapon, but nothing was close at hand. "I sent Vincente after you when you left. I was going to tell you that I would give half of the ranch to you."

His eyes softened, then hardened again. "I wish I could believe you, Margaret. I wish it could be different, but I'm going to have to kill you. You will tell the sheriff. And with you dead, I won't need your charity. I won't be bilked out of my inheritance. I'll have what's rightfully mine."

"Rightfully yours?" She was having trouble forming her words. She couldn't let the drug affect her. "My father built this place up from the homestead it was."

"If my father hadn't died, I would have gotten my fair share without your father's charity."

Her limbs were heavy with a creeping lethargy. "So you killed him and faked your death. How will you explain your reappearance?"

He smiled, but it was a soulless grimace. "No one will suspect me of having anything to do with your death. I'll show up in a few more days, bloody and injured. I'll talk about a drifter taking care of me after being shot by the robbers. Everyone will believe me. And with you dead, the ranch is mine."

Her heart sank. She had no doubt everyone would react with joy at his reappearance. He would be able to move right into the house and take over. Her father had made it easy for him. The will stipulated that if she died without an heir, the ranch went to him.

She tried to look at Vincente, but his face wavered in her vision. "Did you have a hand in killing Pa?"

He shook his head. "That was all Lewis. I'd hoped when the will was read that our father would mention me, even in some small way. I was angry when he didn't."

"And hurt," she said.

He inclined his head but said nothing. She tried to speak again, but darkness crowded into her vision. *No, no!* She struggled to stay conscious, but the blackness claimed her.

DANIEL TRIED TO keep things as quiet as possible when he returned to the ranch. He expected Margaret to come hobbling out of the house any second, but her bedroom window remained dark.

He started for his room, then reversed his steps and headed for the ranch house. Just a peek in on her would set his mind at ease. Inez wasn't around either, and the house was dark. He barked his shin against a table in the entry, then walloped his elbow on the stair handrail but managed to keep from hollering. The steps creaked as he went up the stairs and down the hall to Margaret's room.

Her door was closed. Propriety demanded that he waken her

and not go barging in uninvited. Rapping his knuckles on the door, he called her name softly. "Margaret?" When she didn't answer, he tried again. Again there was no answer. She had to be in her room. Staring at the doorknob, he made a decision to enter anyway. She might have his hide, but he couldn't go to bed until he was sure she was all right.

He twisted the knob and pushed open the door, then fumbled for the kerosene lamp on a stand just inside the door. The light sputtered as he glanced around the room. Empty. The covers were rumpled, but Margaret was not in the bed. If she'd gone to the privy, she would have taken the lamp. Something about the room's disarray alarmed him. There was a broken cup on the floor, along with liquid he assumed was tea or coffee. A dark stain was on the sheet.

"Mr. Daniel?"

He turned to see Inez in her nightgown. The candle in her hand cast shadows on the walls, and her hair was in a long braid over one shoulder.

"Where is Margaret?"

Inez frowned and glanced around. "She was in the bed. My Vincente, he bring her tea."

He pointed out the liquid. "It's been spilled."

"Let me find Vincente." She turned and went down the hall.

Daniel heard her calling for her son without a response. Could someone have come in here and forced them both to leave? His gaze lingered on the liquid on the floor. Why had it been spilled? Kneeling, he touched the fluid and sniffed his fingers. He stiffened at the smell of laudanum.

Someone had taken her. "Send someone for the sheriff! Have him look for Calvin." He leaped to his feet and ran for his horse.

THIRTY-TWO

⌒⌒⌒

Margaret's head pounded and she nearly groaned. She gradually became aware that she was moving. Her eyes were heavy, so heavy. With a great effort, she managed to lift her lids, then shut them again when the pain in her head intensified. Hooves clattered against rocks, and she smelled horse.

When she finally managed to keep her eyes open, she realized she was tied to a horse. It was night, and the moon peeked over the hills. Her head drooped on Archie's neck, and her hands were bound to the saddle horn. A man was behind her, his hard arms pressed against her from both sides. She struggled to push away from the horse's neck and sit erect, but her head lolled on her shoulders. She was so very weak. She couldn't jump off and run if she had the strength—which she didn't—since she wouldn't get far on her injured ankle.

Lewis spoke behind her. "I'd hoped you'd stay asleep."

Everything came flooding back. Lewis had killed her father, and he intended to kill her so he could have the ranch. She felt paralyzed by her situation and by the laudanum still numbing her senses. What could she do to escape? Was there any way she could help Daniel track her? For she had no doubt he would find her gone and come after her.

Moaning, she leaned forward and tugged off the boot on her left foot.

"What are you doing?" Lewis growled in her ear.

"My ankle is pressing against my boot. I need to take it off. I think you put them on the wrong feet." She yanked on her boot.

"You're going to send us both toppling into the mud." He reined in the horse and leaped to the ground, then he grabbed her leg and yanked her boot off.

She winced. "Can't you be a little gentler?"

"I'm sorry to say it won't matter much. You won't be feeling anything in a few more hours." He handed the boot to her and mounted the horse again.

His dark warning tightened her gut. "What are you going to do with me?"

"I like you, Margaret. It's nothing personal, you understand. You've been good to me. There's no other way, though. You have to die. I want to make it look like an accident that happened far from anywhere I might have been."

Her mouth felt filled with cotton, and she licked her lips. "Why would I have gotten out of bed and gone for a ride?"

"Vincente found me injured, and you insisted on coming to assure yourself that I was really alive. Everyone knows how impulsive you are. And how much you loved your cousin Lewis." His tone was almost gleeful. "No one will doubt our word since there are two of us. Vincente will say your horse bolted and you were thrown."

Margaret knew it was all too plausible. "You don't have to

kill me. I'll marry Daniel and move out of the area with him. It doesn't have to be this way."

His fists tightened on the reins in front of her. "I wish that were true. I don't like what has to be done."

They rode for several more minutes before Margaret was sure he wasn't going to answer. The glow of the moon illuminated the path with dim light. The horses reached the beginning of the butte.

He reined in his horse. "We'll have to be careful here. And I want to throw off anyone who might be following us." He pointed to a cleft in the rocks. "I'm going there. Watch her, Vincente. I'll be right back."

Lewis shoved her from the saddle, and she tumbled to the ground, twisting her ankle again. She bit back a moan when she tried to stand. "Could you pour some water on my handkerchief? My ankle is throbbing and I want to wrap it."

Vincente shrugged and pulled out his canteen. He upended it over the scrap of cloth in her hand. Margaret sat down and tended to her ankle but kept a surreptitious eye on her cousin. He took his horse back and forth through the cleft, then he dismounted and kicked some rocks out of the path. She realized they weren't going through that spot at all. He was making a false trail to throw off Daniel. But she would foil him. At the right spot, she would drop her boot to mark which way they went.

She finished tying the handkerchief around her ankle and waited for Lewis to return. Her head was clearing, and she had control of her muscles again. If only she had a gun. When Vincente wasn't watching, she glanced around to see if there was anything she could use as a weapon. The boulders were too large to lift, and the other stones were only pebbles. Nothing that would be useful. She couldn't outrun them. Not with her injury and one foot bare. There had to be something she could do, but she was too exhausted to figure out what that might be.

Astride Archie, Lewis clattered back down the hillside. He wore a self-satisfied grin. "That should fix things."

He held out his hand to help Margaret mount. As her hand met his, she had a flash of inspiration. She yanked hard on his hand and he fell onto the ground. His head struck a rock and he lay stunned. In a moment, she flung herself atop Archie.

"Yah!" she screamed and slapped the horse's rump. Her boot slipped from her hand.

Archie leaped forward, nearly running into Vincente's horse. Vincente made a grab for her, but she fended off his attack and raced up the butte, through the cleft. It was the only way open to her. Lewis shouted after her, but she couldn't make out the words.

On the other side of the rock formation, the trail twisted around a boulder and continued to climb. She reached the top of the butte and looked down into the canyon. It was dark and mysterious at night, but this place was familiar to her. Many times she and her father had rounded up strays in this canyon. There were plenty of caves where she could hide. She had a chance.

She urged her horse down the path to the canyon. Something whizzed by her head, and she threw herself against Archie's neck, then dared a glance behind. She'd be out of rifle range in a few more feet. It would be darker in the canyon too. The horse stumbled, then continued to the bottom of the hillside. She rode hard for the far side where she knew of a hiding place. Glancing back, she saw movement on the slope.

They were coming.

THE BUTTE LOOMED above him. Daniel dismounted and studied the ground. Lots of mud trampled here. And he grabbed up the boot on the ground. He was sure it was Margaret's. His initial elation plummeted. Had they already killed her and were disposing of her body? *Please, God, no.* And who had her? Daniel wasn't sure who had taken her, but he suspected Calvin might have something to do with her disappearance.

He followed the trail up through the cleft. This was unfamiliar territory. He'd never been on this side of the river. Darkness blanketed the canyon below him. There was no movement that he could discern. A coyote yipped in the distance and the chorus was joined by several more. The lonely sound added to his feeling of being watched. Nothing moved except a few locks of his hair stirred by the breeze.

He dismounted and studied the ground. They'd been through this way. Their tracks went down the path into the canyon. Once he was back in the saddle, he urged his horse down the narrow path past prickly pear and cholla cactus. Time had ceased to have any meaning. He had no idea how long it would be before dawn. When he reached the bottom of the trail, he paused and listened. He didn't dare call out in case they were nearby and his voice would tip them to his presence.

The ground was rocky here so no help for tracking them. Which way had they gone? He stared into the inky blackness, praying for a clue. The canyon was vast. He could wander here for days and not find them. Something moved off to his left, and he tensed, barely biting back an exclamation. Sage crunched underfoot. Someone was moving. He stilled the horse and waited, straining to see in the dark.

There was a rush of movement, then a hand yanked him from

the horse. As he hit the ground, the rocks bit into his cheek and arm. A boot pressed his head into the ground.

"I thought you'd come looking for her."

Was that *Lewis's* voice? Daniel whirled and faced two men. Both held guns that were pointing at him. Vincente was beside Lewis.

"You'll be the perfect bait to draw out Margaret," Lewis said.

"You faked your death." It made perfect sense. No one would suspect Lewis of harming Margaret. "You're not the man I thought you were." But Vincente's involvement seemed out of character with what Daniel knew about the man.

Lewis's boots clattered among the stones as he drew nearer. The gun barrel never wavered. "Call for Margaret. Tell her to throw up the sponge."

"I will not. You're the ones who tried to shoot us, aren't you?"

"Of course we are. You're smart enough to know the plan without any explanations. Margaret will come running to save you."

Daniel knew Margaret would take no thought of her safety. The moment she heard his voice, she would give herself up. "Go ahead and shoot me. I'm not going to fall in with your plan." Daniel's hand inched to the revolver in his holster.

Before he could slap his hand on the butt and draw, Lewis poked the barrel of his weapon in Daniel's chest. "Don't move again." He reached over and yanked the revolver out, then tossed it away.

The glint of metal disappeared in the darkness, but Daniel mentally marked the clatter of where it fell about ten feet away by the boulder. His rifle was on his saddle. He had to watch for an opportunity to get one of them.

Lewis gestured to the right. "This way. She's in this canyon somewhere. If you don't call for her, I'll shoot you in the leg."

Daniel stayed where he was. "No."

"I don't want to rough you up, but if you force me to, we'll drag you behind the horse."

"You can't scare me, Lewis. If you kill me, I'm going to heaven. Do whatever you want. I'm not going to help you."

Lewis stepped behind him and shoved him forward. "Move."

Daniel walked slowly, not wanting to get far from the weapons. He might be able to wrest the gun away from Lewis, but he would still have Vincente to deal with. "What's your mom going to say about your involvement in this, Vincente?"

"Shut up," Lewis said.

"What did you promise him, Lewis? Money? If I were Vincente, I wouldn't trust you to follow through. If you'd kill your own uncle and cousin, what would prevent you from killing him? So you shoot us, then kill Vincente, and no one is the wiser. You keep it all then, Lewis. Smart."

The heavy blow from the gun's butt came out of nowhere. Pain shot through Daniel's skull, and he crumpled to his knees. His vision swam and he blinked to clear it. Now was his chance. He slumped as if he'd been knocked out.

Lewis swore. "I didn't hit him that hard. Drag him, Vincente."

Vincente didn't move. "He was making some sense, Lewis. Don't double-cross me. I have made arrangements that if I don't come back, a letter will be delivered to the sheriff."

"I have no intention of killing you, but if you keep talking like that, you might change my mind. Now drag him into the middle there."

Daniel didn't move as Vincente knelt over him. Daniel saw the glint of the gun in his holster. He grabbed Vincente around the neck and held him tight, then grabbed the butt of the gun and jerked it free. In one fluid movement, he shoved the man away and sprang to his feet with the gun pointed at Lewis.

"Drop the gun," he barked.

Lewis reacted by firing his weapon. The bullet slammed into the fleshy part of Daniel's thigh. Fiery pain radiated into his groin and down to his knee, but he gritted his teeth and dove toward the boulder where Lewis had thrown Daniel's revolver. Another bullet sparked off the rock and missed his head by inches. Daniel fired back, but his shots went wild since he was still moving toward safety.

He heard Lewis moving toward him. Peering over the top of the boulder, Daniel saw the man creeping toward the boulder. Vincente was circling around the other way with a rifle in hand. Daniel glanced behind him. He was trapped.

THIRTY-THREE

⟨ ❧ ⟩

argaret waved her hand in front of her face but could see nothing in the inky cave. She'd moved toward the back in spite of her fear that it might be inhabited by snakes or spiders. In fact, it likely *was* inhabited by poisonous critters, but Archie was in here with her, and she took comfort from his soft snuffles and warm body.

She shuffled a little closer to the opening, but not so near that Lewis and Vincente could see her if they came looking. At least Daniel wasn't in danger. And God cradled her in his arms in this dark hole.

Her ankle throbbed, and she wished she could ride out of here. But not with her enemies searching for her. There was only one way out of this box canyon—the way she'd come. And to get there, she would have to cross in clear view of anyone out there. Better to stay here until she was sure they were gone.

And she had no doubt they would leave. Lewis would need to see if she'd escaped. She expected him to lie in wait along the path and send Vincente ahead to see if she turned up at the ranch.

She moved closer to the opening and listened. A coyote

yipped in the distance. The distant hoot of an owl sounded. She poked her head out and stared into the darkness. It was so black, like staring into a cauldron of pitch. She had no lantern, nothing to help her find her way out of the canyon in the dark. Dawn would light her way, but it would also betray her movements to her pursuers.

She inhaled and forced herself to crouch in the opening. Inching out, she tried to make no sound. The air was still and close. Were those voices? The low murmur could be a distant conversation or it could be the wind, if there was any. Or a stream. The sound was too muted to place the source. She took a step outside, then another. Her heart pounded against her ribs and she expected a bullet or an attack at any moment. She clung close to the rocky canyon walls and edged closer to the sound.

A stone rolled away from her boot, and she froze at the clatter of its slide. When there was no change in the murmurs she heard, she resumed her trek around the canyon wall until she was close enough to realize the sound was Lewis's voice. He must be talking to Vincente. If she moved in the opposite direction, she might escape. She started to backtrack when the voice she heard made her freeze. Daniel had come after her.

She edged nearer and came to a place where the canyon wall veered out. Twenty feet away were the dim shadows of three figures. Daniel was sitting with his hands bound in front of him. Lewis sat on a boulder and smoked. Vincente was beside them swigging from a canteen.

If only she had a weapon.

Lewis stood. "I've had enough of this. She doesn't have to hear your voice. She just has to know we're going to kill you." He turned toward her direction. "Margaret!"

For a moment she feared he'd seen her, then she realized he was just calling out to her. She clamped her teeth to keep from answering.

"Margaret, give yourself up or I'll shoot Daniel. You know I will. I don't make empty promises."

"He'll kill me anyway!" Daniel yelled. "Stay where you are!"

Vincente kicked him. "Shut up or I'll gag you."

"Stuff your handkerchief in his mouth," Lewis ordered.

Vincente moved to do as he was told. Daniel whipped his head around, but Vincente pinned him and gagged him.

Margaret's nails bit into her palms. She had to do something, but what? These men had killed once, and they'd do it again. She had no doubt that if she hadn't escaped, she'd be dead now. She'd nearly lost Daniel today, and she wasn't going to stand by and let them harm him.

Lewis yanked his gun from its holster and fired it in the air. "I'm not fooling around here, Margaret. I won't shoot him cleanly. First his foot, then the other, then his knee, then the other. I'll make him hurt."

Margaret's breath came fast. She needed a diversion. There was a rock by her feet. She hefted it in her hand, feeling the weight of it and the balance. She eyed what she could see of the landscape. There was an outcropping to her left, near the cliff. She hurled it toward the target as hard as she could. The noise it made when it struck was louder than she'd expected. The men whirled at the clatter.

"There you are," Lewis said, his back to her now. "Show yourself, and I'll turn Daniel loose." He motioned to Vincente to check out the noise.

Daniel was the only one facing her. His gun drawn, Vincente

advanced toward the spot where the rock had fallen. The rifle was unattended by the boulder Lewis had vacated. Margaret had one chance to save Daniel. She moved as quietly as she could from her hiding spot. Daniel's eyes widened when he saw her, and he shook his head. She put her finger to her lips. The rifle was only five feet away. She had to reach it.

One more foot, then another. Her hand was nearly on the butt of the rifle when her foot slipped on loose shale. Lewis whirled at the clatter and fired. The bullet burrowed near Margaret's foot, and she dove for the rifle.

She rolled over with it in her hand, but Lewis had his gun trained on Daniel. "Put it down or the next bullet is in Daniel's head."

The rifle was pointed at the ground. All she had to do was bring it up, cock it, and fire. But was there time before he shot Daniel? She got to her feet. "Let us go, Lewis. You can have the ranch."

"Drop the rifle." His voice was harsh and unyielding.

Daniel gave a slight shake of his head, the movement so subtle she didn't think the other men saw it. She hadn't heard Lewis cock the revolver. Before she could decide what to do, Daniel rolled off the boulder and into Lewis's legs. A shot echoed in the canyon, but the bullet had gone wild as Lewis struggled to maintain his balance.

Vincente sprang toward the struggling men, but Margaret fired a shot at his feet. "The next one won't miss." She shot again on the other side of his feet, and he finally stopped and raised his hands.

Lewis toppled over in the struggle with Daniel. He started to bring the gun around toward Daniel, but Daniel grabbed it with both hands, even though his wrists were tied together. He wrenched it from Lewis's fingers, then tossed it away.

Margaret ran forward and yanked the handkerchief from Daniel's mouth. "Get up, Lewis."

Her cousin staggered to his feet. His hands were clenched and he started toward her, but Daniel kicked his feet out from under him again.

Daniel held out his hands. "Untie me."

Margaret released the ropes and handed him the rifle. Now that it was over, her legs were shaking. She sank onto a boulder and fought the tears burning her eyes.

Daniel put his hand on her shoulder. "Are you all right?"

"Yes, just shaken." She stared up at him. "How are we going to get them back to the sheriff?"

"I'm going to stay here with them while you ride for town."

She didn't like the idea at all, but there didn't seem to be a good choice. "There's a cave where you can keep them penned up."

"Look, let's just forget about this," Lewis said. "I'll leave and you'll never hear from me again."

Her mouth gaped. "You *killed* my father! You tried to kill Daniel and me."

He looked down and sank onto a boulder.

"I had hoped my mother would never know," Vincente said.

Poor Inez. This would crush her. Vincente had not hurt her father, but he'd fallen in with Lewis's schemes. Kidnapping, attempted murder. He would be sent to prison.

The first rays of the sunrise illuminated the canyon. "Go now," Daniel said. "You can be in Larson in a couple of hours."

She whistled for Archie, and he came running toward her. She wanted to kiss Daniel, to tell him how thankful she was they were both alive. But not with Lewis and Vincente looking on. "I'll hurry."

THOUGH SHERIFF BORLAND told her to go home, Margaret insisted on riding with him and his deputies back to the canyon. They'd released Calvin, who rode off still angry. Her ankle throbbed and her muscles ached. Her bottom ached from the hours in the saddle, and her eyes were gritty from lack of sleep. A hot bath would be most welcome when she got home. But not until she saw that Daniel was safe. She'd prayed constantly since she left him with Lewis and Vincente.

They rode through the opening into the canyon, and she strained to see Daniel's familiar broad shoulders. There was no one in the place where she'd left them.

"The cave is there." She pointed at the dark face of the rocky wall. She urged her horse toward the opening. She dismounted outside the cave. "Daniel?"

What if the two men had overpowered him? Foolish imagination. He had to be here. "Daniel!"

There was movement in the mouth of the cave, then Daniel poked his head out. His face was grimy and pale with fatigue, but she'd never seen a more wonderful sight. "Daniel!" The strong arms she hurtled into provided the safe haven she'd longed for all her life. "You're all right."

His dry lips brushed across her forehead. "No problems. We're all a little thirsty, though."

She left the sanctuary of his embrace and grabbed her canteen off the saddle. He drank it down while the sheriff pushed past him with his deputies in tow. It was over. The sheriff would handle it from here on out.

Daniel slung the canteen over his shoulder and opened his arms. She willingly went back into their safety. "Don't ever scare me like that again. I can't lose you, Margaret."

"And here I thought you were trying to get yourself killed to get out of marrying me," she teased.

His arms tightened around her. "I'm holding you to your promise. Let's not wait. This experience has shown me that life is too short to waste a minute. How long will it take you to get ready? I don't even mind if you get married in your britches."

"Scandalous! Lucy would have my hide. I think I could be ready next weekend with some help from Lucy and her aunt Sally. I might even be willing to learn to use the sewing machine myself."

"I might even try if it hurried things along." His grin widened.

The sheriff and his men ushered out Vincente and Lewis in handcuffs. Lewis didn't look at her as he shuffled past.

Vincente paused. "Tell my mother I'm sorry."

"I will." Margaret shouldn't pity him, but she couldn't help it. He'd been a friend for too long.

The men moved off with Sheriff Borland bringing up the rear. He paused and smiled. "We'll take it from here. You two go home and get some rest. You did a good job here. There's no other woman like you in the country, Miss Margaret. If this had happened to any other female, you and Mr. Cutler would both be dead." He tipped his hat and went to join the rest of the men. The sheriff had brought two extra horses, and the party rode off toward town.

A crow cawed overhead as if to announce that they were alone. "It's over." Daniel bent his head and his lips touched hers.

His lips were dry and cracked, but she clung to him and drank in the unconditional love she felt enveloping her. His arms were the sanctuary she'd always longed for.

If only Pa had lived to see her so happy. She pushed away the thought of dresses and hairstyles and lost herself in the warm lips pressing on hers. The scent of cowboy and horse filled her head and her heart.

This was love. And it had finally found her when she wasn't looking.

IN SPITE OF her joy about her upcoming wedding, Margaret's spirits were dampened by the pain Inez carried. The woman had agreed to stay on in spite of her sorrow over her son's behavior, but she moved through the house with obvious anguish. The days raced by as Margaret made sure everyone in the area was invited. She had no time to figure out a dress, so she decided she would wear her mother's, the one she'd worn to the dance.

Lucy joined her early on the morning of the big day. She had William and baby Carrie with her. "Are you excited?" She put Carrie on a blanket on the floor. William sat down with the infant too.

"I wish I'd had time to get a proper wedding dress," Margaret said. "I'm just going to wear the green dress."

"You look lovely in it," Lucy said.

Inez brought in a plate of tea and cookies. She put it on the table and beckoned to Margaret. "I know what you will wear, señorita. I aired it out when *Señor* Daniel arrived and I saw how he looked at you. Follow me."

Margaret lifted a brow. "All right." She scooped up Carrie and the women followed Inez.

She led them to the attic stairs and lifted the lid of a trunk that had been pushed under the eaves. "Your mamá wore this to marry your papá." Inez reverently lifted a white dress, softly yellowed with age, from the trunk. "She would be proud to have you wear it."

Margaret ran her fingers over the soft fabric. "It seems like a dream somehow." If it were a dream, she didn't ever want to wake from it.

"Oh, it's lovely," Lucy breathed. "It's perfect, Margaret. I'll help you get ready."

They followed Inez down to Margaret's bedroom. Margaret put the sleeping infant on the bed. "I'll take a bath and wash my hair."

"I bring water." Inez touched William's soft hair with a wistful look as she passed.

While Margaret bathed and washed her hair, Inez pressed the dress. When her hair was dry, Margaret held up her arms as Inez slipped the dress over her head and fastened the tiny pearl buttons down the back.

"It is perfect," Inez sighed.

"Leave your hair down," Lucy said when Margaret started to braid it. Lucy combed it, then pulled the top back in a ribbon. "You look beautiful."

And somehow Margaret felt beautiful. God had made her for Daniel, and they were a perfect match. She stood with her head held high and walked to the door.

Daniel met her outside the door. His jaw dropped. "How lovely you are," he whispered. He held both her hands in his and gazed into her eyes.

The strains of "Red River Valley" drifted through the night as the ranch hands sang. "Come and sit by my side if you love me. Do not hasten to bid me adieu. But remember the Red River Valley, and the girl who has loved you so true." The words of the song echoed on the wind.

"That song seems appropriate somehow, doesn't it?" Daniel asked softly. "I never thought to find a woman like you, Margaret. We'll build this ranch into an empire we can give to our children. But even more important, we'll pass on the most important things: faith in God, hope for the future, and unconditional love." He turned and led her toward the door and the waiting friends and family.

With her hand clasped tightly in Daniel's, Margaret knew she was safe in his arms.

READER GROUP GUIDE

1. It's a common thing to greatly admire an older sibling. It's also common for a younger sibling to feel ignored. What were the dynamics in your family?
2. Having a friend who sees the real you can be one of the most rewarding experiences in our lives. When did you have your first real friend like that? How did he or she change your life?
3. Have you ever felt judged for your gender? If so, how did you handle it?
4. Charlie fell in with the wrong crowd because he felt unloved at home. How can we keep ourselves from this reaction in our own lives?
5. What do you think caused Golda to head down the wrong path?
6. Margaret was quick to make assumptions about others. On what criteria should we evaluate other people?
7. What makes you feel safe? Is this true safety or just an illusion of safety?
8. Margaret's worth was tied up in how she looked and in her status. Where do you find your worth? If it's based on an illusion, what can you do to change it?

ACKNOWLEDGMENTS

My friend and cheerleader, senior acquisitions editor Ami McConnell, loves change. Me, not so much. When publisher Allen Arnold called to tell me he was taking a ministry position and leaving Thomas Nelson, I was crushed. But Ami is right, and change can work out well. I adore Daisy Hutton, who took over as publisher for Allen! She's the right person for the position. She's handled the transition with such grace and wisdom, and I'm so thankful we have her. Thanks, Daisy!

My team is a dream to work with. I can't imagine writing without my editor, Ami. I crave her analytical eye and love her heart. Ames, you are truly like a daughter to me. Marketing and publicity director, Katie Bond, is always willing to listen to my harebrained ideas. I wouldn't get far without you, friend! Fabulous cover guru Kristen Vasgaard works hard to create the perfect cover—and does. You rock, Kristen! And, of course, I can't forget my other friends who are all part of my amazing fiction family: Natalie Hanemann, Amanda Bostic, Becky Monds, Kerri Potts, Jodi Hughes, Ruthie Dean, Laura Dickerson, Heather McCulloch, and Dean Arvidson. You are all such a big part of my life. I wish

I could name all the great folks at Thomas Nelson who work on selling my books through different venues. I'm truly blessed!

Julee Schwarzburg is a dream editor to work with. She totally gets romantic suspense, and our partnership is a joy. Thanks for all your hard work to make this book so much better!

My agent, Karen Solem, has helped shape my career in many ways, and that includes kicking an idea to the curb when necessary. Thanks, Karen, you're the best!

Writing can be a lonely business, but God has blessed me with great writing friends and critique partners. Hannah Alexander (Cheryl Hodde), Kristin Billerbeck, Diann Hunt, and Denise Hunter make up the Girls Write Out squad (www.GirlsWriteOut .blogspot.com). I couldn't make it through a day without my peeps! Thanks to all of you for the work you do on my behalf and for your friendship. I had great brainstorming help for this book in Robin Caroll and Cara Putman. Thank you, friends!

I'm so grateful for my husband, Dave, who carts me around from city to city, washes towels, and chases down dinner without complaint. As I type this, he has been free of prostate cancer for a year, and we're so thankful! My kids—Dave, Kara (and now Donna and Mark)—and my grandsons, James and Jorden Packer, love and support me in every way possible. Love you guys! Donna and Dave brought me the delight of my life—our little granddaughter, Alexa! She's talking like a grown-up now, and having her spend the night is more fun than I can tell you.

Most important, I give my thanks to God, who has opened such amazing doors for me and makes the journey a golden one.

Libby arrives at the Tidewater Inn hoping to discover clues about her friend's disappearance. There she finds an unexpected inheritance and a love beyond her wildest dreams.

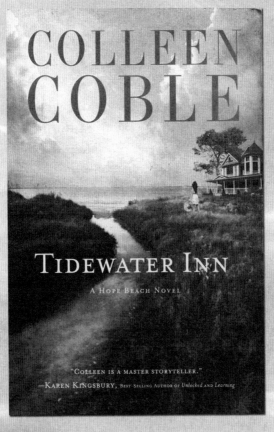

The first novel in the Hope Beach Series

THOMAS NELSON
Since 1798

ONE

L ibby Holladay fought her way through the brambles to the overgrown garden. She paused to wave a swarm of gnats away from her face. The house was definitely in the Federal style, as she'd been told. Palladian windows flanked a centered door, or rather the opening for a door. The structure was in serious disrepair. Moss grew on the roof, and fingers of vine pried through the brick mortar. The aroma of honeysuckle vied with that of mildew.

She stepped closer to the house and jotted a few impressions in her notebook before moving inside to the domed living room. The floorboards were missing in places and rotted in others, so she planted her tan flats carefully. She could almost see the original occupants in this place. She imagined her own furniture grouped around the gorgeous fireplace. She'd love to have this place, but something so grand that needed this much repair would never be hers. The best she could do would be to preserve it for someone else who would love it. She itched to get started.

Her cell phone rang, and she groped in her canvas bag for it. Glancing at the display, she saw her partner's name. "Hey, Nicole," she said. "You should see this place. A gorgeous Federal-style mansion. I think it was built in 1830. And the setting by the river is beautiful. Or it will be once the vegetation is tamed." Perching on the window seat, she made another note about the fireplace. "Nicole? Are you there?"

There was a long pause, then Nicole finally spoke. "I'm here."

"You sound funny. What's wrong?" Nicole was usually talkative, and Libby couldn't remember the last time she'd heard strain in her friend's voice. "Are you still in the Outer Banks? Listen, I heard there might be a hurricane heading that way." She dug into her purse for her jalapeño jellybeans and popped one in her mouth.

"I'm here," Nicole said. "The residents are sure the storm will miss Hope Island. The investor is really interested in this little town. And we have the chance to make a boatload of money on it. It's all in your hands."

"My hands? You're the one with the money smarts."

Nicole was the mover and shaker in Holladay Renovations. She convinced owners to dramatically increase the value of their historic properties by entrusting them to Libby's expertise. Libby had little to do with the money side of the business, and that was how she liked it.

"I think I'd better go back to the beginning," Nicole said. "Rooney sent me here to see about renovating some buildings in the small downtown area. He's working on getting a ferry to the island. It will bring in a lot more tourism for the hotel he's planning, but the buildings need to be restored to draw new business."

"I know that much. But what do you mean 'it's in my hands'?" Libby glanced at her notes, then around the room again. This was taking up her time, and she wanted to get back to work. "We're doing the lifesaving station for sure, right?"

"Yes, I've already seen it. We were right to buy that sweet building outright. After you get your hands on it, we'll make a bundle *and* have instant credibility here. I've started making notes of the materials and crew we'll need. But I'm not calling about the renovations. I'm talking a lot of money, Libby. Millions."

That got Libby's attention. "Millions?"

"I stopped by the local attorney's office to see about having him handle the paperwork for our purchase of the lifesaving station. Horace Whittaker. He's got both our names on the paperwork now."

"So?"

"The secretary gasped when she heard your name."

"She knew me?"

"The attorney has been looking for a Libby Holladay. Daughter of Ray Mitchell."

"That's my dad's name."

"I thought it might be. I'd heard you mention the name Ray, but I wasn't sure of the last name."

Libby rubbed her head. "Why is he looking for me? My father has been dead a long time—since I was five."

"He died a month ago, Libby. And he left you some valuable land. In fact, it's the land Rooney thought he had agreed to purchase. So we're in the driver's seat on this deal." Nicole's voice rose.

Libby gasped, then she swallowed hard. "It's a hoax. I bet the attorney asked for a fee, right?"

"No, it's real. According to the secretary, your father was living in the Outer Banks all this time. And Horace has a box of letters Ray wrote to you that were all marked *Return to Sender*. It appears your mother refused them."

Libby's midsection plunged. Throughout her childhood she'd asked her mother about her father. There were never any answers. Surely her mother wouldn't have *lied*. Libby stared out the window at two hummingbirds buzzing near the overgrown flowers.

"Do you have any idea how much money this land is worth?"

Nicole's voice quivered. "It's right along the ocean. There's a charming little inn."

It sounded darling. "What's the area like?"

"Beautiful but remote." Nicole paused. "Um, listen, there's something else. I met a woman who looked like you a couple days ago."

Libby eased off the window ledge. "Who is she?"

"Your half sister, Vanessa. You also have a brother, Brent. He's twenty-two."

"My father married again?" Libby couldn't take it all in. This morning she had no family but a younger stepbrother, whom she rarely saw. Why had her mother kept all this from her? "What about my father's wife?"

"She doesn't seem to be around. But there's an aunt too."

Family. For as long as she could remember, Libby had longed for a large extended family. Her free-spirited mother was always wanting to see some new and exciting place. They had never lived at the same address for more than two years at a time.

"You need to get here right away," Nicole said. "There are a million details to take care of. This is the big deal we've been praying for, Libby. You will never want for anything again, and you'll have plenty of money to help your stepbrother. He can get out of that trailer with his family."

The thought of buying her stepbrother's love held some appeal. They weren't close, but not because she hadn't tried. "I can't get away until tomorrow, Nicole. I have to finish up here first. We have other clients."

How much of her reluctance was rooted in the thought of facing a future that was about to change radically? She never had been good with change. In her experience, change was something that generally made things worse, not better.

Her partner's sigh was heavy in Libby's ear. "Okay. Hey, want to see Vanessa? She'll be here in a few minutes. There's a beach cam out by the lifesaving station, and I'm supposed to meet her there. I'll send you a link to it. You can see her before you meet her."

Libby glanced through the window toward her car. "I have my computer in the car." She tucked her long hair behind her ear and gathered her things. "What does Vanessa think about our father leaving prime real estate to me?" She left the house and started for her vehicle.

Nicole cleared her throat. "Um, she's pretty upset."

"I would imagine. What did you tell her about me?"

"As little as possible."

"I don't know if that's good or bad."

"I wouldn't worry about them. She and her brother are fishing for info though. She mentioned lighthouse ruins and I asked for directions. She offered to show me, but I went out there by myself yesterday. I'm still meeting her today because I knew you'd want to know more about her."

It sounded like a disaster in the making. "I have so many questions."

"Then come down as soon as you can and get them answered. Wait until you see Tidewater Inn, Libby! It's really old. It's on the eastern edge of the island with tons of land along the beach. The inn was a house once, and it is a little run-down but very quaint. It's hard to get out here. Until Rooney gets the ferry approved, you'll have to hire a boat. You're going to love it though. I love this island. It's like stepping back in time. And I've even seen some caves to explore."

"No road to it from the mainland?" Libby couldn't fathom a place that remote.

"Nope. Boat access only."

Her phone still to her ear, Libby opened her car door and slid in. The computer was on the floor, and she opened it. "I'm going to have to get off a minute to tether my phone to the computer. Send me the link to the harbor cam. Don't tell Vanessa I'm watching."

"When can you get here tomorrow?"

"It's about two hours from Virginia Beach?"

"Yes."

Libby doubted she'd sleep tonight. It would be no problem to be in the shower by six. "I'll be there by nine."

She ended the call, then attached the cord that tethered the phone to the computer. She would use the cell signal to watch Nicole's video feed on the larger screen. Then she could watch and still take any calls that came in. Her skin itched from the brambles. She established the connection, then logged on to the Internet. No e-mail yet.

She owned property. The thought was mind boggling. No matter what condition it was in, it was a resource to fall back on, something she hadn't possessed yesterday. The thought lightened her heart. She stared at the grand old home beside her. What if there was enough money from the sale of the inn to allow her to buy a historic house and restore it? It would be a dream come true. She could help her stepbrother. She could buy some Allston paintings too, something she'd never dreamed she could afford.

A woman pecked on Libby's car window, and Libby turned on the key and ran down the window. "Hello. I'm not an intruder. I'm evaluating this gorgeous old place for the historic registry."

The woman smiled. "I thought maybe you were buying it. Someone should restore it."

"Someone plans to," Libby said. What if it could be her instead of her client?

The woman pointed. "I'm taking up a collection for the Warders, who live on the corner. They had a fire in the kitchen and no insurance."

Libby had only two hundred dollars in her checking account, and she had to get to the Outer Banks. "I wish I could help," she said with real regret. "I don't have anything to spare right now."

"Thanks anyway." The woman smiled and moved to the next house.

Libby ran the window back up and clicked on her in-box. An e-mail from Nicole appeared. She stared at the link. All she had to do was click and she'd catch a glimpse of a sister she had no idea even existed. Her hands shook as she maneuvered the pointer over the link and clicked. The page opened, and she was staring at a boardwalk over deep sand dunes that were heaped like snowdrifts. In the distance was a brilliant blue ocean. A pier extended into the pristine water. The scene was like something out of a magazine. She could almost feel the sea breeze.

She clicked to enlarge the video and turned up the speakers so she could hear the roar of the surf. Where was Nicole? The pier was empty, and so was the sea. A dilapidated building stood to the right of the screen, and she could just make out a sign over the door. Hope Beach Lifesaving Station.

Then there was a movement on the boardwalk. Nicole appeared. She smiled and waved. "Hi, Libby," she said. The sound quality was surprisingly good. The sound of the ocean in the background was a pleasant lull.

Libby had to resist the impulse to wave back. Her partner's blond hair was pulled back in a ponytail under a sun hat, and she wore a hot-pink cover-up over her brown bathing suit.

Nicole glanced at her watch and frowned. "Vanessa is late.

Like I started to say earlier, I didn't want to wait on her to see the lighthouse ruins, so I went out there alone. I have to show it to you. Wait until you see what I found. You'll seriously freak! Hey, give me a call. This pier is one of the few places where my phone works. Isn't that crazy—an entire island without cell service. Almost, anyway."

Libby picked up her cell phone, still connected to the computer. They could talk a few minutes. Before she could call, a small boat pulled up to the shore. Two men jumped out and pulled the boat aground. Nicole turned toward them. The men walked toward her. There was no one else in sight, and Libby tensed when Nicole took a step back. Libby punched in Nicole's number. She watched her friend dig in her bag when it rang.

When Nicole answered the phone, Libby leaped to her feet and yelled, "Get out of there. Go to your car!"

Nicole was still watching the men walk toward her. "It's just a couple of tourists, Libby," she said. "You worry too much." She smiled and waved at the men.

Libby leaned closer to the laptop. "There's something wrong." She gasped at the intention in their faces. "Please, Nicole, run!"

But it was the men who broke into a run as they drew closer to the boardwalk. As they neared the cam, Libby could see them more clearly. One was in his forties with a cap pulled low over his eyes. He sported a beard. The other was in his late twenties. He had blond hair and hadn't shaved in a couple of days.

Nicole took another step back as the older man in the lead smiled at her. The man said, "Hang up." He grabbed her arm.

"Let go of her!" Libby shouted into the phone.

The man knocked the phone from Nicole's hand and the connection was broken. The other man reached the two, and he plunged a needle into Nicole's arm. Both men began dragging Nicole toward the boat. She was struggling and shouting for help, then went limp. Her hat fell to the ground.

Barely aware that she was screaming, Libby dialed 9-1-1. "Oh God, oh God, help her!"

The dispatcher answered and Libby babbled about her friend being abducted right in front of her. "It's in the Outer Banks." She couldn't take her eyes off the boat motoring away from the pier. "Wait, wait, they're taking her away! Do something!"

"Where?"

"I told you, the Outer Banks." Libby looked at the heading above the video stream. "Hope Beach. It's Hope Beach. Get someone out there."

"Another dispatcher is calling the sheriff. I have an officer on his way to you."

"I'm going to Hope Beach now."

"Stay where you are," the dispatcher said. "We've got the sheriff on the line there. He's on his way to the site. Don't hang up until an officer arrives."

She had to do something. Anything but run screaming into the street. Libby looked at the computer. She could call up the video, save it for evidence. But the stream had no rewind, no way to save it. If she could hack into the site, she could get to the file. The police could save time and get the pictures of those men circulating. With a few keystrokes, she broke through the firewall and was in the code.

Then her computer blinked and went black. And when she called up the site again, the entire code was gone. What had she done?

"*The Lightkeeper's Bride* is a wonderful story filled with mystery, intrigue, and romance. I loved every minute of it."

— CINDY WOODSMALL —
New York Times best-selling author of *The Hope of Refuge*

ABOUT THE AUTHOR

Author photo by Clik Chick Photography

RITA finalist Colleen Coble is the author of several best-selling romantic suspense series, including the Mercy Falls series, the Lonestar series, and the Rock Harbor series.

Visit ColleenCoble.com